The Concrete Sea

John Dalton

**Tindal
Street
Press**

First published in Great Britain in April 2005 by
Tindal Street Press Ltd
217 The Custard Factory, Gibb Street, Birmingham, B9 4AA
www.tindalstreet.co.uk

A CIP catalogue reference for this book is available
from the British Library

ISBN: 0 9547913 2 0

Typeset by Country Setting, Kingsdown, Kent

Printed and bound in Great Britain by Clays Ltd, St Ives PLC

mys
F
DAL

b16983944

Acknowledgements

Thanks to Joel Lane, Emma Hargrave and Alan Mahar for their editing help. Thanks also to Beulah and Antonio up there in the hills outside Montego Bay.

I

Is that the guy? The one wearing a beige overcoat. Eurasian eyes beneath scribbles of black. A folded newspaper that could hide anything. Don Avoca loitered by the railway station doors and lit up his last fag before the journey ahead. He kept well to the side where there was shadow and a pillar he could duck behind.

Or is that him? Gaunt face with ginger hair and black suit. The guy who looks like he's from a grim Atlantic isle with maybe more than a bible for a weapon.

Stations. Where strangers converge. Dressed up bodies of all kinds bustling through. Streams of egos and personality; unknown thoughts and furtive dreams daily whirling beneath the camera's gaze. Who would you suspect?

Maybe that guy? Small, big-eared and balding. So innocent and unassuming, how could you see danger in someone like him? Eyes – wet and slippery eyes.

Don couldn't do anything but cross the forecourt to catch his train. Pass those that lingered by the news stall, muffin shop and flower seller. Wrapped up in themselves they might be amid the vanilla and carnation smells, but there could be one person on the look out for an escapee. A casual bump, a silenced gun to the ribs and then POP. Don cursed the paranoia he felt.

It was the rumours, the malicious tittle-tattle from sods who like to stir it that brought on the panic. Would've been all right otherwise, only flashbacks of blood to cope with. God, the talk that was doing the rounds.

He took the plunge. The floor was thin ice, the sky a flash of wings through black girders. The people, he forced himself to think, were walking frailties to be brushed aside.

Don Avoca did make it to the train. He found himself an empty set of seats with a table. No one had got him and he was safe. He eased his bulky shoulders back into the upholstery and ran fingers through his thinning black hair. The train felt good. He had a new job to work on and a new place to go to. With a flicker of enthusiasm, he put his hand on the bag beside him and thought of getting the case file out. Fingers wavered, though, and pulled back. He looked instead through glass at the station platform. The strangers were standing still now with their unknown thoughts. Like himself, they were neither here nor there. Don sighed. The observation unsettled him. Right, fifteen years as a PI, maybe one of the best in the north, but what do I really have to show for it? He felt his shoulders stiffen. Familiar feelings of self-doubt were beginning to stir. The fears, the tug of apathy on his sleeve that was making every effort a little bit harder. Don straightened himself up. No, it shouldn't be that way this time. Get a grip, he thought. The journey, the murder investigation he was heading to – this job had an edge, it was personal.

The train shuddered and started to move. Don was relieved. He heard the rhythmic clunk of the wheels begin to build up speed. No more neither here nor there, but actually going places. He leaned back in his seat and yawned, tried to imagine that his past was really slipping away. The city, Manchester, that had become suffocating and over-familiar. His flat on the third floor that he'd only half lived in. Don shivered. A home layered with grime, where blood seeped beneath the doors and his cupboards were full of bones. He yawned again. Too long a time in one place, too many splinters under his skin.

He glanced at the window. Images blurring now – bricks and blocks of grey, smears of green and flickering shafts of light. He smiled grimly. Like doing a runner, he thought, shaking off the shit and heading to a new future. He closed his eyes. The pull and the rhythm of the train was bringing sleepiness. He felt safe enough to let go and drift. Hopefully, no mind-barging phobias would haunt him, or fretful thoughts lodged down deep. The clatter and bucking of the train could drown out such things. Don could listen to cacophony and ride on obliviously. No chance to think – just dream. Dreams, there'd been so many of late and he felt he could almost drown in them.

There was something strange about the guard. There was something strange about the train. It had no roof. Up above, bright blue sky and white puffy clouds streaking across at speed. The train appeared motionless.

'You goin Stratford, is you, me dear? Right. Change at Birmingham.'

The guard was a small chubby black guy who hadn't shaved that morning. He wore a bright yellow uniform and a yellow peaked cap, the shiny visor catching the movement of the clouds. Don could hear his heavy feet shuffling along the aisle.

'OK, sir, goin all the way, are we? You ticket is in order.'

He moved on and up towards Don. The noise of his feet was irritating.

'Ticket please.'

Don's hand strained and fumbled before finally sending a ticket slithering across the grey plastic of the table. The guard picked it up, his smile dimming slightly. His bleary eyes looked closely at the piece of card and his smile went completely.

'This is one hell of a ticket you got here, man.'

'Wha?'

'There ent no station call dis, man. I mean, RE-TRI-BUTION?'

'Er . . . I don't get you.'

'Dis don't seem like a ticket at all, more like mystical chart. Shit.'

The guard began to look closely at both sides of the card, his eyes suddenly intent and slightly startled.

'Man, ent seen one a dese in a long time. You wanna know what I see, man, eh?'

Don shrugged self-consciously as if to say it wasn't anything to do with him. He began to look around the carriage and his mouth remained gobbingly open.

'Where the fuck am I?'

'You wanna know what I see, man, eh? I see two skeleton, man, one in a past an one in a future. An I tell you, dis train, it don't go to no Retribution, an it don't fuck wid skeleton, so jus sit tight, right – an get off at Birmingham.'

The guard put the ticket down and moved on. There were no more people in the carriage, but at the passage doors he stopped and turned. He gave a narrow-eyed glare at Don, looked skywards and then drew out a harmonica. Stevie Wonder licks filled the air as he moved off and out to the next carriage.

When he awoke, Don didn't open his eyes. In fact, he squeezed them more tightly shut. The dream was disconcerting. It was like the old stuff that came out of cracks in the wall. He took a deep breath. He had to get rid of it all. He really must get a grip. Another deep breath and he forced his eyes open. The train must've stopped and picked up passengers. One sat opposite him. Don froze and almost closed his eyes again. A guy, thin face and shaven head. An insolent face that did not flinch as Don stared.

Jesus, is this the guy? Did he follow me at the station and get on the same train? Is he now checking me out, flaunting himself, trying to put the shits up me, making me suffer until the time for dispatch finally comes? Don forced himself to look away. Rain on the window and fields smudged like paint.

'Fuckin boring, eh? That's train journeys for yer, bloody crawls through nothing an always late.'

'Yeh, guess so.'

The guy looked belligerent and spoke in the same way. Was this because he knew Don and was the one, or was it just his normal way? He did have the word PUNK tattooed above his hairline.

'Lost me Walkman, that's the bugger. Paper took five minutes to read an now the mobile's run outa juice.'

'It's a bad scene when you run out of juice.'

'Sure is.'

Don began to relax a little. The guy seemed like a punk rocker, an ageing one, probably harmless, the sort of guy who showed his affection with a punch.

'So, you going Brum then?'

'Yeh.'

'And me. Just got out the fuckin nick, haven't I? Gotta go to this fuckin hostel and hang around till I get my own place sorted. Fuckin hanging around, that's all I've fuckin done for the last three years.'

'Right . . . lousy situation. So what did you do to deserve all that?'

'Crack. I was fuckin flogging, mugging and flying on the fuckin stuff, so much so I didn't know where the fuck I was or what the fuck I was done for. Mad, paranoid stuff, I tell ya.'

'That's drugs. Screw with your brain.'

'Too right there, and I've been truly gang-banged.' The punk looked straight into Don's eyes, seemed to think for a moment and then said, 'Er, don't know if you realize this, mate . . . but you were talking in your sleep.'

'Yeh?' Don felt a flicker of embarrassment.

'Yeh.' The punk maintained his gaze and chewed at his lip before he spoke again. 'That word you were muttering – just don't do it, mate. It's never fucking worth it. Believe me, I've been there and back again many times and it just ain't fucking worth it.'

'Hey' – Don wriggled in his seat awkwardly – 'I really don't know what you're on about.'

The punk continued to stare and chew at his lip. He raised his eyebrows and nodded his head as if to say 'You know'.

Don pushed back in his seat and checked the window view again. Still slurries of rain but now there was blurred brick and concrete behind it. They were approaching the city. He had felt OK about the chat with the punk. Now he felt disturbed. He didn't want things dragged out into the open. He wanted to leave his past behind, hoped he could leave himself behind. Fresh words on a blank sheet.

'It looks like we're there.'

'Bout fuckin time.'

'Well, good luck in sorting your new life out.'

'It'll be all right, as long as I don't run into fuckin you.'

The punk grinned, a gawky kind of smile, and proffered a hand, a stiff thrust towards Don, which Don rather awkwardly took.

'Right, and the same sentiments. Here's to never seeing you again.'

Don smiled grimly to himself. Yeh, there's a future for you, a place where passing acquaintance evaporates and perfect strangers disembark.

'Just don't the fuck do it, eh,' he heard as the punk disappeared from view.

*

For a while, Don kind of liked being a stranger in the city. Leaving the station and walking the rain-washed New Street to his hotel, he felt comfortable just looking out and taking in the fresh scene. All those familiar shops and the cameras that watch over them. The grand civic architecture. A catatonic iron man standing by a fat stone lady taking a bath. No interaction either way was a relief and he almost felt he was on holiday. He wondered whether he should check out tourist information. What cities are for, what the whole world is. Not many places on earth now that aren't a tourist attraction, he thought. For a man with itchy feet, the future could be OK. He carried on through the rain, with darkness falling and city lights turning on. Just some other place, a respite place, as long as he chose not to think why he had come.

Once in his hotel room, however, with its four walls and his baggage on the bed, the relaxed levity began to crumble. Early winter night had fallen. Unpleasant thoughts popped up out of nowhere: There's blood behind the door, Don, and someone wants to pay you back. Wherever you are, you know they can get you. Don forced himself to open his suitcase and put his clothes away. The mundane action helped to soothe his nerves. He pulled out a folder of notes, which he put on the bedside table. Then out came a gun, a small snub-nosed number, which he wrapped in a sock and stuffed under his clothes. A bag of plastic wrist ties followed and were put in a drawer. From the folder of notes, he then pulled out a photograph. A young woman, barely nineteen, her head tilted, her smile coy, looked at the lens with ease and optimism.

Don propped the photo against the bedside lamp and promptly turned away. Something rarely looked at beyond a glance, he tried hard to keep the image superficial, just a young woman, and so avoid the implicit pain. He surveyed the room. Bland, small and, like so many hotel rooms, slightly spooky. All those previous visitors – who they were, what they got up to and what ghostly traces of them might be left behind. He walked over to the window, the out-there place that would be his tomorrow, and looked out at the city night. Stretching to the horizon – grids of stars, rivers of light and block on block of deep labyrinthine shadow. *Something pernicious out there.* Don looked back at his empty single bed and felt a shiver of fear.

2

A phone was ringing some distance away. Don tried to figure out where it was. The dream he was in, or reality?

He was squatting in bushes by the side of a railway track with a gun in his hand. Across from him, in the sands, some kind of war was being fought but he couldn't see anything of it, only thick black smoke billowing on the horizon. He could feel the menacing presence of a man behind him. 'Shit scene, man,' the guy croaked. 'Keep coughing up blood and the bastards don't give a toss.' Don cringed, was scared of what the man might do, but then felt himself struggling, maybe swimming skywards –

The phone sound became very loud. Don jolted his head, his eyes flooded with daylight and finally his hand went scrambling for his mobile.

'Yeh.'

'Fuck, I've woken you, haven't I, Don?'

'Er, could still be dreaming, I guess.'

'Nah, all too real I'm afraid. You want me to ring back?'

'The damage has been done, I reckon.'

'You sure?'

'Go on.'

'So, you got yourself settled in there, Don, got a reasonable room, not too expensive I hope, and a bit of a breathing space. Well, space anyway. Guess there ain't much breathing you can get in a city.'

'I'm all right, Pat, don't worry.'

'Just ringing to check on your welfare, mate, like you've lost those fears about being followed and all that. You know me.'

'Yeh, you're worse than a parent, and you're a controlling bastard, checking up on your workforce.'

'There is that, Don. I may owe you one but it's costing me a packet this and I didn't get where I am today by being slack on the dosh.'

'This is mutual, Pat. You know I'll do what I can for Kate.'

'Sure, don't doubt it. So it's the Lee woman this morning?'

'Yeh.'

'She did all right last time so I hope she isn't pissed off that I've sent you down. I don't want to – you know, people do take offence – I hope she still co-operates. She can have a day's fee just for that.'

'I'll soon find out.'

'And, you know what I mean, you haven't, like . . . ?'

'Pat, you are a control freak, really. You want to know what shirt I'm going to wear today, like will I choose the right colour?'

'No, don't be touchy, I didn't mean to –'

'I told you – fresh start, new patch, no past. As well as I can, I'm not going to be that Don any more, I threw it all away at the station.'

'OK, OK, fair enough, I won't mention it again.'

'By the way, if you ring the hotel, you ask for Cherry, right, room 19.'

'Right. I'm supposed to get that, aren't I? Oh well.'

*

Don double-checked that he'd locked his room. He glanced down the corridor. Nothing disconcerting, just morning, a window of bright morning. It brought a smile. The four walls and the bed, that sweaty venue of a squirming night could now be forgotten. He ambled towards the lifts, clicked slow time with his fingers and let the shreds of his dreams fade away. *But you'll never really get rid of me, never, or what I gave you.* Once on the ground floor, he could've been any old hotel stranger grabbing coffee and cold toast in the buffet lounge. He checked out his surroundings. Not ideal. Very open plan. The hotel seemed to run a lot of business meetings and small conferences. People were in, out and loitering all the time. Anybody could walk in, someone specific could, someone who was out to do harm to Don. He'd have to consider a change. But not another poky bolthole like his hotel room. Better to be shot than have the past catch up inside your head. He gulped down the last of his coffee. The large glass doors of the hotel beckoned, glowed with daylight like they were an opening into the sky. No chance.

Don sighed as he stood on the hotel steps and looked around. *Cities – seen one, seen em all. Lived most of a life in them. Probably got brick dust and car fumes in my veins. By now I may well have brain deformities.* It was the usual bustle of cars and people, the grind and slosh of a workday morning. He strolled off through drizzle and began to look for a taxi, a stranger among strangers and so comfortably anonymous. It was now a question of getting into gear. The start of a new case, the quest and the challenge. It should be a moment for optimism before the difficulties and tension seep in. This was his thing, the skill he possessed. He pushed against lethargy, that niggling sense of darkness, and gazed expansively at the city sights. Eyes went soaring up the rippling glass of the Hyatt

Hotel. They looped along rooftops and jumped cloud space to the slim wedge of Alpha Tower. He didn't see the aluminium post lodged in the middle of the pavement and bumped right into it. He looked up. A camera pointed down at him. He felt a sudden and unexpected fizz of anger as he stared into the lens. Shit. Somewhere up there, behind the technology, stuffed in a room, is a snooper. Have you clocked me yet, got the screen I'm on? Well, here're two fingers for you. Don smiled. I tell you, what you cannot see and what you cannot know. I'm a pervert. I want to sodomize the queen. I want to blow up Parliament. Huh, got you there, eh? Can't read minds yet. He moved on. A taxi rank was in sight. He was glad. Suddenly he felt queasy about the idea of deformities of the brain.

Metropolitan Investigations lived in a converted factory a couple of miles outside the city centre. It was a solid Victorian pile and the terracotta trim gave it an edged glow. Don trudged up the stairs, walked down a long, empty corridor before he finally found the office. Before entering, he took a deep breath and imagined himself wiping clean a pane of glass. In the first office there was an empty reception desk. He looked around. To his left, a black guy was leaning on a water dispenser and chatting on a mobile. When he clocked the visitor, a finger pointed to another door. Don went through.

'Found the place OK, huh?' said a small and serious-looking Jackie Lee.

'The taxi seemed to go in a sort of round-about way.'

'Yeh. It ain't exactly High Street, but it's cheap. You wanna coffee?'

'Sure.'

It was a small office with overgrown pot plants and pic-tures of jazz artists on the walls. Sanders, Ranglin,

Hancock – faces Don could relate to. Jackie Lee had quite a collection of paper piles – files, books, letters and the like, which seemed to occupy most of the flat surfaces. Don looked out the window. Barely fifty metres away, a stilted motorway stood. Traffic streaming endlessly into the city, churning spray across a blurred skyline with gloomy clouds overhead. Jackie brought in the coffees and Don took a seat on the other side of her desk. He just managed a view of her between the paper and computer console.

'How you want to go with this? You want me to talk you through or just show you the files?'

Don eased back in his chair and took a sip of coffee. He began to feel insecure. Many miles away in a strange place on a bleak and dismal morning. That other long corridor, rattling door handles like alarm bells in his head and the door he should never have opened. Things were tugging at his fresh start. He quickly leaned forward.

'I don't know how I want to go with it, Jackie. You know, you – you sort of had the case before and I don't want to just trample in.'

There was another aspect to his unease. Him feeling edgy, yeh, but Jackie too, sitting back and quietly checking him out. She was good looking. A tan, almond-shaped face with a small mouth and a nicely curved nose. Mixed race, he thought. She had a calm presence, but a suspicious one too. And why not, thought Don, don't even trust myself. He tried to figure out her narrow eyes. Sadness was it, or fear? Don saw something else too, an affliction his own eyes had, lousy sleeper.

'Kate Connor,' she said. 'I really did want to sort that case, really did want to find her.'

'Yeh?'

'I guess I got involved, and it was a bastard of a shock when she turn up dead.'

'Right, and a lot worse for Pat Connor. I knew Kate too, she was a good kid. So, there's a lot of – what shall I say? – a lot of motivation backing this up.'

'Yeh, I can see that. I heard from Pat, and of course I'll take any money that's thrown my way, but I'd be happy to help out whatever, really.'

'That's nice. OK, I guess then we've got ourselves off to a good start, yeh?'

Jackie smiled for the first time. A forced one perhaps but still quite a beamer. Don was slightly taken aback. He shuffled nervously in his seat and thought of having a fag.

It was a big case fifteen months before. Kate Connor, university student, had disappeared off the face of the earth. The local newspapers took it up in a big way for this was no potential runaway or drop-out girl. This was one decent, level-headed, conscientious girl. A hard-working student of psychology, a non-drinker whose leisure pursuits were painting and playing the flute. She lived in a hall of residence and seemed totally straight. Jackie didn't believe that she was, she felt that she had to have some kink but it was hard to find. Maybe a touch of virginal provocativeness, a tease, but Jackie didn't really know. The only lead with an angle was Kate's friendship with Bridie Chariot, daughter of Mal, peddler big time of dope. But she didn't get any further. Bridie was at the university doing art, but she seemed to keep well out of the way of her dad and was as straight as Kate. Nothing else moved the investigation along.

'There must have been some fuckery, obviously was, but I couldn't find any hint of it, and it really pissed me off. And now . . .'

'Yeh. This line of business, you can hit a brick wall and it gets to you.'

'Certainly got me.'

Jackie suddenly looked away and stared at the window. Don sensed a switching off within her, a disconcerting absence. He looked again at her eyes. Sadness maybe, and perhaps a touch of the haunted too. He squirmed. Fuck, bit like looking in the mirror.

After some time, and still looking at the window, Jackie spoke. 'Don, how bout I show you where she was found?'

'Sure.'

'I kind of get fed up at being in the office.'

'Yeh, I know, rooms and paper, what they do to you.'

Don followed Jackie down the long corridor, descended steep stairs and went out into drizzling rain. Getting going did feel better, tagging along with this attractive stranger, sleepless eyes and a corpse in common. They got into Jackie's Fiat, which was parked under the rumbling motorway, and headed off into the sprawling maze.

'Shit, I just hate this weather,' Jackie groaned.

'Yeh, makes me wanna keep my head down. Mind you, a lot of things do these days.'

'You been in this business long?'

'Around fifteen years.'

'Solo?'

'Now, yeh. I worked for the Thwaite Agency for a few years but split. Guess I wanted to pick and choose.'

'Fair enough. So you don't do none of the drudge stuff.'

'Depends what's on offer. I kind of have a lot of regular clients now, like Pat, and that's good. You been doing it long?'

'Bout ten. Found myself working as a civilian in police intelligence, not nice, an then this guy Baz Weston, he offer me a job at Metropolitan an I jumped at it.'

'Now you're the queen of the pile, huh?'

'Nah, only temporary. Baz got himself sick a while back, so I'm just minding the shop.'

'Well, you seem to be minding it pretty well.'

That smile. As Don looked over, Jackie turned on her nice smile, perhaps sincerely this time, and she coyly laughed. Don felt something go for a bit of a bump inside.

'Right, not bad,' she said. 'I'm always up for a good compliment.'

It must have been half an hour's drive before they came to it. A slow drive through nameless suburbs that soon made Don feel cut adrift and lost.

The 'slang hole' was an old sand pit that lay at the back of an abandoned foundry. It was the name the local kids used. The boarded up factory was due for demolition but the presence of toxic waste on the site had caused a delay. The hole itself was also securely fenced since much poisonous waste had been dumped into it. With other factory land surrounding, it was a forgotten area unknown to most. An ideal place to dump a body.

'So how do we get in then?'

'Ain't easy, I tell you. It's good job I got me jeans on. Just follow me, eh, an watch your step.'

Jackie, followed by Don, went to the side of the foundry railings. There was a gap between the foundry and the concrete block wall of the next factory. It was not much more than half a metre across.

'Jesus.'

'Good job we're a fairly skinny pair.'

'Have we really gotta go down there?'

'What? Is the man saying he don't like to get dirty?' Jackie looked at Don with mock seriousness.

'Go on.'

It was a squeeze, a long squeeze between two walls and over ground clumped with weeds, bricks and old paint cans. Rain dripped off dead plants and the wet ground soon soaked into Don's shoes. At the end, they came to a high metal gate, freshly bolted.

'Great, and now?'

'The gate, it had been forced open before the police

recovered the body. But you have to ask yourself how the fuck a body was got down here in the first place.'

'With a pile of difficulty.'

'Yep.' Jackie turned sideways and lifted up a foot. 'OK, mister, give us a hitch up, and don't worry, I'll give you a pull up from the top.'

'You should've warned me about this, you know.'

'Not one for the outdoor life, eh?'

'Only the out door of the offy.'

The pit had steep sides. There were winter-dead weeds and brambles; lopsided trees and bushes; and walls of exposed red sand all around the crater. Rainwater trickled in gullies that wound down through the undergrowth and mist. Bad vibe place, Don thought. Sets alarm bells ringing. Maybe once upon a time I would've kicked out at the elements, but now? When will I ever get free from having to do this shit? He sighed and gritted his teeth. To the left, like a tongue of vomit, was the jumbled outpouring of foundry waste. Old iron ingots, sand castings and rusting metal drums stuck amid a tangle of twisted and splintered wood. Jackie nimbly led Don down. She picked out solid clumps to stand on, used branches as supports and zigzagged her way through the detritus. Don slipped frequently, cussed even more while Jackie quietly smiled.

'So did the police bring you down here?'

'Nah, checked it out myself later, after they told me what they'd found.'

'You needn't have done that. I mean, this is some really lousy excursion we're on.'

'I told you, the way I feel bout this case.'

It was easy to see where Kate's body had lain. A large circular area had been completely raked away. The branches and shrubbery that had been cut back still showed their wounds. Don stopped at the perimeter. He felt sadness come into him. *So here she lay, fifteen months, cold and alone. Felt the last of the leaves on her and bore the frost and snow. Her ivory cheeks had a whole summer of sun and nestled silently in the flowers. Come autumn again and heavy boots shook the ground and it feels like I've lost two instead of one.*

'She was found just over there, by that stump, what was left of her. I guess the rats and foxes and stuff had their fill, and then the flies and all that. Doesn't bear thinking bout.'

Don didn't say anything. He stood pale faced and stared at the patch of ground.

'She had no clothes on. There was a half-inch hole in the back of her skull.'

'Jesus.'

Jackie walked into the circle and crouched down. She fingered leaf mould and twigs and looked as if she were about to sob. Don hunched into his coat. He wasn't sure what he was feeling. A grim closeness to it all but then, somehow, this place seemed far away, like a painful memory hidden deep in the landscape of his own mind. The idea of a fresh start began to seem just a delusion. Eventually, he walked over to Jackie and put a tentative hand on her shoulder.

'S'all right,' Jackie muttered. 'Bit taken aback that this place still gets to me.'

Don then looked nervously up at the rim of the pit, at the trees, rubble and bleak walls of sand. He shivered. *A nightmare venue. Some awful space you cannot escape from, cannot avoid the feeling of death; and up there on the rim, within the shapes, faces will lurk, coldly curious faces that will always haunt you.*

'One other thing,' Jackie then said. 'They found traces of small bones in her throat – fish bones.'

'What you mean, like fish-and-chip-type bones?'

'No, like goldfish or something like that. They're not sure, but it wasn't the sort of fish you'd eat.'

'Weird.'

Don got a sudden glimpse then of iridescent fish cruising the shallows of the Corrib River, slivers of eloquence amid the murk, and the bones seeming like a thought fragment from a killer. He went wandering, head down, his feet scuffing at fallen leaves and damp grass. He guessed the police had done their fingertip search but he felt he had to do something, if only just to get a feel of the place. Jackie followed him aimlessly. She looked pale, edgy, and clearly wanted to leave quickly.

'I did a look round. The way we came in had to be the way they brought Kate in, cos there's big fences all round the rest of the place.'

'Could've fell from the sky.'

'That wouldn't surprise me.'

'The police reckon she was killed here?'

'After all the time that's passed, they don't know. I guess she could've been.'

Don walked beyond the cleared area and began to foot-sweep the soggy leaves. This was the kind of place he might've gone down when he was a kid, maybe make great piles out of the leaves and hide within them.

'So who would know about this sort of place, Jackie?'

'The guys who worked at the foundry, I guess, maybe other factory workers and the odd local person. I dunno, the local kids?'

'And the police have been checking on that?'

'Yeh, but unless you can make a connection.'

Don found himself looking at conkers on the ground, most black and rotting but some still had a chestnut sheen. There was another kid thing.

'Was it kids who found her?'

'Nah, some surveyor, checking out the costs of site clearance. Don, you think we should go now?'

'Yeh . . .'

Don was looking down at the ground, vaguely aware that there was something odd in his line of sight. He couldn't quite work out what it was.

'OK, let's split.'

He turned to go, but then stopped and looked back down. He picked the object up. Sodden and weatherworn maybe, but he reckoned he knew what it was. He walked over to Jackie.

'Huh-uh, you've found a conker. Well done, Don.'

'I don't think this is a conker. Look at the size and shape of it.'

'OK, so it's a squashed one.'

'No, I reckon this is a sea bean. They wash up on the beaches and you can buy them at those shell shops in seaside towns. Come all the way from the Caribbean apparently, across the Atlantic.'

'What, like my father?'

'They float along with the Gulf Stream.'

Jackie frowned. 'Is this some kind of rise?'

'No, on the level. I know it because I had one myself one time, as a paperweight. They're good. You can fiddle with them, you know, like worry beads. I used to rub my thumb into that ridge there.'

Jackie took the bean off Don and gave it a dubious inspection.

'Don, what the fuck is it with this situation? Fish, and now this. We're a hundred miles from the sodding sea!'

3

They sat by the window in a café on a busy trunk road. There was a huge wooden horse head hanging on the wall as well as a poster celebrating Galway's victory in the Gaelic football cup. The decorations couldn't hide the flaws. The cracks across the walls and the skirting board rotting away. The smell of damp and grease triggering retch impulses in Don's throat. He looked at heavy lorries rumbling through rain out on the highway as his thumb rubbed the familiar groove of the sea bean. It was polishing up well, just a few black weathered bits to work on. Don found himself avoiding looking directly at Jackie.

The ghost of the girl in the slang. Would've liked to have sat with her, winter cold or green spring. But not her really. That other girl, my girl, who has gone away to windy shores and whose words have grown distant and strange.

'What you think then, Don?'

He finally turned and looked at Jackie. One sympathetic light perhaps in the murky landscape. He nodded his head back into the café and grimaced.

'Some lousy situation, huh?'

'Yeh, workers' caff. They'll all be in for their egg sarnies in a bit.'

'Right, but I meant the other too.'

'I know, but that place, I don't want to think about it.'

'You OK? Back there, you seemed a bit . . .'

A frown then and Jackie's eyes flashed panic. 'I'm fine.'

It was a door-closing statement. Whatever curiosity Don had about Jackie's feelings over Kate's death, he was not about to be enlightened. He turned to the window and the churning traffic. A hundred square miles of concrete and brick. All the crime it hides. He sighed.

'I'm really gonna need some help, Jackie.'

'I told you, I'm happy to do it.' She smiled. 'You should speak to Bridie first. She was the one where the trail ran cold last time. I could probably set that up quick if she's still in the same set-up as before. Shall I?'

'Sure.'

'Give me a couple of hours and I'll ring you.'

'Yeh, that'd be good.' Don stayed with the business. 'So what's the set-up at your place, many people there?'

'We got a couple of guys. One's the heavy who does the writs and stuff and another's hot on surveillance. Apart from a part-time secretary, there's just me and I do the investigative side, though Baz would normally do a lot of that too.'

'I hope you aren't gonna be too stretched.'

'Nah, we'll manage. Meantime, you should maybe get yourself some wheels or something. It ain't gonna be easy moving around.'

'Right, it is down to me, isn't it? Work, what I'm here for. I should get off my arse and do it.'

'I wasn't, you know . . .'

'I know, but it isn't such a bad thing for me to get a push in the back.'

'I'm kind of tempted to ask, you know, this case – is there some sort of edge to it with you?'

It was Don's turn then to show panic in his eyes.

'But I won't.' Jackie smiled, shrugged and sat back. 'Anyway, Avoca, what kind of name is that?'

'Irish. My lot, they started way back on the west coast, moved east and then ended up in Lancashire. Lots of travelling, towns and cities.'

'Right. Well, I'm half Brummie, half Jamaican. My father Earl, he was the restless one, back in the Caribbean right now.' Jackie bit her lip and looked cautiously at Don. 'Maybe . . . maybe we should meet up later. You're a stranger in town, might like the company, and you can fill me in on what you find out.'

'That's very nice of you.' Don smiled.

'Hey, I reckon that's the first time you've done that.'

The car-hire geezer had a bad attitude. Surly. Didn't give a damn. 'Have whatever car you want, they're all a load of crap. As long as the paperwork's done, what do I care?'

Don went with the mood. 'Management bad, is it?'

'Tight tossers.'

'Pay hardly worth wiping your arse on?'

'Too right. This is one of three jobs I've got.'

'Not much time for the girlfriend.'

'What girlfriend?'

The chance to moan made the geezer almost helpful. He said he'd get a car round to the hotel within the hour. Don wished him a win on the lottery and then hauled himself out into the drizzle. He began the short stroll back to his hotel. His clothes were still sodden and his shoes smeared with mud. A hundred square miles of concrete and brick. The thought scared him. It brought on a wobble, as if he was faced with a huge mountain he knew he could never climb, or maybe couldn't be bothered to try to any more. Don gritted his teeth and suddenly wished it would rain harder, wished for a raging gale to take away the pangs. He quickened his pace. The streets were less crowded because of the weather and he could put some resolve into his walking. *These intervals, these empty moments when time goes slack and you've got nothing to distract you* . . . Up ahead, he saw the silver post with the spy camera.

'Right, so what am I thinking now? D'you think I'm guilty? I tell you, I fucking am, mate. I've done something terrible and the bugger still haunts me.' Don stopped in front of the post and sneered up at the lens. He thought of getting out his gun and shooting the camera, start a one-man campaign against all snidey spying eyes. But then he thought of windmills and Don Quixote and the goddamn mountain reared up again.

A quick shower at the hotel helped. So did the phone call from Jackie, telling him she'd fixed up a meet with Bridie and suggesting they go for a meal later on. Don felt he had something to keep him on track. He left his room and headed out to the hire car. Maybe Jackie was OK, he thought. Maybe her smile might do some good. On the driver's seat of the silver Nissan was a scrawled note from the geezer: DON'T LET THE BASTARDS CRACK YOU UP!

Bridie Chariot wasn't living in a hall of residence any more. The red on her bank balance was starting to haemorrhage. So, when her mum left husband Mal, Bridie went to live with her. Musical chariots and, no doubt, a lot of heartache to go with it. Don didn't want any of that, additional undercurrents of emotional stress, and he hoped his queries about Kate wouldn't be affected by them. The doorbell he pressed played a melody, he didn't know what. Mum appeared at the door. A defiant look, scornful maybe, but a vulnerable sag in the shoulders too. Don followed her into the plum and cream living room and enjoyed the luxurious give in the sofa when he sat down.

Sally Chariot, in her forties, was a slim, trim woman with greying auburn hair and a large nose. She had quite a distinctive and proud face, though it seemed Don's presence made her nervous. A forced bored yawn and nail picking greeted him as she sat down opposite.

'Bridie'll be here in a minute.'

'I'm glad she'll see me.' Don focused on her fiddling fingers. 'Did you meet Kate?'

'Oh yeh, a couple of times. When I was with Mal. Bridie brought her round.'

'Nice kid, yeh?'

'Very.'

Bridie then slipped lithely into the room. Tall and thin like her mum but not much more resemblance. A small beige face with spiky hair, black with shafts of bleach around her temples. A pair of large glasses beamed over at Don. She looked like an owl that had just fluttered down from a tree.

'Hi.'

Don felt uncomfortable. Nineteen, was she? Not much older than his own daughter. Those phone calls he got beginning with 'Hi'. Don pushed back the thought and started off by expressing his condolences. Then he said they had another chance to find out what happened to Kate and he'd appreciate some help.

'Been through it so many times in my head,' Bridie replied, 'you know, what happened, and was it anything to do with knowing me. I can't come up with anything, really. Like I said to that other investigator, Jackie, I saw her the day before she went missing, we had coffee in town and went shopping.'

'Right. It was a horrible thing, anyone would just rack their brains about it.'

'Yeh . . .' Bridie looked over at her mum and shrugged a little. 'And I can't help feeling guilty, even though, you know . . .'

'Sure.' Don felt his own feelings surge a bit. 'So, when you said "anything to do with knowing me" you sort of thought that she might have met someone, in your circle as it were, and that this might've led Kate off into . . . ?'

Bridie swallowed. 'Yeh, I guess that's it. I mean, I can't think of anything else. Kate really was straight.'

Sally Chariot then stretched an arm from her chair over towards Bridie. It wavered mid-air and her bony fingers flapped a little as though they were wings. She turned to Don, her expression hard. 'My husband, my ex-husband, has a somewhat unconventional job which means he meets a lot of dubious characters.'

'I guess that's one way of putting it.'

'OK, he's a villain. But give him his due, he never brought it home, which is why I stayed with him so long. But bad types did turn up and Bridie and me, we did wonder whether one of the shits spotted Kate when she visited us. She really was a bit of an innocent, that girl.'

She was, Don knew. An innocence he'd always found hard to square with her ruthless father.

'But you couldn't make a connection?'

'No.' Bridie sighed. 'She only came round a couple of times and there was never anyone there. I just didn't want anyone to meet Dad really.'

Those words came at Don like a punch. The soft sofa suddenly became more swamp-like and Don was sinking, feeling weak and wondering where the fuck he could find support.

'You don't look so good, Mr Avoca.' Sally's words didn't sound sympathetic. Don got the sense that she was at the stage, in the aftermath of the ex, where she felt all men could go and rot.

'Call me Don, eh, and I'm all right. I knew Kate too and it gets to me sometimes.'

'Yeh, well, bitter tears, part and parcel of life.'

'Nothing else you can think of? At the university? The way Kate was?'

'Not really, it was all checked out a year ago. The one thing about Kate is she was a bit of a sucker for lame ducks and lost causes. She wanted to help people and maybe she ran into someone who she thought she could help and it all went wrong.' Bridie turned her lips down, shrugged and pushed her glasses into place. 'But I can't remember anyone like that.'

'Mmm, doesn't look that great, does it?'

'Mal, you should check out my scumbag ex, you'll get a long line of suspects there.'

'OK, I get you. By the way –' Don knew he was going to sound bizarre '– do either of you keep fish?'

Perplexed faces stared mutely back.

'Doesn't matter.'

Don left then, back out into the alien sprawl. He was thinking he wanted a phone call beginning with 'Hi' or a warm shoulder to embrace – not even in dreams . . .

A westerly wind whipped marram grass into a frenzy. Don stood up shivering and aching all over. The sea was getting rough. A gale was coming. Don felt his face, felt unfamiliar hair straggling his chin. His overcoat was full of holes and grimed with mud and salt. Up out of the pebbles and sand he staggered and then he saw the young woman. She stood firmly set against the full blast of the wind, watching waves and a heavy grey cloud heading for the shore. Don stumbled his way towards her. The clatter of pebbles made the young woman turn. Shock on her face, then fear, and then she was gone, whisked away in the blink of an eye.

Jackie switched the car headlights off and pulled up the hand brake. Suddenly the lights of the city glimmered forth, a vast field of flickering, a crop of light stretching across the murky depths below. Don undid his seatbelt and tried to relax. The sudden view had unsettled him. It was like he'd just stepped outside himself and, upon looking, couldn't find out where he was. Just a pinprick of light somewhere in that lot. He shivered.

'You're not cold, are you?'

Jackie was hunched up, searching through her handbag. The car felt somewhat cramped.

'Ner . . . just jittery. Coming up here, it's slightly disconcerting.'

'Thought you might fancy some breathing space, that's why I come.'

'I don't like space, nasty things tend to fill it.'

'Ha, you could be right there but – a little bit of this might chill you out.'

Jackie pulled a spliff from her handbag.

'Really, Jackie, that is naughty, and forward. I mean, how'd you know I'd be into that stuff?'

'What? In our line of business and you're gonna tell me you ain't?'

The rain had stopped and streaks of mist were coming up over the brow of the hill. Don shivered again. Winter. Cold bones and chattering teeth. Winter was shit.

Earlier, they'd eaten at the Karachi Diner, a pink and silver fast food joint. Not Don's idea of a meal but it served as a halfway meeting point. As he'd chomped into halal burgers and paratha, he'd told her of his meet with Bridie. Nothing much to tell. Back where it was a year ago. Just the prospect of stumbling ahead blind and hoping something gives. Jackie had seemed sad, staring out across the road to the empty forecourt of a petrol station. Don had looked at it too, a concrete square of neon light and gaudy colour, a plastic flower calling for the itinerant, like moths, to alight. An in-between place similar to Don's situation.

'Shit, let's we two go for a drive.'

'You don't like staying still for too long, do you?'

'That's me, itchy feet.' Her reply was coldly terse.

'Me too, I guess.'

And so, with dusk falling, Don squeezed into her car and they went off across the city and into the night. Don felt relaxed in the darkness, watching the cosy glow of tail-lights and seeing the city unravel like the moving backdrop of a video game. But Beacon Hill was a wrench. No more lights and buildings. Steep, narrow roads. Glimpses of dead bracken and branches and then nothing, just headlights in the featureless dark. The city, gone, only to reappear dissociated, like an abstract chart of the night sky.

Don waited for his share of the spliff and wondered what Jackie had in mind. Friendly but far away, the enigma of Jackie Lee. The journey had been mostly silent, just Dolphy on the CD player, 'Hat and Beard', jaunty percussion sounds stepping through the brash wailing horns of a city at rush hour. The spliff came. Don inhaled hard and felt the buzz immediately. He smiled and tried to ease back.

'This is a bit strange, Jackie, like we're teenagers or something.'

'What, out in daddy's car for a secret blow?'

'Yeh, with your first romance maybe.'

'Nuzzling up with a bit a lovers' rock.'

'Yeh, but we're getting on now. We should be in a nice warm house watching froth on the box or playing Scrabble with the spouse. Weird . . .'

'Sounds like, for you an me both, we been through that and maybe want more. I just needed to get out of that, Don. It eats you up.' Jackie gestured towards the city. 'It's like you never stop, and while you rush round busting your arse, things brood away inside. Before you know it, you're a goddamned zombie.' She took back the spliff and smiled wistfully. 'Besides, it ain't bad to think back sometimes.'

'Getting sentimental scares me.'

'Come on, Don, don't shy off from what makes you feel good.'

'Right.' Don eased further down in the seat. 'So whatever did happen to lovers' rock?'

'It turned bitter and started to rap.'

Don did get a little vision then. Rooms, twenty-year-ago rooms with the lighting low and the air layered with smoke. Good vibes on the sound system, good vibes in the eyes of all the cool cats who lounged and laughed, innocently feeling maybe that nothing could get through to them. A time when you think you're there, but really it's only the start.

Jackie coughed and then turned towards Don. Her face was suddenly very serious. 'Ringing you up today, at the hotel, to tell you about the Bridie meeting – the hotel people, they didn't know Don Avoca.'

'Ah, right . . .'

'A description got me through to a Mr Cherry. It's nice to know that you like jazz but tell me, Don, why the hell are you using a false name?'

Don felt a flush of sweat on his brow and a tightening of his jaw. This little attack had him completely thrown. He was annoyed that she'd got him off guard, smug and stoned – and impressed.

'Fuck, I wondered what was going on here, friendly spliffs and all.' He fumbled for convincing bullshit. 'It's a bit of a tricky one, Jackie. It's about Pat Connor and I used the alias as a precaution . . .' The blood, don't tell her about the blood. God, not even sure of the truth myself. 'Pat, like he's no angel and he's got conflicts going on. People, they know I work for him and this was just a way of not drawing any attention down here. It was his idea.'

'What sort of conflicts?'

Don wriggled. He didn't want to say any more. He was beginning to like Jackie and this could fuck it up. But it was too early to be open, and hard.

'Rival economic interests in the building trade, the dodgy deals people do to secure tenders,' he waffled.

'Sounds bullshit to me.'

'I don't think I should say any more, it's his business.'

'Shit, Don, I don't like this. I didn't expect fuckery from you and this is making me suspicious now. Like, you know, could Kate's death have anything to do with Pat or these dodgy deals?'

'No way.' He paused. 'Mind you, I can't say I've ever thought about that angle.'

'Shit, Don, I'm pissed off you not being straight with me.'

'Sorry. But one thing, right, there may be shadiness from where I'm coming from, but with Kate, it's down the line serious, nothing iffy attached.'

'I ain't convinced.'

Don winced and silently stared ahead.

'I better take you back to your car.'

'We still co-operating?'

Jackie sucked her teeth and turned on the ignition. A blast of headlights blew away the city view and began to swerve over the featureless dark of the hill.

'I'll stay on board, Don, but you're going to have to prove yourself, and do some explaining too.'

Don cursed to himself. He searched in his pocket for the sea bean and got his thumb digging into its gentle groove.

4

He couldn't get out. Each time he tried to climb the steep bank, sandy earth gave way and he slid back down. Don was losing strength. But he had to escape, and not just for himself. Down, behind and in the shadows, he felt sure someone else was with him, someone who was in deep trouble. Don became aware that he was shouting. He couldn't hear his own words but certainly felt his increasing panic. Then he heard, 'Hold on, I'll find you, I'll get you out.' These words were from above. A hand appeared over the rim of the hole. 'Come on, man, there's someone you should see.' Don found himself being hauled up. His mouth choked with the sand that poured over him. He coughed harshly, and then, in the blink of a dreaming eye, he was walking down a road, a kind of scrap-yard avenue. This time, he knew for sure he was not alone.

'We didn't get that other person.' Don's mouth was dry and he could feel the grit in his teeth.

'There was no one.'

'I'm sure someone was –'

'Just dead fish.'

Don couldn't shake the feeling off.

'Maybe they're in that lot, stuck in a wrecked car and about to be squashed.'

'You're a fraud, Don.'

'Are we there yet?'

'You're a devious bastard.'

'No.'

'Really, though, you're just an empty shit.'

'Fuck off, you can't see what's inside me.'

'I am inside you. Just go through that door.'

Through the doorway was a steep set of stairs. Don, effortlessly this time, climbed upwards, past shimmering walls and over steps that made harsh shadows beneath his feet. Then he stood in a long corridor, one that stretched away like a deep well into blackness. Don was scared. Something was coming up and out of that dark. He pulled open a side door and quickly stumbled through. An empty room, bare floorboards and the half-light of dawn. Don looked around. Something was still not right. Slowly, like an insect creeping up his neck, he felt fear squirm back in. That feeling again, he was not alone and something was in the shadows. He then heard the breathing, over in the far corner, like a thumb rasping a comb. Fear burst right through and he became rigid. The breathing became louder, throatier and close. 'I blew it before.' Don heard that thought as if it was actually spoken. He turned. A thin white face with pleading eyes confronted him. Don shied back but the face kept coming. It rose up and hovered. Then it opened its mouth. Blood, a gob gush of warm blood splattered down.

Rain again, and Don was in the car trying to work his way through looping expressways that led north of the city. The windscreen wipers were working hard – squeak and thud, three frames a minute – bleak scenes of bumpers, brake lights and stained concrete. Don was trying to be just-a-body, a functionary focused on destination only. But it wasn't easy. The night-before spliff had left him groggy and each thud of the wipers made his head wince. And he knew he was riding more than just the car. Somewhere, not far back, a torrent was gushing down the street, a flood surge of lousy dreams and unwanted memories. But there was something else that alarmed him even more. Half an hour back, when shaving in front of the mirror, he heard a voice. Not, he thought, his voice, but more like words eavesdropped by an open window. *'Face facts, you will have to do it, Don.'* It was out of nothing, clear as a bell and in his head. Scary. So Don was running, grimly thrusting the car through the wet, hoping he'd reach Mal Chariot's place soon.

Mal owned a club called Garvey's. Nothing much to shout about, a small-time drinking den with dancing girls and live gigs at weekends. The guy at the door told Don that they had plans to 'Mek it the firs black lap dancing she-bang.' He also told Don that Mal was out down Paradise having his morning coffee.

Don hunched up and sloshed his way down the street, hoping he'd out-run the flood and was getting back to normal again. He quickly pushed through the doors of the restaurant and shook himself down. The Paradise was obviously an evening joint with its low lights and thick curtains.

Don headed towards the shadowy rear where a couple of guys sat. In a large glass tank on the left, fish the size and shape of small plates swam. It seemed he was expected. Jackie was still smoothing the way. Mal sat with a balding Asian guy. This guy had a surly look on his stubbled face and a dirty shirt on his bulging gut. Don was told this was Ahmed, long-time business partner of Mal; but Don only got to exchange wary glances. The guy took himself off as Don sat down.

'Can't be bad if you fame precedes you, eh man?'

'What you mean? Right . . . Jackie's been in touch.'

'Yeh, but a guy who work for Pat Connor too.'

'You know of him, huh?'

'Sure, I get news from up north. I'm a player, ennit? You gotta tread careful whatever you do, so it pay to keep in touch wid what a go on.'

'Saves me some explaining, I guess.'

'You can't blame a man wantin revenge for im daughter death.'

Mal was a big guy, but his muscular frame was on the wane. His once good ebony looks were slipping down into cheek gullies and his short, cropped hair glinted grey. Don felt comfortable with that.

'I saw your ex yesterday. She kind of recommended you.'

'Bet she did.'

'Thought you might know nasty types who'd do harm to a nineteen-year-old.'

'Sally don't miss a chance to dig the knife in. You see Bridie too?'

'Yeh. Seemed to be on her mum's side, I'm afraid.'

'Tch, she a come back to me in time. She dat age man, self-conscious, rebellious, an ungrateful for what her father im done.' Mal's dismissive shrug didn't hide the hurt. 'You got kids, man?'

'Yeh, a daughter like you, she's sixteen.'

'An is you on good terms?'

'Haven't seen her for ages.'

'Fuck . . .' Mal pulled out a packet of fags and gave one to Don. His back seemed stiff and creaky. He blew out his first drag with vehemence. 'Shit scene, eh, two abandoned dads an Pat Connor los im girl for good.'

Don felt that, the sadness, and he felt disconcerted by Mal making the observation.

Hi, how's the big city treating you, Dad? I can hardly imagine it now. How's this for a comparison? Today we went out on the Minch for a field trip. We were on the look out for basking sharks. Their great mouths gobble up the Gulf Stream and reach us about now. No luck. Just a pair of cheeky seals scrounging for scraps. Isn't that the way of it?

Don cast a glance over at the tank and watched the flat fish endlessly circle. Yeh, some comparison.

'Silver dollars.'

'Wha?'

'The name a dem fish.'

'Really.'

'Dat's Ahmed for you, even im fish are money. I tell you, man, the guy look like a tramp but im worth a million. Can't break the habit. Come here dirt broke, go for years savin all im penny, an even now, when rich, im can't bring imself to waste money on new clothes and ting. Dem fish an im sons are im only indulgence.'

Don watched the fish for a few moments more. He kind of liked the jerky movements they made and could see why people kept them to relax by. He also thought about what lay in Kate Connor's throat. He turned back to Mal. 'So, Mal, you ever meet Kate?'

'Briefly, jus the once, at home when she was leavin. Did'n say anytin. She seem shy an mebbe a bit scared, like a mouse.'

'Big bad Daddy.'

'Could be, but she seem nice enough. Me did see her once wid Bridie down the club too an dat was it. Dere's nuttin me can add now to what me a said before, cept a course ita sad she been found dead.'

'So, then or now, there's no connection you can make with your scene and Kate that might have led her into trouble?'

'No, man, but me can't guarantee that there weren't no connection. Me don't know all that a go on.'

'Do you know guys around who might pick on a girl like Kate?'

'Fuck, man . . .' Mal eased back in his chair and massaged his neck. He took in a dose of fish therapy before speaking. 'Me know plenty crazy types but always keep dem at arm's length and dem never get close to me private life. But there mebbe is one guy you shoulda check out, gauge im reaction, cos im is a nutter an me would'n put anytin past im. But me got no other reason to mention it, right?'

'I'll try anything at the moment.'

'Im call Khalid. Me do business wid the guy, reluctantly, watchin me back all the time.' Mal shrugged. He got a pen out and wrote on a napkin. 'Dis im number, tek it or leave it, man. Me can't tink a damn all else.'

'I'll take it, crumbs and all.'

Don eased up out of his chair. He felt reluctant to move. There was a wet city outside. Silver dollars and time spent with a crook in Paradise seemed quite a bit better.

'Thanks for your help. I might come back to you some time.'

'No problem, man. Dat murder was bad an it need sortin.'

'I know it.'

'An don't forget to tell Pat that me help, you know what me sayin?'

'Sure, you want to keep sweet with him.'

'Me hear dat im been havin trouble up on im own patch an blood is bein spill.'

Don stiffened. The word 'blood' shot through his defences and sent sparks spluttering through his nervous system. Mal surely couldn't know? Don put a huge effort into appearing unconcerned. 'Nah, that's all sorted.'

All Don's reluctance was suddenly gone and he quickly slipped away into the cold anonymity of the streets.

*

Charcoal skies had ceased to give off rain, but clouds still hung low and wisps of them swirled around the tall buildings. Don was having lunch in some canalside restaurant, avoiding the hotel room and voices that spoke out of nowhere. He sat by the window with a view of brick walls and rippling black water. No one was outside. Smoke drifted from a moored barge. Don ate without enthusiasm as he thought back to Mal and the pain on his face when he talked of his daughter. A feeling he knew only too well.

Eighteen months ago, that was when his ex and Melanie went up to Skye. Of course they'd split up a few years before that, but then he'd seen his daughter a lot. Skye was a shock, but there was little that Don could do. He stared at the canal. Lunchtime and everyone had their lights on. They flickered and fragmented on the black waters. He did go up there once. A day-long journey up into wilderness, through endless mountains and swathes of water; a meandering ordeal across a strange and morbid landscape. It was a mistake. Tense conversations, blame and the emotions of unhealed pain. He thought he remembered a kind of retreating love-look in Melanie's eyes as though a process of grieving was well underway. But Don's main memory was of the sea. Standing silently yearning, listening to the waves and looking at that vast and lonely horizon.

Don pushed his food away half finished. He was getting maudlin, soon more pressing anxieties would start to niggle and he'd be on the run again looking for distraction.

'Hello there, Jackie. Don here. Thought I'd give you a buzz and tell you the latest.'

'Yeh? Well that's OK.'

'Been to see Mal. Not much has come out of it, though it turns out he knows of Pat Connor.'

'That don't surprise me.'

'The only thing he suggested was I see some geezer called Khalid. Not any good reason for it, other than the guy would be quite capable of doing harm to a girl like Kate.'

'Don't know him.'

'I can but try. I guess it's just a case of turning over stones, stirring waters and hoping something pops out.'

'Be careful. Mal, in many ways he's all right, but you can't trust the guy that much. He might have a reason of his own to finger this Khalid.'

'Yeh? Well, thanks for the tip.'

'You ain't out the doghouse yet.'

'Guess not, huh? So . . . how bout I buy you a drink later?'

'I dunno, Don.'

'I'll try and make it bullshit free.'

'Hah, really? I suppose it's a start. Let me think about it and I'll ring you later.'

'I'll give you my mobile number . . .'

Back in the hotel room again, those four small walls and a window view of concrete. Don was glad for the conversation but a restless night was catching up on him and he felt tired. He lay on the bed thumbing the sea bean, trying to think about the job and the angles he could seek to check. That photo of Kate Connor propped up on the bedside cabinet: so much time had passed and memories were fading. The image now was a skeleton in a strange and forgotten place. Don struggled to connect the two and was fearful of what emotions might surge when he finally did. His thoughts were interrupted. His arm eased over to the ringing phone.

'How's it going, Don?'

'Wet as Manchester.'

'Right, and cold too, yeh?'

'Only with the leads I'm getting.'

'Guess it's going to take some time.'

'Reckon so, Pat. I checked out someone you might know, a guy called Mal Chariot.'

'Yeh, the dad of Kate's friend. I know of him – drug dealer, keeps to himself – but I don't reckon I've had any direct contact.'

'He wasn't much use really, but he did sort of set me thinking.'

'Oh yeh?'

'I guess it's a question that has to be asked, you know, about your enemies.'

'Fuck, what about them?'

'Would there be someone who'd want to hurt you by murdering Kate?'

'Shit, Don, that's a bastard of a thing to think.'

'Why's that?'

'Well, you know, it bring things right to my door, for fuck's sake, and that ain't nice to contemplate.'

'You've never thought about it?'

'Fuck, Don.'

The phone went silent. Don sensed edginess and imagined Pat running a hand over his balding head as he always did in a taxing situation. The receiver rustled back to life.

'OK, yeh, it did cross my mind. At the time, when she went missing, I got into a right state, thought about everything as anybody would. I even thought she might've been kidnapped by some shitface who'd send me a note asking for dosh. Nothing did come of course, and then, well there was no one I was seriously in dispute with. The Halligan problem happened after.'

'But you don't really know for sure?'

'Shit no, how can I? I'm gonna have some doubts and feel lousy because of it.'

'I wish you'd raised the possibility right at the start.'

'Don, I really don't think my business has anything to do with Kate's death.'

'Go through it in your mind, Pat, one more time, just in case. There might be some little connection you might have missed.'

'If it'll make you happy.'

'It will.'

'By the way, Don, the reason I rang, there's something I maybe should tell you.'

'Huh-uh.'

'It's rumours, OK? But some of my guys, they've been picking up whispers from Halligan associates.'

'Oh no.'

'Don't worry, it's just small talk and I'm checking it out now.'

'What they saying?'

'That trouble we had, they just can't accept the fucking verdict. They're getting more uppity and making plans, you know, about what to do about us.'

A dockside. Silhouetted crane jutting over oily water. Cast-iron bollards growing out of the quay and further down, amid the darkness, the looming prow of a ship, its triangular shape puncturing the faint glow of the night sky. Don hadn't been to the docks in ages. In front of him was a tide gate, two doors of solid steel, a foot wide, that cut across the lapping reach and joined the quay to a yard heaped with twisted metal. Don shivered. He was alone and he felt worried. What was he doing there? Waiting for someone, or searching? He found himself walking towards the tide gate. The feeling was there that someone, or something, was lurking in the heaps of metal across the water. He just had to go. But the gate, it had but one low down rail and on either side, ten feet below, was the black drowning deep of the dock. Don feared such watery places, he could not swim, but yet he was now on the gate, on his hands and knees inching across the void. Halfway across, doubt struck. His senses told him someone was behind. Don, crouching down, felt there was a man in the shadows watching him. The hairs on the back of his neck rose and he froze midstream. He even somehow thought he saw the gun as though he had eyes in the back of his head. But then something else began to move. Water was gurgling and the tide gate beginning to turn . . .

Don thought he caught sight of clouds through the hotel window. He was conscious of sweat and that his body was twisted into a strange shape before he let himself be pulled back down.

Sunlight on crystal-clear water. Don could see the blue sky and white puffy clouds moving silently along like an armada of balloons. He realized he was floating, floating on water and this proved a happy surprise. So maybe he could swim after all. 'What the fuck . . .' Don let his head rest on this liquid pillow for some time, would've been content to stay that way if it hadn't been for the feeling that there was something or someone swimming below him. He smiled, effortlessly turned, and then drifted down into the water. It was equally amazing. The fish that swam about him were wonderful. Yellow, blue, orange and silver; stripes and paisley patterns; and every shape you can squash a circle into. Don swirled around in the water with ease, sought to touch the jaunty fish, but then he felt his back hit something. He turned smugly, his hands felt glass and he saw his own face in front of him. He didn't like the way he was smiled at.
    'You're a fraud, Don.'
    'Fuck you.'

'You know you will have to do it.'

'I don't want to think about that.'

Don closed his eyes and wriggled around in the water. He slid further down the glass to where it was darker. When he looked again, someone else was on the other side. This guy was frantically tapping.

'You wanna know what I see, man, eh?'

It was a black guy. He had an unshaven face and wore a yellow cap.

'I tell you, man, you is a nasty piece a work an you need sortin.'

'Go away.'

'Skeleton an blood, dat is what me see, man, an a whole lot more. You is fucked up.'

'I've seen you somewhere before.'

'An I seen you, man, walkin dem streets wid you bad thoughts an murder in you heart.'

'There's nothing you know about me.'

'Yeh? I know you wanna bugger the queen, dat's one thing. I know you a plannin violence an anarchy an woulda best be lock up in a madhouse.'

'Fuck you.'

'We a watchin, man. You ain't gonna get away wid it.'

Don squirmed further down the glass wall where the dark was total. It seemed like he'd escaped but there were things in the dark, unseen things that poked and nibbled at him. He heard something like the sound of a whale. It could have been himself screaming.

He was sprawled almost horizontally across the bed with the cover trapped between his knees. His brow was drenched in sweat and his mouth parched dry. He groaned and hauled himself upright. The sea bean still sat in his hand. It wasn't his intention to go to sleep, just to rest, and now he felt totally disturbed. He stared at the bare walls and it took some time to work out where he was. Fuck, don't think, don't linger, he told himself. Get out the gun, grab a coffee in the lounge and then seek out the Khalid geezer. Before another thought could form, Don took his own advice.

5

Meridian Apartments had a locked iron gate across its entrance and an intercom system where you had to punch buttons and ask for access. Don did this, feeling resentment as he stooped to the mike, his eye on a camera that poked its lens right onto him. This was once a factory area full of rattling machinery and oil-smeared guys snatching time out for a Park Drive buzz. Now it was a fenced enclave for the rich. Don could see the end of the road where the railings ended and, beyond, what seemed like a council estate – low pay and state benefits land. Khalid responded on the intercom and the gates opened. Don smiled at the craziness of it all and then got into the hire car, ready to park up among the more prestigious marques that littered an inner quadrangle. He then hauled himself through a red-brick arch, authentic factory remnant, and up brand-new steps to flat 27.

Khalid was brusque at the doorway, a man on the move slotting Don in on his busy schedule.

'Be with you in a min, mate, on the phone, and getting me dinner together.'

Don went into a bright kitchen and stood by the window. Dusk had fallen, a cold dusk full of drizzle and bleary city-centre lights. Don could see a canal below him, where sky reflections swam beneath a film of mist that draped the water's surface. Another bad dream place, a place where people might dump unwanted pets. Khalid bustled back into the kitchen. He plonked a wok down loudly on the cooker.

'Smart place you got here, right in the heart of it all.'

'Can't says I notice it much.'

'No? Trendy canalside apartment? You've got to appreciate what you're paying for.'

'For business, mate, that's what I got it for, that and the clubs and the four miles it gets me away from my ex. The canal, fuck, who cares?'

'Right . . .'

'Don't give much of a toss about it, me. I mean, have you seen the neighbours? Opera snots! Rich fucking accountants who're into fucking gyms, theatre and antiques.'

Khalid lined up a selection of vegetables on the work surface – mushrooms, pepper, spring onions and okra – and drew a gleaming knife out of a wood block. He was a short, stocky guy; very muscular with a round brown face. Don couldn't get much of an initial make on him. He talked a lot but didn't seem like a nutter.

'Not much of city bloke anyway, grew up on the Callow Estate, me. You're surrounded by fields up there.'

Khalid began to chop.

'You could wander the fuck all over and run wild. And we were wild I tell you. Get out the old air pistols and hunting knives and it were like we was fucking guerrillas in Afghanistan. Bagging ducks, chickens, even got a fox once. Remember that, cut its head and tail off for trophies, still got the fucking skull somewhere . . . must be at my ex's.'

With thick clumsy fingers, Khalid began to pile the vegetables into his wok, along with oil and soy sauce.

'Course, that were before we got into drugs and stuff, beating up other gangs, gutting old ladies' cats.'

Khalid cast a glance over at Don. He winked and then grinned. The smile, that was the first thing that wasn't right, a forced leer more like. Don got a good look at his eyes and he found himself easing back. Crossed slightly, looking at Don's shoulder, and an expression that irked, a kind of spiteful defiance. Don checked out an exit route.

'You've gone beyond me, Khalid. I'm not from around here.'

'So I hear.' Khalid shoved a wooden spoon into the steam and sizzle and began to stir. 'You better tell me what that fucking Mal has sent you down here for.'

'I'm sure he told you, about Kate Connor, the young woman who went missing over a year back and has recently turned up dead.'

'Must say it didn't ring any bells.'

'Yeh? But you thought you'd see me anyway?'

Khalid yanked open the freezer door with a hairy forearm. A packet of frozen prawns got torn apart and dumped into the wok. The ice doubled the steam. 'Fuckin Mal, the guy's past it,' grumbled Khalid as he stirred. He turned and gave Don an off-centre glare.

'I said I'd see you cos fuckin Mal said it'd be good for business, you having connections or whatever. So I'm seeing you, right?'

'You don't remember anything at all about this girl, friend of Bridie, around when Mal was still with his wife?'

'Always precious bout his soddin family and now look what's happened. Girls, mate, I see em by the thousand.'

Khalid grabbed the wok handle and tossed the contents around. He grabbed a prawn to test if done and then piled the food onto a plate. Still standing, he picked up a fork and began to shovel away.

'You don't know, then, any guys on the scene who might go too far with a young virgin?'

Khalid shook his head as he wolfed the food. Don felt irritated and sickened.

'I mean, are you into young virgins?'

Eyes narrowed, but Khalid replied, 'Fuck no.'

'What are you into, then?' Don tried to sound conspiratorial.

'White trash mostly.'

Khalid scooped up the last of his meal. The fridge door was quickly opened and a can sprung by a thick finger. He took a large swig of lager and belched. The snidey smile returned.

'I like to fuck white woman cos they're hot an easy an got no shame.' Khalid raised a hand and rubbed his greasy fingers together.

'Mal said you were a charming guy.'

'Doing me bit to corrupt the infidels. Shoot em up, bang em after.'

'Right, so you're on a mission.'

'A duty, mate, and I take the honour serious.'

Don began a slow edge towards the kitchen door. The 'nutter' Mal spoke of had appeared, that, or the guy was doing a major wind-up. Worth a further nose, he thought, but cautiously, behind his back. Khalid's crossed eyes and bellicose manner, they made Don feel odd about himself, like he was no better and had his own sordid agenda. *You will have to do it!* Those words didn't speak in his head this time, but he was conscious of them all the same and they made him more uncertain.

'What you looking at, mate?'

'Eh?'

'Are you giving me the hard eye? Worse, are you fucking judging me?'

'N-no, just thinking about where I might try next.'

'No you weren't. You were thinking I might be the guy who did that girl in, you were putting me down as scum.'

'You've got it wrong, Khalid.'

'I hear voices, man. It's a gift I have, hear em from all over and I'm hearing them in you now.'

Khalid began to move towards Don, his beefy arms hanging loose, and those flawed eyes probing.

'I'm just doing a job, mate.' Don put his hand on the gun in his pocket and moved towards the front door. 'No angle, I promise you, but to check things out.'

'Yeh, I sensed something first off. You're an evil fuck, I reckon, an you better get out quick before I screw your head off.'

'Don't worry, I'm off.'

Still staring intently, Khalid stopped and put his hands on his hips.

'I fucking well know it now . . .'

'Well, see you, and thanks, Khalid.'

'YOU'RE ONE OF THEM.'

Don didn't want to think what the last words meant. They touched some nerve within. He was relieved when those iron gates opened automatically and he could escape.

He did manage to set up a meet with Jackie. She was working late, bad sign, and his offer gave her an excuse to leave the office. Don was pleased. A night in the hotel or some bar on his own was a bad prospect – those things going on inside himself. They met up at the Black Swan. Near his hotel but in the back streets away from the club hustle. A basic working-class boozer with brewery ornaments and fake beams. A few regulars propped up the bar as Don ordered a vodka for Jackie and a ginger beer for himself.

'That's a surprise. Thought you'd be a whisky man.'

'I'm trying to cut down.'

'How bad is it?'

'I'm not an alky if that's what you think, but I can overdo it once I start.'

'Can't leave the pub without being pissed.'

'Your classic binger.'

Jackie's body was nicely draped in a simple black dress. She sat opposite, ran fingers through her pink-tinged hair and then exercised her shoulders a little. Don tried to ease up too. All that he saw, it felt good, but the tenseness in his jaw was hard to shift.

'You sounded edgy on the phone. How was it with this Khalid bloke?'

'Not nice. A real pile of shit that guy. He ended up threatening me.'

'You touched a nerve.'

'Yeh, it was all a bit weird.'

'You think that was because of Kate?'

'I dunno, it's possible and I wouldn't rule it out, but I reckon the guy's nuts anyway.'

'I'll ask around, see what I can find out.'

'That'd be good. I guess it's worth working around the Mal and Khalid situation and maybe going back to Bridie too, without her mum present.'

'I could do that.'

'Yeh?'

'If you don't mind.'

'No, but I thought . . .'

Jackie avoided Don's gaze and took a sip from her drink. He could sense she was still pissed off with him but was apparently keen to stay with the case.

'Spoke to the boss today,' he said cautiously, 'bout his enemies and possible fuckery up north. He said he'd gone through all that and felt certain his circumstances had nothing to do with the murder.'

'You believe him?'

'Can't see why not. Why would he send me down here if he felt something might come back to haunt him?'

'Send you down with a false name.'

'Yeh, right . . .'

Jackie's eyes were back to probing. It was Don's turn to

check out the bar's décor and sip his drink. Could he tell her the whole truth yet? Nah, he thought, might put her off.

'It's really no big deal,' he said. 'There's this spat going on, been going on for about nine months, between Pat and this group of toughs run by John Halligan. Threats and counter-threats, you know the kind of thing, so Pat's being careful.'

'Huh-uh. How far are you in with Connor?'

'Maybe a bit more than I should be.'

'That ain't good practice now, is it, Don?'

'No, but in a way, this Kate business, if I can sort it, I can restore the balance and be more choosy.'

'You mean he'll be eternally grateful to you.' She pulled a face. 'Now where have I heard that before?'

'Situations, Jackie, don't we all have them?' Don ventured a smile. 'Though I can't say I know anything about yours.'

Jackie leaned back in her chair and smiled calmly back. Don almost met it full on. His eyes were growing in confidence, noting the curve of her chin and a small mole that nestled close to an ear.

'That's a pushing boundaries remark, Don.'

'You've been curious enough about me.'

'Just checking your business credentials.'

'Oh, right, but don't you think that sounds just a little bit boring?'

'And you reckon other things about you will be anything less?'

'Woh.' Don began to think he should've had that whisky. 'Anyway, you started it, took me up that godawful hill and got my defences down.'

'That was still business, Don . . . well, most of it.'

'Straight up, though, Jackie, it'd be nice to get to know you a bit. I've been here, what? Two days? And it's all been a bit sad and miserable. Jesus, it's rained most of the time. Friendliness with a lady would be welcome, that is, if you're free or whatever. See? What do I know about you?'

Jackie picked up her drink and took a sip. She seemed seriously thoughtful at first but then Don thought he detected a glimmer of a smile.

'We both have the same look in our eyes.'

'Yeh.'

'But you're a guy who's just passing through.' There was a hint of playfulness on her face.

'I guess that is true.'

'Looking for a little fling, are we? Something you do on all your cases?' The smile was fully apparent now.

'Of course, it's standard procedure.' Don smiled back. 'Really, I'm being straight up here.'

'I dunno, Don. As you say, "situations" . . .'

'Think about it.'

Jackie leaned forward, put her elbows on the table and rested her head on her hands.

'Yeh, well, it's been a long time, things have happened, Don, and I don't know where I'm at with this. And of course, you, you've still got a firm entry in my bad books.'

'Shit, the complications of life.'

'Terrible, ennit?' Jackie sighed. 'Yeh, well . . . maybe I am doing too much work.'

Rain was back, a cold, wind-driven rain that stung Don's face as he returned to the hotel. The kind that couldn't be ignored, coming at all angles, with sudden cruel surges at street corner and alleyway. But he did all right at blanking it out. Warm stirrings within. The difficult search, the threats and the voices, they'd been blown into darkness and Don was smiling with the honeycomb city lights. A blunder. As he turned and walked towards the bustle of Broad Street, up ahead three men got out of a car. With no words and no fuss they moved swiftly towards him. He had only the briefest chance to register danger and none to react. Hands grabbed at Don. Something flew half hidden in the dark like a bat and – *crack!* He saw a blast of light before his eyelids sagged and his legs went wobbly. The hands gripped him painfully like pincers. He heard a muffled voice – 'Take him over there' – and his feet scuffed the pavement as his sagging body was hauled away.

When he came to, Don was in a subway, a dingily lit concrete hole, the walls scrawled with graffiti. His eyes tried to focus on the swirls of spray paint, tried to pull out a word to make some sense of, a solid pronouncement he could grab hold of, but it was all blurred and unintelligible. Two men were holding him up against a wall. A pallid stubbly white guy on his right, a wiry Asian guy on his left and Khalid pacing up and down in front of him. He was mumbling, punching his hand and looking up at the dim lights of the subway.

The Asian guy leaned his head close to Don's ear and started whispering. 'Just take what comes, man, an don't try an fight it.'

'Wha?'

'Don't know what you done to upset him, man, he just get crazy sometime, but he go apeshit if you resist.'

'Fucked if –'

'Stay cool an take it.'

Khalid was working himself up into a state. He punched his hand harder and kicked the wall. Then he shouted 'Shit fucker! Shit fucker!' and strode over to Don. The crossed eyes were burning fiercely as he scowled and bared his teeth. 'You fuckin hell are one of them, fuckin dushman!'

'Look –'

'Soon as you'd left, I was convinced, knew you had the voices, knew you were out to screw me. I fucking knew it!'

'Khalid, I –'

'Shut up, arsehole! Just listen to this, right? I know when a guy's got the ghosts, got evil voices in his fuckin brainbox. One of my talents, right, a gift, and I know I have to put their bastard lights out. Me, I should never've let you go, should've done you there and then.'

Don saw phlegm dripping from Khalid's mouth and noticed his eyes were not only askew but somehow disconnected, that they lolled uselessly while some other inner eye was at work. He was at a loss as to what Khalid was on about but yet felt queasy, almost guilty.

'So, punishment time, dushman, time to learn your lesson – YOU DO NOT WALK WITH GHOSTS!'

Khalid sent a fist thundering to the side of Don's head, whipping it back against the wall and making his ears explode with pain.

'This one's for the nasty arrogance you have.'

A punch to the jaw this time, jerking Don's head against the Asian guy's shoulder. Khalid raised his fist again and he thumped right on the nose.

'For the fuckin bitchy anger you got.'

Blood smeared Don's face and his eyes became pools of bleary water. He tried to dig his fingers into the arms of those who held him, get some focus and maybe a solid hold from which he could lash back.

'You think that the guy he had enough?' The Asian guy sounded worried.

'Shut up!'

Khalid then wound back and sent a fierce blow burrowing into Don's solar plexus.

'The worst fucking voice of all, you blaspheming shit!'

Don sagged and gagged for air, a high-pitched whine came from his mouth and his face went a sickly grey. The guys holding him let him slip down to the floor as he desperately sought to grab some air. He clutched his stomach and then felt the gun in his trouser pocket.

'You really got the bastard sorted, sent them ghost voices flying.'

'It isn't that easy. This dushman needs a mark.'

Khalid pulled out a knife, leaned down and prodded the blade towards Don's cheek.

'You done enough, boss.'

'Shut it.'

Don flopped his head towards the grimy, black floor where he saw fag ends and a cellophane straw wrapper. He struggled to work his hand into his pocket, felt the rim stretch hard and burn his skin until his fingers brushed against the gun butt.

'Th – there's something you should know,' he managed to mumble.

'Eh?'

Don shifted awkwardly around. His hand went full into his pocket. He violently tugged out the gun, thumbed off the safety catch and fired. All three men around him jolted backwards. The bullet had hit the far wall but it was the concentrated noise that had most effect. His sight was still blurred and the bells of the whole nation were ringing but Don didn't give a damn. He fired randomly around the subway, bullets screaming and ricocheting all over the place. When the fifth one was discharged and the smoke began to clear, Don found himself alone in the concrete hole. Through the dinginess, he looked at the wild scrawls of graffiti, strangely quiet and peaceful compared to the raging cacophony inside his head.

6

A bar packed with a hundred people, all talking, was an onslaught Don could do without. A gabbing orchestra compressed in a room, players fuelled by alcohol and soloists performing in shriek and guffaw. Don listened to the sound and compared it to starling flocks assembling for the winter. He felt a sense of estrangement. He was sitting mute and the noises he made were in his body. The throbbing sound in his ear, the gurgling in his stomach and the painful creaks that sounded when he moved his head. Don was eyeing up his second double whisky. He sat on a stool at the corner end of the bar counter, away from the crush of punters and their insatiable booze demands. He'd been there about ten minutes and was conscious that closing time was near. Post-attack, this spot and this succour had been his only aim. He'd staggered back through the streets, braved concern and distaste at hotel reception and then got cleaned up in his room. All this effort done with one goal – get pissed. Don picked up the double and downed it. Then he pulled out a tenner and waved it at a slim-line barmaid who seemed in danger of wasting away. She would be some time. The pub was a large hall segmented into seating areas, all parts packed, playing frantic conversational tunes at full throttle.

The Khalid onslaught had been pushed to the back of Don's mind, for the most part. It was all a question of enduring the pain and ensuring he got his reward. But he couldn't ignore it entirely. Flashbacks alighted in his thoughts and tried obsessively to stay. The question 'why?' was more dogged than most. Was it some kind of city thing? he thought. Like a random attack, muggers or hungry druggies and Don being in the wrong place? Loonies are out there uncared for in the community. But that didn't account for Khalid's personal insight. Had Don said something like *'I will have to get you'* without realizing it; or thought it, and had mad Khalid somehow read his mind? Did this confirm Don's worst fears? When his musings got this far, Don would try to shake his mind free. He'd try to think a little further back, to the early evening when he was in the pub with Jackie. Now wasn't that one gem of a possibility? This was when the smiles came, painful smiles and certainly booze induced, but he would know then that his evening's goal had been reached.

'Looks like you've found your spot.'

'What was that?'

'Like to be on the edge of a crowd, do you?'

'Right . . . always.'

'Same with me, got to have my bit of space.'

The woman standing next to Don had long blond hair and gold caps on all her front teeth. She looked to be in her forties and she struck up the conversation with Don as though she'd known him always.

'This place is a bit like a bear pit, you have to fight to get a drink and get heard.'

'What did you say?'

'I said –' The woman rolled her eyes. 'Ha-ha – you're a funny geezer.'

Don raised his glass. 'A few of these helps.'

'Let me get you another.'

'You sure?'

'Yeh, why not?'

The woman was chubby. Large bra-less breasts hung low beneath a black T-shirt over which she wore a shiny red shirt. Don got a fair whiff of perfume and thought of baubles at Christmas time.

'Most of this lot in here are barely legal drinkers, ain't it, so us older ones should stick together.'

'They shouldn't allow youth, should they? We should be the last generation.'

'Now there's a thought.' The woman managed to get her drinks order in, four in all, before she turned back to Don. 'The name's Lily by the way.'

'Don. Pleased to meet you.'

'So how come you're sitting here hiding in the corner?'

'I'm a stranger in town.'

'Oh right, a mystery man.'

'That's it, and you?'

'Guess I'm local, though I've done my share of travelling round. I'm here with a couple of friends. You could join us if you like.'

'That's nice of you.'

'In fact, we're going to a party in a bit. You could come along too.'

'I'm overwhelmed.'

The couple that Lily was with hardly gave Don a look. A smirk from the bald guy with an earring, a frown from the lady hiding beneath a cowl of black hair and green eye-liner. They were in the middle of an argument. Don couldn't hear what it was about. He picked up his whisky and tried to get words flowing with his new friend. This seemed important, a way to ride the booze whizzing through his bloodstream, a way to stop any self-conscious thought.

'So what do you do, Lily, in this big city?'

'Me? Make clothes by day and break hearts at night.'

'Yeh? I hope you do the latter in a nice way.'

'My lovers die smiling. What about you, what's the mysterious stranger doing here?'

'Sort of tourist. Come to see all the wonderful CCTV cameras you got.'

'Huh-uh . . . a violent activity, is it?'

Don fingered his face. 'To be truthful, I do bad things by CCTV cameras to see whether the guys watching clock me . . . it got a bit out of hand today.'

Lily shook her head in disbelief.

'Really, and if they don't clock me, then they get the chop.' Don smiled, painfully.

'Daft, totally, but what's it matter? Let the booze do the talking, eh.'

And the drink did talk in the ridiculous ways it does until it was time to leave for the party. Lily grabbed Don's arm as they reeled behind the moody couple, out into damp air and down a gloomy side street to a parked car. Don and Lily heaved into the back and helplessly lolled against each other. The bald guy shot the car off excessively fast and very soon front-seat nigglings restarted.

'Anyway, Dawn, it's always you who tries to manipulate things.'

'No it's bloody well not.'

'You know it, sneaky you are sometimes.'

'Oh yeh? Well, you just stick your head up your arse and pretend nothing's happened.'

'No, I don't . . .'

Lily put her arms around Don and nuzzled her face into his neck. 'Been like this all evening,' she whispered. 'Drives you mad.' She then nibbled his ear, undid his overcoat and put an arm around his waist. Don began to feel engulfed. Perfume, embracing hands, sour words, dark confinement, fast-flowing city lights – his woozy head began to spin. *You got the ghosts, Don, I can see it, you got those evil fuck voices and I tell you – you do not walk with ghosts!* Don responded to Lily's clinch, squeezed hard and kissed her forehead.

Up front, Baldy was still driving fast and his dialogue had become blunt and vicious: 'Stupid bitch!' 'Snidey bint!' 'The fuck why I bother!'

'*But you will do it, Don. Hide or evade as you may, you've done it before and you'll want to again – pain demands it.*'

'No, no, no way will I do that.'

'What was that, Don?'

'Eh?'

'What you just said?'

'Shit, I think I've just drifted off.'

'Daft, totally, so give us a proper kiss.'

Lily brought her head up to Don's, but before he could get to grips with scarlet lipstick and gold-capped teeth, the car swerved left and then shuddered violently to a halt.

'Well, here the fuck we are,' Baldy said, 'so let's get pie-eyed. Jesus, I need it!'

Out of the car, Don took in a few big gulps of cold air as he heard rainwater drip off trees and muffled music coming from the semi in front of him. A typical residential area. Don felt he could be anywhere. Then Lily grabbed his arm and they slouched towards the house.

'So, Don, tell me, do you always talk in your sleep?'

'Wouldn't you like to know?'

'Yeh . . .'

Inside, it was back with the booze orchestra, frenetic collective noise, backed up this time by dance music and people snogging on stairs. Don and Lily dumped their coats on a large pile and headed for the drinks. A meandering squeeze through to the kitchen, Don getting glimpses of bare shoulders, chortling mouths and glazed, smiley eyes. In the kitchen, Lily grabbed a half-full bottle of vodka and a couple of paper cups.

'Well, we don't want to have keep coming back in here.'

They eased their way into one of the living rooms where the music was low and most people just talked. They claimed a corner and Lily filled the cups generously.

'You seem in quite good shape, Don, from what muscles I could grope.'

'I do all right.'

'You've got a bit of – what do they call it? – charisma.' She slurred the last word badly.

'I promise you, I'm totally germ free.'

'Ha, so what d'you really do?'

'I told you, undercover investigator. I try to find out what people really think.'

'Well, that'd be a damn hopeless job.'

'Too right, I can hardly work out what I'm thinking.'

Don noticed there was a fish tank in the room, a small one where frilly little fish danced around plastic leaves and a plaster skull. He watched for a while but his sight began to blur. The vodka was beginning its corrosive journey around his veins.

'You married, Don?'

'Nah, you?'

'Nah. Tried it once a long time ago but found I like my freedom best.'

'Sounds good, if you can cope.'

Lily gave Don a sour look. 'There's no easy way with anything, is there? I guess I like to see myself as a traveller. You know, to see that when shit happens, there's hassle, but opportunity too, you know, when you have to move on. Fuck, I'm rambling, talking a pile of shite.'

'No, sounds a good philosophy, that's something I could go with.' Don took a shot of booze and raised his eyebrows. 'Been to a lot of countries, have you?'

'Lots.'

They both smiled and began to kiss. Their bodies lurched

and they held their drinks cautiously away from them. Don enjoyed the touch, the surge of feeling, and he tried hard to get lost in passion. It worked for a while. Then the voices from the people near by suddenly seemed to rise in volume and he found himself getting distracted.

'You can tell he's playing at it, more concerned about the audience and winning money than the relationship.'

'Could be the future, that.'

'Well, there's enough cameras around.'

'Imagine just doing everything on the basis that you're being watched.'

'Horrible.'

'Some people are empty headed enough to enjoy it.'

'For some people, it proves they exist.'

Don eased up on the kissing and looked around him. He didn't like what he saw. Faces were doing weird things. One was stretched and balloon-like. A woman's nose became a snout, feral and sniffing at the air. Another guy, the pupils in his eyes slithered inwards so he had the cross-eyed look of Khalid. Don shook his head and exhaled loudly.

'You all right, Don?'

'Feeling the booze, I reckon.'

'Let's go and dance, work some of it off, eh.'

They did. A push through to the next room and they found space to get a groove going – a lumbering and unco-ordinated one. The music came from a chart compilation, vaguely familiar tunes that Don might have heard in a supermarket. But there was rhythm, so he could hold onto Lily and try to effect some movement. He looked at her eyes – cornflower blue, definitely sharp, and also self-contained. She had a pleasant smile on her face and her cheeks were burning red.

'Don't do this much, do you, Don?'

'I have my moments.'

'Mind you, it is hard work.'

'I'm not entirely sure where my body is.'

A few more songs and Lily began to sag. She suggested a break. Don was glad, for though the rush of alcohol had eased, the world around him still seemed fluid. People and objects shifted shape as though seen through water. More staggering through crowds until they managed to collapse on an empty sofa.

'Shit.'

'Phew.'

'Been a long, long day.'

'Give us a cuddle.'

Don put his arms under the red shirt and began to massage Lily's back gently. Comforting, but odd. Who was this woman and what was he doing with her? Don yawned. He tried to think back to Jackie but couldn't, just became aware of the pains in his head. He looked at the room – strange, and the people – equally strange, and then he thought of the house in an unknown place in a strange city and he felt utterly lost. Don tightened his embrace and buried his head in shadowed flesh.

Don was floating, his whole body outstretched on still, dark water. A canal perhaps. He could see swirling mist, dancing vapours that glowed with coloured lights and occasionally parted to reveal thickly knitted clouds. Could he lift up off the water, or be sucked from it by the power of that dense sky? Then a man with a balloon face came into view and said 'Welcome'. Don was in a room lying on the carpet. There were people everywhere and he had to struggle up to avoid being trodden on. A party, a mad party where bodies jostled and sprawled, maybe a crazy drugs party. He felt exposed, looked around frantically and found himself face to face with Khalid. 'You're an evil fuck.' Khalid took a vicious bite out of a burger, then licked a greasy finger and stuck it up in Don's face. The

63

*room went into a liquid swirl. Don felt nauseous. He was
angry and wanted to move but someone was holding him,
breathing hot air down his neck. Don pulled, struggled
and wrenched himself away. He began to squeeze through
bodies, bodies bigger than him and stubbornly assertive.
Then another glimpse of Khalid. With a young woman on
a sofa, Khalid had his greasy fingers between her legs. The
cross-eyed one looked over and laughed. Don began to
fight the bodies – stepping, falling, crawling. He had his
gun out, but failing, always he kept failing to get a clear
shot.*

'Don!'

'Er, yeh . . . ?'

'Wake up now. I'm going to call a taxi.'

'Right.'

Don was conscious of Lily easing him to one side. He
smiled blearily and tried to prop himself upright on the
sofa but the urge to return to dreams was compelling. His
eyes failed to stay open as Lily left the room.

*Was he back at the party? There was something going
on behind a door but the room he was in was empty.
Almost. As Don went to try the door handle, a voice
spoke out of nowhere. 'You will have to do it.'*

'Nah.'

'I'm telling you, you go through that door and you'll do it.'

'What do you know?'

'More than you think.'

'Who are you, anyway?'

'A friend.'

'You're that bloody camera snooper, right?'

'The fuck I'm not.'

'Don! Come on, you dopey bugger, I've got a cab outside.'

'I don't like snoopers.'

'What? Jesus, Don, let's get you up. You need fresh air.'

Don's eyes eventually focused on the scarlet and gold of

Lily's mouth. He sniffed her perfume and allowed himself to be pulled up by her.

'Come on, luv. We'll get you home, give you a strong coffee and then I'll let you have a Lily special.'

'Sounds good.'

'More than.'

The rush of cold air was a shock. It felt as though his sweat had suddenly frozen and he'd be dead in seconds from Arctic exposure. He gladly rushed to the cab and back into Lily's arms. The car drove off into the damp night.

'D'you ever talk to yourself, Lil?'

'Sure, all the time.'

'And do you ever answer yourself back?'

'What? You're daft, totally, you are. But I guess I do in a kind of way.'

'That's encouraging.'

He was swimming with the fishes. Some fast-flowing river, a kind of aquatic motorway, where lines of silver fish swam with the current, their big yellow eyes like head-lights in the flow. Don joined in with the traffic and heard the fish talking.

'You gotta be careful.'

'Too right.'

'Cameras, sensors, detectors, even satellites in the sky.'

'Ain't a fish in the sea they can't find.'

'Talk about endangered species.'

'Fuck yes, dangerous to speak or move.'

'Think, even, they're working on ways to tap your thoughts.'

'Shit, we'll have to switch off our minds.'

'Huh, hardly worth existing . . .'

'Come on, Don, you sleepy sod, it's moving time again.'

'Fuck, I hope this's the last time.'

'Certainly is.'

Don held onto Lily as they left the taxi, hauled up a

short path and entered a small block of modern flats. The lift doors were already open, so they eased in and Lily punched a button.

'Nearly there.'

'Blimey, swanky, this lift's got carpet on the walls.'

'Nothing special, probably a mistake by the carpet fitter.'

'I reckon you're a mermaid, Lily.'

'Me? Ner, like most women, I end up saving men from drowning.'

'Well, I reckon I'm in your power, which I probably shouldn't be.'

'It's the way I like it.'

The lift doors soothed open and across the hall Lily opened the door of flat 31. Don headed straight into the living room and the black leather sofa that looked so inviting.

'Right, it's the special for you.'

He entered the reception room. It was a sparse place with bare floorboards and a musty smell. He saw Melanie sitting by the window, her head half in shadow and a magazine on her lap. There was nothing he could think of to say, so he shrugged his shoulders and gave off a tight smile. Melanie's look was briefly scolding and then indifferent as she turned back to the magazine. Don moved on, opened another door and then walked into a long corridor. There were maybe a dozen doors he could try but he knew the one he had to go to.

'I told you you'd do it.'

'Who says I am?'

'Come on, Don.'

'It's just a job and I'm entitled to defend myself.'

'You've got him cornered. You know he'll attack.'

'So?'

'So, you know beforehand what will happen – that's premeditation.'

'Who are you really?'

'The name's Cory.'

'Right, well, bugger off, Cory, and let me do my job.'

Don moved down the corridor. It would be the third door on the right. As he put his hand on the knob, Don crouched down. He eased the door open, crab-walked his way in and then pushed the door closed. There was nothing he could see in the dark but he heard breathing all right. A throaty, uneven sound came from the far corner. Don pulled out his gun and primed it.

'This is the end of the line, Mick,' he then said softly. 'No way out. Ten seconds, OK, I'll switch on the light and then we'll walk out to my car.'

The breathing grew in intensity, it transformed into frantic sobs and then Don heard a yell. A shadow loomed through the dark towards him. When he saw the knife and the pale smudge of Mick's face, Don fired. There was no sound. Don leaned back against the wall and watched Mick's face begin to float towards him. It took a very long time. Dead eyes looking at the ceiling and a mouth churning around as though chewing gum. Then, above his head, there was a groan and blood exploded. Don yelled in horror, tried to duck away, but the blood came down, great globules of it splattering into his open mouth. Before he could retch, he swallowed . . .

'That's it, Don, wake up now. Time for Lily's special pick-me-up potion.'

Don opened a cautious eye, conscious he was breathing hard and sweating profusely. He saw a half-pint glass with some sort of black liquid in it.

'It'll make you feel strong, Don, full of fun and frisky. Right? And then, you're going to come with me to my bed.' Lily's mouth had grown in size. It seemed huge, a scarlet grotto glistening with gold.

7

Brief dream memory. Empty white bath and a small fish in the bottom wriggling its life away. Don distinctly heard the sound of a tail slapping the smooth surface. Then he opened an eye. Teddy bear on the bedside table. A tangle of male and female clothes. Images of the night before slotting into his mind – Lily, her place, the party – like cash cards into a machine. Don struggled over onto his back and looked at the ceiling. Those plastic stars that glowed in the dark. Then he glimpsed forward at the window. A dingy winter sky and a tree down to its bare bones. 'Shit.' Don was inclined to close his eyes again, but sleep and dreams, there'd be no better solace in that. He groaned and sought to take stock. Various body pains – Khalid. Headache and buzzing noises – booze. Perfume taste in the mouth – Lily. Feeling like crap – my life. Don tried a smile but even that hurt.

'Shit,' he repeated.

'You've only yourself to blame.'

Don froze. Not from the room, not even from his lips. He put his hand to his face and squeezed.

'You went walking with ghosts.'

No doubt, the voice was inside his head, just like that previous time, out of nowhere and clear as a bell. Don tried to hold himself still, relax, clear his head and hope for silence.

'What you did last night, Don.'

Shit, fuck, it's got to be an aberration, he thought. Over-indulgence and getting stressed out. If I just get on with things . . . With great effort, Don got himself upright and winced. A large chunk of pain jolted up his spine and cannoned into the top of his head.

'This has got to be rock bottom,' he moaned. 'What the fuck? Where the fuck? Jesus!'

As he began to brace himself for the haul to the vertical, he saw a note under the teddy's foot. He sighed and reached over.

Dear Don

Gosh, you were a wild animal in bed last night. W-I-L-DDD! Don't get me wrong, I did enjoy it but I wouldn't want to do it too often. There's a taxi card attached. Feel free to make breakfast and stuff. May-be we could meet up again and take it real slow.

Your luscious Lily (remember?)

Don did manage to get going. He did so cautiously, as though any untoward movement might trigger off an alarm, thinking maybe he was suffering a temporary error of con-sciousness, some synaptic glitch in his circuit-board brain. It was all strange. The four wigs on white polystyrene heads on the dressing table. A life-size china Dalmatian by the living-room fire. The large photo of a well-endowed nude dude in the hall. And in the bathroom, wall-to-wall mirrors, where Don saw his haggard face fly off into infinity. This view really freaked him. Which fucking one is me? He began to think he might still be dreaming and rushed off to find the phone.

'Reckon I need some kind of fucking reality check.'

'At last, you're catching on.'

'No, no, I'm not listening to this.'

'I'm just what you make me.'

'Well, that's comforting to know.' Don bit his lip and cursed himself for actually talking back.

He managed to get a taxi booked, eventually, after he'd had to say he didn't know where he was and had gone scrabbling round for an envelope with Lily's address. Then he was out as quickly as possible, forsaking food and ignoring the thought of leaving a note. The flat was another bad vibe place he wanted to hide deep in his memory. So there he was, standing on an unknown street in cold drizzle and staring at a bare tree. He felt scared, tried to blank out his mind and just be an aching, hungover body.

'You can't ignore me, you know, I could be your saviour.'

'Sod this, I've got a job to do, got to pull myself together, got to get rid of – you!'

'No point in being nasty.'

'God, the job, what is the damn job?'

A white private cab then drew up and a dour Asian driver beckoned Don in. He gave the name of the hotel and then sank down in the back seat, relieved he would be getting to somewhere familiar. He peered out of the window. Fuck, look at it all. Houses, shops, factories; people on streets and endless, criss-crossing car journeys; clusters of lives merging in and out of each other and repeated infinitely. All because you're born in some situation and have to get on with it. Shit, if you had a choice at birth, would you want to just fit into that? Don didn't like these ideas. Things didn't appear solid any more and he didn't seem part of what he saw. He hitched himself up in the seat and fumbled in his head for a more positive thought. History. The word just popped out. Don shifted around. He felt uneasy. Those ideas he'd had about leaving his past behind, the closed door and the trauma beyond. Did he really think he could just run away?

'It's got to be the case, I've got to admit it, I did kill someone.'

'*Ner, you can't do that.*'

'And why shouldn't I?'

'*It would be a big mistake.*'

'Who are you to tell me what to do?'

'*You'll just make a fool of yourself and miss the point entirely.*'

'Shit, I'm talking to you, aren't I? Acknowledging your damn existence.'

The cab driver up front then turned his head. Don got a view of grey stubble and a half smile.

'Weren't talking to me, were you, mate?'

'Well . . .'

'Just talking to yourself, eh?'

'Erm, I guess . . .'

'Don't worry. Me, I don't bother, I get all sorts. In fact, I do it meself all the time.'

Don didn't get much of a look when he arrived back at the hotel. The staff probably already had him down as a sleazeball, so were staying cool and letting the in-house dick keep an eye on him. Don didn't mind, in fact he welcomed the attention: there was someone out to get him and the hotel dick could watch his back. In his room, he went straight to the bathroom. Not a great place when you're feeling like crap. Switching on the light in the windowless room set off the vicious drone of an extractor fan. The mirror inside was shadowed and poky. Don looked at it. The image he saw seemed leathery and bloated, scuffed and bruised, with the eyes of a frightened animal. Nothing to do with me. Don shied away, undressed and turned on the shower. Don't think of myself as looking like that. The water was good, the heat sting of it, the drench and the noisy flow. It drowned out thought and enabled him to massage his body into the shape he knew it should be. By the time he began to dry off, he felt almost normal and ready to face up to the job. Almost, because he was still frightened of setting off an unsettling chain of thoughts. The decision was taken for him. The phone rang. Don went over, eased himself on the bed and picked up the receiver.

'Wow, the man is finally in.'

'Jackie.'

'I've been trying to get you all morning. You had your mobile turned off.'

'Really, and what is the time?'

'Jeez, you go off on the town after you left me last night?'

'Was it only last night?'

'I see, sounds like you've been on a serious bender.'

'I wouldn't know where to begin.'

'How about I wake you up with some of my news.'

'Open my eyes, Jackie, please.'

'Tch. It's not a lot but I did do a follow up with Bridie, on her own, first thing at the campus. Seeing you had got her thinking again, she did manage to come up with one little snippet.'

'Great.' Don was relieved. He hung onto Jackie's words like they were part of a rope pulling him back into the world.

'You know she was talking of lame ducks? Well, Bridie remembered that Kate had been a bit friendly to this duffer, some guy with learning difficulties who hung around one of the game arcades that Mal has a finger in.'

'Er, I just about get that.'

'Yeh, well, I don't know much more, cept that Bridie had a friend at this arcade that she visited and Kate would often go with her.'

'I'd say that was worth a follow up.'

'Beggars can't be choosers. I've also sent out some feelers on this Khalid guy. Might get something back later.'

'Shit, don't mention him.'

'What, you had more contact?'

'The bastard beat me up last night.'

'God! You should've rung me.'

'That was only the start.'

'You OK?'

'Yeh, just a few bruises. Look, let's meet up for dinner later, I reckon there's a lot to talk about.'

When Don put the phone down he realized he had the sea bean in his hand and that his thumb had been working the groove all the time he spoke. He smiled. Yeh, comforting all right, just like worry beads – and he stacked a pillow behind him and sprawled out fully on the bed.

'Listen to me, you is one seriously fucked up man an you need help, professional help or else the shit gonna hit the fan.'

'Nah, I've got it sorted.'

Don was in the back of a car, seemingly squashed right into a corner and tucked up like a ball. In the driver's seat, far away and looking down at him, was the Snooper, the brim of his yellow cap hiding his eyes.

'You don't get it, do you? You is conning you self. You is livin a lie. Me a tell you, when the time a come, explosions, man, death an explosions.'

'I told you, I know what I'm doing.'

'Ha!'

This was a different voice, a woman's, and it came from the passenger seat.

'Leave it be for the moment eh, Lil? Let me a try to talk some sense into him.'

'Bloody hell, why should I leave it be, that bugger, he was like a mad animal with me. I've got a bruise here, a scratch somewhere personal and, well, talk about jack-hammers.'

'Lil, cool it, eh, the man him ent well an we gotta go easy, mek him see the full extent of him sickness.'

'Fuck that, let me sock his bristled kisser.'

'Lil, forget it. Me and you huh, later, I'll gi' you such a sweetenin you'll feel like honey drippin off a silver spoon.'

'Oh, Horace.'

The phone rang again and woke him. Don shook his head, felt pain and cursed. He let the phone ring into silent submission and then reached over for a fag. The room felt exactly like what it was, a nothing place, an expensive rented doss hole, one tiny little niche in a bloody great anthill. He looked at the window, darkness falling. Once more the phone rang.

'Yeh?'

'Hey, Don, guess who this is?'

'Hopeless at guessing, I'm afraid.'

'This is Lil. You remember, from last night?'

'Oh, right . . .' Don wondered whether he could just cut the line.

'Thought I'd see how you were, you know, given the state you were in.'

'I reckon I might've just been dreaming about you.'

'Really?'

'So how come you found out where I am?'

'Nothing sinister, Don. This morning, all the contents of your jacket had spilled out on the floor. Hotel matches and your wallet. I'm afraid I snuck a look, found out you really are a private investigator.'

'I used to think it keeps the wolf from the door.'

'So, are you OK, survived me and the booze?'

'Slowly crawling back to normal, Lil.'

'I was wondering whether we could meet again, you know, no big deal, just a sober, friendly chat?'

'I dunno . . .'

'Bet you got a lot of stories to tell.'

'Well . . .' Don squirmed next to the receiver, felt vaguely guilty and surveyed the room. 'Maybe, when I got the time . . .'

'Great, I'll ring you in a day or so.'

Jackie had suggested some curry house down by Holloway Head. Do the best lassi in town. Fine, if you like the stuff, which Don didn't. Still, the Moghul Palace was as good a place as any and better for being in a different patch of town. He was glad to escape the hotel. Disturbing dreams, menace in the shadows and now Lil. Along with his gun, Don brought the sea bean. He arrived early, took a beer at the bar and tried to focus his thoughts on Kate Connor. The emotion of the case was clear but the detail of it all stayed foggy and distant. Jackie arrived, rain glistening in her hair and crimson gloss on her lips. More emotions stirred as Don took her coat and a waiter sat them at a table with a window view of a shining highway.

'Well, you look good, like a flower in the morning dew.'

'Gosh, Don, are you feeling all right?'

'Don't ask for any self-analysis.'

'Got a blackened eye, and is that cheek a bit swollen?'

'That's what you can see on the surface.'

'I mean, are you really OK? You seem different.'

Don shrugged. 'Maybe I'll tell you all about it later.'

A waiter came and took their order. Vegetarian for Jackie, chana dhal and spinach, along with the jug of lassi. Don stuck to lamb, naan and beer.

'I feel more optimistic today, Don, about this case.'

'Your help is totally appreciated. I don't feel as if I've done much yet.'

'Two ways forward maybe. One, find this lame duck by checking out the games arcade; and two, there's this Khalid guy.'

'Shit, don't mention him.'

'What did happen?'

'God, I could – grind his head into pulp.'

'Don, come on . . .'

Jackie looked alarmed. He quickly told her of his encounter. The crazy talk of ghost voices, his henchmen and the violence in the subway. 'Had to use my gun to scare them off.'

'God, that is bad . . . From asking around, I think I might have the names of those two other guys. His lieutenants or whatever.'

'Yeh, well, you'd certainly want to work round Khalid. Total nutter. Wild and dangerous. The one guy, though, he did kind of seek to protect me and I'd certainly want to meet him again.'

'There you go then, Don, progress; we're on our way.' Jackie smiled and Don noticed the way her lower lip pushed forward and made a cute little cushion he wouldn't mind nibbling on. 'So, are you going to tell me what else happened last night?'

Don leaned back in his seat and was glad when he saw the waiter arrive with the food. As the dishes were laid down, Don ducked around the waiter's arms and grinned sheepishly.

'I guess I can't remember too much actually, Jackie. After the attack, I just wanted to get blasted, went into a pub, got drawn into some party crowd and found myself this morning in the back of beyond sleeping on somebody's floor.'

Don winced inside. He shrugged at Jackie, ripped up a naan and began to eat. Jackie smiled to herself and did the same.

'Yeh?'

'What?'

'What you're thinking?'

'What should I think, Don?'

'Tell me.'

Jackie looked Don straight in the eyes. He saw the pain, maybe hunger too but also hardness. Don began to feel uncomfortable, unsure as to which part of her he was now talking to.

'I don't inspire confidence?'

'Let's say you ain't the most professional guy I've met.'

'I'll take that as a compliment.'

'I don't really know much about you, do I?'

'There is something I wanted to tell you.'

'I'm all ears.'

Don mopped up the sauce with the last of his naan and took a big swig of beer.

'Don't do it, Don!'

Shit, the voice. Don squirmed inside. Not now, he thought desperately. Go the fuck away!

'You just don't know what you're doing.'

Don grinned to hide his discomfort and then pulled out the sea bean. He pressed really hard into that groove and found that he was tapping his foot on the floor.

'I didn't give you the whole truth about back in Manchester and I guess it partly explains the way I am.'

'Go on.'

'You'll regret this, you stupid sod.'

'There's been this to-do between Pat Connor and this Halligan guy. Pat reckoned his gang were systematically ripping off his building sites, you know, heavy equipment, timber, even bricks, so he put me onto it. It was true. So we went to his office one night but it was Halligan's brother who was there. He reacted badly, a fight started and, well, I ended up shooting the guy.'

'Jesus!'

'It was awful. He rushed me with a knife, I had a split second to react –' Don sighed. 'The gun went off, the guy stalled and then flopped on top of me. At the end, as he died, he belched out all this blood and it went all over me. A horrible scene.'

'Now you've done it.'

'That sounds really terrible. I can see how you might feel fucked up.' Jackie put her hand on Don's arm, a frown of sympathy on her face. 'What happened after that?'

'There was an inquest, my response was seen as self-defence, all the evidence was in our favour and so no further action. Of course, Halligan didn't see it like that, which is why I have to watch my back.'

The proverbial load went tumbling down to the floor and Don became almost giddy with relief. Fuck you! he screamed silently at his unwanted voice. He took hold of Jackie's hands. The touch brought some sort of completion to his confession.

'Don Avoca, fuck, you're a bit of a surprising one.'

'There's probably more.'

'No more, thank you, for tonight.'

'And then there's what lies in your startled eyes.'

'Shit, hold it, mister, I want something light and frothy now, like a sorbet and real cream in my coffee.'

'Hmm, I'll go with that – and more likewise.'

Jackie smiled. It was a relaxed smile and Don thought he detected a hint of knowingness. He felt encouraged enough to lean over and peck her cheek.

'Don't think you've heard the last of me.'

8

Well, Don thought, why not? I am an outsider. It was a new morning. Cloud level near zero. A dark, damp, chilly day, the same as the last, the whole city caught in a dull weather malaise. But Don didn't mind. He'd had a no dream, deep sleep night and it was back to business whatever the environment. He was thinking of that cab ride and his morbid view of the sprawl. Those clusters of lives merging and repeating themselves infinitely. Could be on another planet, another species. Only the history inside your head makes any sense of it and even that's dodgy information. He was driving north again, searching for the Beyond the Galaxy games parlour, checking shop façades, looking for something lurid and neon. There was no doubt his chat with Jackie had worked wonders. He'd even had a full-on kiss when they'd parted. But Jackie was out on other business all day, so Don resolved to pull his finger out and show her he wasn't all hopeless. An early phone call to Mal Chariot had set him up.

'So, Don, you is still workin on you los cause.'

'Isn't that all there is to life?'

'Ha, reckon I might go wid dat, s'long as dere's bread to mek it feel all right.'

'I mentioned you to Pat. He's happy you're helping and there's just a little more help you can give if you don't mind.'

'I ent chargin feh words yet if dat's all it is.'

'That's all it is. One, I just want to check with a woman called Carmelita, about her meetings with Kate, and I was wondering whether she's still at the same place?'

'The Galaxy – yeh, sure.'

'The other thing's more touchy, about Khalid.'

'Everytin's touchy bout Khalid, did'n I a tell you dat?'

'Not exactly, not in fine detail, like how he spits out knuckles when he talks.'

'Oh shit, you musta spooked him. Some people, whoever they are, they jus spook him.'

'Reckon I must have one hell of a spook factor. Anyway, he's got a lieutenant, a sort of sane tough that Jackie reckons is called Shafaq.'

'Yeh, I know Shafaq.'

'I'm fairly sure I could have a normal conversation with this guy.'

Mal provided Don with a list of Shafaq's regular hangouts and then he finished the chat with an open invite to Garvey's.

'Jus the place for a cold winter night, nice girl, an leave you guns at the door . . .'

With its Day-Glo pink façade and silver lettering, Beyond the Galaxy exploded out into the damp winter light of the high street's dowdy shops. Don parked up and headed into the zone of escapism and alien encounters. It looked like it was too early for most space punters, with just one over-aged geek blasting shit out of foreign forces on a shoot-em-up machine. Don eased his way past the video screens and flashing bandits and headed for the change counter at the back.

A black woman with slanting eyes and a wide mouth was reading the paper and barely looked up as Don approached the grille. 'What you want, dear, tens, twenties or fifties?'

'Me? Nah, I don't like machines, just can't get on with the buggers.'

'No point a comin in here then, it all we got.'

'Cept for you, Carmelita.'

She did look then, raised eyebrows and wary eyes.

'No, I'm not the taxman or any other interfering official busybody.'

'Well, that nice to know, but it don't mean I appreciate some stranger comin in an knowing me name.'

'Right, so I guess I'd better explain.' And Don did, what Bridie said and his contacts with Mal.

'Well, that is goin back a bit, ennit?'

'I've recently figured out that history is important.'

'Yeh, but whose version a it?'

'Good point. How about yours and what you remember of Kate?'

Carmelita put the paper down and put her arms on the cash shelf in front of her. She looked up at Don, her eyes still wary but also weary and bored.

'I don't tek too much notice of what a go on here, cept for lookin out for cheats or trouble-mekers. It ent wise to do so cos, dese customer, them up to all kind of shit an this is jus a job for me, yeh?'

'Right.'

'But Bridie, it nice when she come to see me. We have we a chat an she bring in cake sometime. I remember the Kate girl but she never say much at all.'

'What about this "duffer" bloke that Bridie mentioned?'

'Ricky Smith. Total pain in the arse.'

'How so?'

'I know him half-dere an can't help it, but him was such a nuisance. Him talk to me all the time, try beg money for the games them, badger customer an always fiddle wid the machine.'

'How'd he turn up?'

'Dunno. Him mum on her own an workin, an Ricky him on disability allowance wid a bus pass. Reckon him just ride around an find place to pester.'

'Doesn't still come here?'

'Oh no, him banned. The lump threw a fit one time. Shit, I was scared I tell you. Don't know what a trigger it, but him big lad, him kick in screen, pick up one machine – sling it right across the room! One time when I happy to get the police in dem.'

'Never seen him since?'

'Never want to.'

'No idea where he is?'

'Lock up in a funny farm I hope.'

It was some sort of a lead. A mentally disabled guy prone to violence. But how would you find him? The name Smith, and then the guy wandering round a hundred square miles of brick on endless buses. Don shrugged. Something to think about later. His next concern was to find Shafaq. This action had more of a fresh edge to it, just like the bruises, that still ached. Don dug out his *A–Z* and planned an itinerary. Café Nico in Cape Hill was first. He nudged into a line of crawling traffic. It was going to be a long day.

'You didn't like that woman mentioning the funny farm, did you?'

'Oh, fuck.'

'Near the bone that.'

'Jesus, I thought I'd got rid of you.'

'Always kidding yourself.'

'Whatever, you don't exist.'

'Not nice words are they, "funny farm", just because someone's head is fucked up.'

'Certainly not nice having you in my head.'

'You could end up in one, Don, the way you're going.'

'Fucking hell.'

'Don't go on resisting. Just do the job, find the bastard killer and then let me take over. I know you're insecure and feel like a nobody but it won't be much longer before you can just shrivel up and hide.'

Don felt a sudden surge of misery and frustration. Drizzle had started once more. The wipers he set off reinforced feelings of confinement. He felt a desperate urge to yell out loud.

'Shit. What do I have to do to get rid of you?'

Don tried hard to focus on his driving, shoulders hunched over the wheel and his jaw clamped tight. His ears buzzed and he had a vague sense of feet scampering through dingy rooms within his brain. He stayed in this fearful rigid state until he did find Café Nico. Escaping the car was a relief. In the street, in the open, he felt troublesome things could scatter, maybe, like rats caught out in the light. The café itself was a very functional place. Bare white walls, yellow plastic furniture and a clean glass counter where you could buy the usual fry-ups, kebabs and a rather sad selection of bharjis. The only gesture towards decoration was a stuffed pike in a glass cabinet on the wall next to the menu. Don looked up at it cautiously.

'Did it wink at you?'

'What?'

It was a middle-aged Cypriot guy who spoke. Don guessed this would be Nico.

'You don't have to worry about Elvis. It's just the way the light hits the glass eye, some people think it winks.'

'Nico, right? Well, I wasn't too worried about the fish, and Elvis, he is dead anyway, isn't he, but –' Don checked himself. What the fuck am I saying? He put a hand in his pocket and sought out the soothing sea bean. 'Sorry, I've only popped in to see if Shafaq's been around.'

'Not today, no, he sometime come in for late breakfast but it's a couple of days now since he did.'

'Right . . . well, thanks anyway.'

Before he left, Don did sneak a quick look at the pike. Did it wink? The fuck it surely did.

Don kept the sea bean firmly in his hand. He held it tight, pressed against the steering wheel as he headed towards his next port of call. DM Autos was owned by Shafaq's brother, a back street garage in Winson Green; one of 'those' places no doubt, but Don didn't care – he was on the run again and hoping his torments couldn't keep up. Shafaq's brother didn't prove helpful, even when Don used Mal as a reference. He was a scrawny guy with tight skin and pockmarks beneath his stubble. Blank eyes and oily hands just said 'I don't know shit' and he was back under the hood doing engine surgery. Don had one last place to try and he knew he'd be expected. The bro would no doubt phone ahead. But Don wasn't bothered, he knew he just had to keep moving. He turned onto a ring road. This went through a more open expanse of the city with tall blocks of flats sprouting out of windswept green, a view of the centre and the Telecom tower shrouded in a murky haze. Something from Beyond the Galaxy, he thought, some video death scene where wooden warriors splattered pixels of blood and grunted with gun-cum. The Monument Arms finally came into view.

Don picked out the face straight away, a quizzical cool look that had stuck with him because of the nature of the occasion when they last met. Shafaq sat relaxed in a chair by the window, wearing lush blue training gear and supping lager from a bottle. He raised his eyebrows and smiled when he saw Don, as though this was just any old encounter. Don thought better of a drink. He sat down nervously, tried to shake off bad thoughts and look stern. It wasn't easy. Shafaq just smiled knowingly.

'You wanna drink, man?'

'No thanks.'

'Didn't think I'd see you again, till me bro rang, that is.'

'Thought I'd just run, yeh?'

'When them get into Khalid's bad books, most people do.'

'I'm stubborn.'

'Yeh, an spunky. That gun you pulled, it put the shits up us all.'

'I got no gripe with you, OK, Shafaq, in fact you seemed to try and help, but Khalid . . .'

'You want a bit a re-venge.'

'Not exactly, I just want to check the bastard out. I don't know if you know, but I'm a PI working on a case and Khalid may be part of it.'

'I got some garbled shit about that. It didn't make much sense. He seemed more pissed that Mal had set you onto him. Me, I just let it ride, I only do it for the money.' Shafaq fingered a thick gold chain around his neck.

'What is it with Khalid? I mean, we'd only just bloody met.'

'Which version you want? The nuts one? The holy Joe? The paranoid druggie? Fuck, I could go on, man, but I guess no one really know. He's all right most of the time, then every so often something flips him. From a business point a view that ain't so bad, you know, scares the shit outa punters, an our rivals.'

'Surprised you weren't tooled?'

'We are when we have to, you just surprised us, but you've got to be careful with guns these times. Them're gangs out there just shooting themselves up and bringing unnecessary pressure. Besides, Khalid, if he had one all the time . . . you know what I'm saying?'

'I could've been one of many victims.'

'Right.'

'Seems like you're a good influence on your boss.'

'I'm in for the business, none a this pride an power shit. I wanna make a big whack an fuck off outa it.'

Don looked around the bar. It had a kind of bright country air about it. Floral curtains, light brown wood and corn dollies hanging on the walls. Incongruous compared to a city view of the railway, shiny rails slithering into the bowels of misty concrete. Don also saw that there were cameras honed in on the bar. He shuddered and instinctively hunched up.

'Fucking spy cameras in bars.'

'Yeh, there to stop dealing. This use to be one big venue. Like living in a goldfish bowl, I know, but I ain't too bothered, makes it more relaxing for me, somewhere on our patch I can come an not get hassled for a score.'

'Right, so what about when Kate Connor went missing, were you around?'

'Yeh, I remember it, but it didn't seem anything to me. I know Mal was vex cos of the attention it was all getting. But I'm cool, I keep outa shit.'

'Not much help there.'

'I might know a guy.'

'Better.'

Shafaq smiled then and looked casually out of the window.

'OK, it'll cost me.'

9

'How's it going up there then, Pat?'
    'Like an Irishman's hurricane, dreary and dead boring.'
    'Pretty dreary down here too, but I guess not boring.'
    'You managing to make some progress then?'
    'Some movement, yeh, a couple of leads.'
    'Great, Don, I knew you'd come up with something.'
    'Too early to say, but I'm gonna have to use the company cash card, if that's OK.'
    'Well, we expected that. What we talking about?'
    'For this one, two hundred.'
    'Jesus, these snitches are getting inflationary.'
    'You should've heard what he was first asking for. And of course, it may lead to nowt.'
    'It's gotta be done though, eh, Don?'
    'Yep. So tell me, any more movements on the Halligan front?'
    'Well, still fucking rumours going round. I wish they'd come and have it out with me. The latest is they're looking to see you, thinking that since you're freelance, you might dish some dirt.'
    'Shit.' Don felt stirrings of panic, a sudden flush of sweat on his brow, and he wondered if he'd become complacent. 'Stuck in a field in a thunderstorm.'
    'What? Hey, don't worry, mate, they don't know where you are.'

'Are you sure? I mean, it's going to happen, Pat. They're going to come for us at some point.'

'No, Don, don't be so paranoid. We just keep quiet, sit it out and I'll keep you posted.'

'This place, there's enough deep shit as it is for me to step around.'

'So how are you keeping, Don? You're not, I mean, you haven't . . . ?'

'Nah, I'm OK.'

'I hope so. We should keep in touch more often.'

Don gazed at the phone on the bedside table. Not much of a way to communicate. Alive enough when speaking to someone. But now merely a lump of plastic in an empty room. He looked around. Nothing at all to relate to. A sense of dread began to seep into him, a fear that silence would rupture with stranger voices. He went to the window. In the dimming light, he saw flat concrete roofs, aerials and air conditioning machinery. Beyond, a barrier of stone towers obscuring the horizon. He looked upwards. A lone seagull was flopping across the dismal sky. Don watched its slow progress, focused hard on the faint speck of life, outsider and scavenger like himself. The silence behind him was growing in intensity – it felt charged up, buzzing and ready to break. He pushed his head against the window as the seagull disappeared from sight.

'I've got to get out of here,' he moaned. Too late.

'You know you'll have to do it.'

'Fuck off.'

'You'll kill again. You've tasted the blood.'

'I had the health tests for that and I was OK.'

'Don't be an arsehole, you know what I mean – you've got the taste and want to do it again.'

'No way!'

'Reckon I know you better than you do.'

'You're just a figment of my imagination, that's all, something that's got out of control.'

'Weak and feeble.'

'Fuck, why do you sneer and nag all the time?'

'Because I'm the best friend you've got.'

'No you're not! I don't know who the fucking hell you are and I don't know where the fucking hell you've bloody come from!'

'South America.'

'What!' Don started to pace around the room. He folded his arms tightly, kept his head down and carried on talking to himself. 'I've never been anywhere near South America.'

'Neither have I. I was born here.'

'This is ridiculous.'

'I'm a British born, South American fish. Corydoras Paleatus if you want my full name. You can call me Cory.'

Don stopped walking and burst into laughter. 'I don't fucking believe this.'

'I'm a British born, South –'

'Yeh, yeh.'

Don sat down on the bed and continued to laugh.

'Pleased to meet you, I'm Don. I'm a – shit!' Don slapped himself on the head. 'This is not at all funny.'

'I was discovered by Darwin, apparently. Well, not really, I was around a long time before him, but, you know, white Western discovered, when all that colonial exploitation shit began.'

'Shut up!'

'It's funny how we all end up together in the same place, a city somewhere miles from where we –'

'Shut up!'

Don slapped himself on the head again. Then he did it with both hands. He continued, increasing the rate and force of the slaps. His head soon began to ache and his ears to ring, and the old pains from the Khalid attack throbbed too.

'That's like banging on the water pipe to stop a leak.'

'Go away!'

'Things might go better if we co-operate.'

'What?'

'Me being foreign to you, wouldn't you like to find out more?'

'Fuck this.'

Don pulled himself off the bed and rushed into the bathroom. He turned on the shower full blast and quickly stripped. The water was on cold but he dived in anyway, the shock to his body making him cry out. 'Go away, go away,' he chanted, grabbing gel and roughly washing himself. He worked particularly hard at his hair and head, forcing his fingers into his scalp as though they could dig out the affliction. It did have some effect. No more voices, just a ringing sound like pylons in the wind and the extractor fan droning away. Don got out and dried himself down, rubbing hard with the towel. He picked up the sea bean as he dressed and clenched it tightly. Still no voice. Instead, a fear and expectancy about the silence which almost felt worse. What next? Don then remembered the cash he needed. He fumbled for his coat. Anything was better than his hotel room, even a dark, sodden evening in the city streets.

Winter darkness was complete by the time Don got outside. He teetered on the pavement in the sodium glare and knew straight away what he saw wasn't real. This was a movie – of city lights, glistening tarmac, misty, blinking car indicators barging slow crawl through urban highways. He could almost hear spooky jazz coming in low with the camera and the hard undertow of a rap rhythm begin to phase in. He felt like a refugee in someone else's story. He hunched up and took off along the street. The pavement, like the road, was busy, but he didn't look at the people. They were – smug arseholes, drug hustlers, brain-dead creeps, desperate beggars, sad consumer clones, scheming sharks, empty exhibitionists, star-struck morons, conformist snitches, power-mad cheats – the list grew longer by the step as Don weaved through the flow looking for a cash machine. A hundred yards on and he saw the hole in the wall. He fumbled for his wallet and got out the plastic. The machine seemed sinister when he faced up to it, metal orifice, silent screen and the thought of a hidden camera watching him. Don felt nauseated by the way the plastic was sucked in, a greedy and grabbing motion, but then came panic. Could he remember the code? He went 5837.

Your personal number has not been recognized. Please try again.

He tried 5387.

Your personal number has not been recognized . . .

'Shit!'

5738.

Your personal number . . .

'Now you've fucked it. Without a number you're nothing in this world.'

'Go away!'

5783 . . . 5873 . . . 8537 . . . 7358 . . .

'What the soddin hell was it!'

'You're really in trouble, Don, if you can't manage to do the job. I don't like that.'

Don slammed his palm down onto the keypad. He gave the screen a bang and the wall a kick. The plastic card spat back out. Don grabbed it, squeezed until it made grooves in his hand and then decided to quit. The number would come to him, he thought, things like that always do. Back into the pedestrian flow he went, trying to remain calm and vacant and hoping that normality would resume. It was a strain. People, awkward bastards, got in his way. He began to think of hitmen again, of the malicious and mercenary who might lurk in the crowd. Coming up to a side street, he bumped right into someone. A bloke with black overcoat and silver hair. Business type.

'Get the hell out of it,' Don fumed.

'Hold on, you bumped into me.'

'You shouldn't be here.'

'I've got as much right to be here as you.'

'Huh, you've got no rights, you're just a rat on a tread-mill like everyone else.'

'Really.'

Don looked down the road. Ahead was the silver post with the cameras on. He pointed at it.

'There you are, there's the authorities making sure you behave like a timid fucking rodent.'

'You're mad.'

'Don't you call me mad.'

'That's it, Don, assert yourself. You don't want to take shit like that from anyone. That was a comment too far.'

Don pushed the guy in the chest, forced him back into the shadows of the side street where there was no camera's gaze.

'I don't take that kind of shit from no one, especially prats like you.'

In a split second, Don saw his fist flying, a reflex that he couldn't control, and then the man fell, became a writhing heap on the wet pavement.

'Well done, Don, the bastard deserved that.'

'Shut it.'

Don stood over the man in disbelief. He looked around anxiously. No one seemed to have noticed. Pedestrian faces just followed their noses, firmly locked in the regimented flow. Don stooped down. The man's wallet had dislodged from an inside pocket. He picked it up and saw a wad of cash.

'*Go for it, go on.*'

'Shit, I can't just – I'm no robber.'

'*Don, you screwed up with the machine and you need money. Fuck it, can't you see, it's likely this git's loaded anyway.*'

Don didn't dare think about the cash machine, so he grabbed the money and merged back into the crowd.

Something seemed to pull him together. The shock perhaps at what he'd done or some remission in his brain. After a panic dash past streams of faces and a rush for the shadows of the back streets, Don found himself by a block of flats. He began to feel calm, and bewildered. When he saw the phone box, he knew what he needed to do. He got out his mobile.

'How's it going, Jackie?'

'Don. I was wondering when you'd ring. You got on OK?'

'That's a good question.'

'You made progress?'

'What is progress?'

'Oh, don't like the sound of that.'

'This is a hard case to get to grips with.'

'Feeling down, huh?'

'You could say that. I reckon all this poking around is getting to me.'

'I get the same way, Don. Work, eh.'

'How about a drink with you?'

'Sorry, can't tonight, got an evening call. But tomorrow, well, I got most of the day free.'

'Great, reckon I need a dose of good looks and sanity.'

'Mmm, still not doing too bad with the compliments. So, Don, did you get any of that stuff which some people might call progress?'

'Right, now can I get my head round to remembering that?'

As Don peered up at the lights in the block of flats, rain began to fall. He saw drops become trails on the glass of the phone booth, catching light and looking like gem dribbles. His thoughts seemed liquid too, a jumbled flow of strangeness out of which he was able to pick sign-post names – Carmelita, Ricky Smith, Shafaq. He hoped they made some sense to Jackie. He rang off then. The last name, he had to meet him and he had an unwanted wad of cash, real sordid money, to offload as quickly as he could.

Don picked up the hire car, anonymous tin and plastic box, and joined the thousands of other mobile boxes in the late evening crawl. He followed a slow trail of red and amber along a concrete gully and then went left through terraced suburbs until he found the Saddam Hussein Mosque. He parked up by a row of shops and walked back. Shafaq appeared out of a silver Audi, now wearing a black NYC cap and long leather coat.

'I reckon that pub where we met would've been better.'

'Told you, that's my patch, and this ain't business I want anyone to know about.'

Don stared at the six-lane highway beside him and the huge stilted overpass with its shiny river of cars. The shops were all heavily shuttered and the mosque had steel grilles over narrow windows. No one was walking. He felt for the comfort of his gun.

'Sort of exposed.'

'Don't worry, man, it's just a meeting place, somewhere on the way to somewhere else I'm going.'

'Isn't that the same old story?'

'Sounds like you need a holiday, man. Maybe I can help. A bit of blow, a few pill or a nice fat arse. Just ask, man.'

'I'm all right.'

'You look like shit.'

'Let's do the business.'

'You got the cash?'

Don nodded. Shifting the money in such a short space of time, he hoped the whole episode would just disappear from his mind.

'OK, this guy, right, he's worried about sticking his neck out so it's gotta be totally hush-hush.'

'What's his name?'

'Mitch, an he'll meet you tomorrow or the day after, you'll get a message as to where and when.'

'That it?'

'The guy doesn't have a diary or shit, you have to get him when you get him. It'll be worth it, he's been round the block a few times.'

Don discreetly counted out the money. 'Better be worth it, Shafaq. I tell you. I'm on a short fuse at the mo and if any fuckery comes, it's in your face I'll blow.'

'Just trying to hustle a living, man, that's all.' Shafaq looked uncomfortable and his eyeballs went roaming. Don also looked around, saw the highway again, with its swarm of cars and the cold, damp hostility of the landscape. A few minutes more, he'd be back in that procession and heading for his hotel. The thought scared him and he stalled for time.

'So tell me, Shafaq, what's the shit between Mal and Khalid? I reckon they don't like each other.'

'They don't. It's just drug politics. Mal, he's a middle-man and Khalid wants to slice him out the loop, go to the source, which is a guy called Ahmed. Khalid's just pissed off at paying extra but Ahmed won't cut Mal out, long-time pals and all that. Them working on a deal now so the friction's higher.'

'The trials of business, huh.'

'At least them ain't shooting each other which some crews do. There was one big gun show right here a while back. Burger Bar Boys and the Johnson Crew, two teenage girls got killed.'

'Shit.'

'Some git went apeshit with a machete round here too.'

'A real cheerful place.'

'That's why you got so many fucking cameras.'

'I was trying not to notice.'

'They don't put up shrines or flower gardens, just fucking cameras. But don't worry, man, we just having a chat, ain't it? Free country and all that. Anyway, Khalid, he may be one mad fucker, but we ain't stooped to shooting up innocents.'

'Right, fists and blades are so much better.'

'Shit, you just got on his wrong side. Besides, you've gotta gun.'

'I don't like em, never used to have one, but with mad violent types and druggies tooled, you've gotta have protection.'

'You're just like a fucking cop really. They're all armed around here.'

Don didn't argue. The talk of weapons escalation was starting to spook him, like it was a confirmation of some general madness, like even if he did sort his head he'd still be walking through a nightmare.

'Second thoughts, Shafaq, how bout a blow and a few skins to send me on my way?'

'Right, sure, a little bit of chill-out holiday coming your way.'

He left Shafaq then and got in his car. The hotel room, though, wasn't his destination.

Don rolled a fat blow in the car, then just drove, aimlessly, for several hours, all around the city. It was an overly slow crawl. He imagined he was off to see his daughter way up north. Warm thoughts, a present maybe on the seat next to him and some kind of hope in his heart. Then he tried to picture Kate, alive, before the elements ate her up. A smiling Kate who he would somehow magically reassemble and bring back to now. Crime and pain erased by aromatic reverie. A cosy fissure in a metal box where he could escape the stress. Don didn't know where he drove, just followed those endless ribbons of black road with their white lines, hieroglyphic signs and arching sodium glow.

10

He *was driving his car although he could see no road. Hands, two hands on a steering wheel that gently rotated. Don's head was on the passenger seat, in some way severed, just sitting there and looking up at what flowed overhead. Streaks of cloud. Fragments of girders. Lamp posts strangely awry, and a solitary seagull circling. 'You can't get further from the truth.' The voice spoke out of nowhere. Don was hiding. The car was drifting through somewhere dangerous, one of those bad vibe places. It felt safe just being a head, out of sight and passing through. He felt cosy and snug. All he needed to do, it seemed, was to get rid of the head and then – bliss? But things began to change, like the road was getting bumpy, and he was rolling around. This was alarming. He had nothing to hold onto, nothing to hold on with and the movements were becoming more extreme. He was bouncing!*

Don cried out and on the ceiling he thought he saw – *Fast-flowing black clouds and an alleyway where mounds of scrap cars were stored.*

'Ent that weird?'
'Sure is.'
'Friend or parasite?'
'Dunno, mutual aid, maybe.'

Don was watching fish with the Snooper. They were lying down as on a river bank but the water was vertical as if contained in a tank. The large green fish with vicious teeth and a sparkling diamond eye, it had its mouth wide open, and some little nipper fish the size of a thumb was eating food off the big fish's teeth.

'Bad luck, if when it's finished, it gets gobbled.'

'Man, an who would clean it teeth den?'

'There's one born every minute.'

'Fuckin cynic. That's them bad voices in you head mekin you do bad things.'

'Don't start.'

'You gotta be tol, man. You really should do nuttin when you got bad voice. It only the good ghost gods that permit retribution.'

'Who the fuck have you been talking to?'

'The Khalid guy, im have redeemin features.'

'You snooping little bastard!'

Don got up on his knees. He saw his hand reach down and grab the face. He squeezed. Fingers sank through skin. The skull collapsed like a rotten melon.

Sweat stuck Don's body to the sheets and almost stopped him from turning. On the bedroom wall he thought he saw – *Fast-flowing black clouds and crowds of people panicking like buffalo on the plains.*

Don was by a block of flats. He stood alone in the half-light and dipped his hands into a shiny pond. There were things beneath the dark surface. Slimy shapes entwined together. He thrust his hands deep into the morass, sought to get a grip and then pulled. The stench made him cry out and jerk his head back. He let go immediately with just a glimpse of what he'd held – things white and bloated, an intestinal mess and a human hand . . .

Daylight glare – and he sat up straight away. Saw the window with its foaming skies. Don's eyes drilled into that cloud reality and the escape it offered. Slowly, feelings of repulsion began to subside. He stayed rigid. It was taking a long time. Things were still not right. He glanced sideways across the room. Something was there. He could hear a rustling sound and a high-pitched moan. And then he saw it. Quick as a flash, a small round shape moved beneath the carpet and headed straight for him. 'For fuck's sake!' Don yelled and jumped out of bed. Two minutes later he was dressed and out of there.

Back in the concrete corridor of the expressway and on the run again. Shifty eyes scanned the backs of cars, lost hubcaps, litter and the white scars of erosion in the dour grey walls. There was no rain, yet. So Don was back where he was a few hours ago but this time he was off to see Jackie and a tense fear gripped his insides.

'*I don't know why you bother, you're in no fit state to try.*'

'Spose you had to come, Cory. Though in a way, I'm kind of glad to hear from you.'

'*Wow, progress!*'

'Don't be sarky, you slippery little fish. I was sort of hoping – God, I'm crazy – I was wondering whether we could come to some sort of arrangement.'

'*Er, what you on about?*'

'Well – I really must be mad – but, I'm going to see Jackie, like I've got work to do and it's hard you popping up and mouthing off at all sorts of unexpected times.'

'*Nothing to do with me.*'

'Come on, I'm only asking you to keep your gob shut when I'm with other people. You can gabble away whenever you want otherwise, I can just about handle it.'

Don took a feeder road going right. He was nearly at

Jackie's office. Sweat was making his hands slip on the steering wheel.

'*This isn't a game, you know, there are important things I have to take account of, the snoopers might be out to get you and there're those bad habits I have to watch out for.*'

'Cory, give us a break, I can't tell people I've got a talking fish in my head, now can I? Have a bloody nap or something, clean my teeth while feeding, do whatever fucking fish are supposed to do.'

'*Huh. I'll think about it . . .*'

When Don entered Jackie's office, he almost felt pleased with himself. He'd hit back at the victim shit, was seeking to get some control. The good feelings rose when he saw Jackie's smile and heard her singsong 'Hi-ya' greeting. She was trying to flick through a pile of files on her lap – difficult as they kept slipping and sliding around. As she shifted legs to try and hold them, he saw her skirt edge further up her beige thigh.

'Can't think of a better morning view.'

'OK, you keep going.'

'What else is there on this dismal day but the hope that bright sparks might fly.'

'Gosh, what have you been up to?'

'You really wouldn't want to know.'

Jackie looked straight at Don then, sleepless, probing eyes meeting his and a brief moment of sad frailty before the look turned away and her voice became assertive.

'Don't say such things.'

'How about I make you a coffee?'

'More like it, I'm always in need of pampering. And when you've done that, maybe we should check out the progress you made.'

'Right.' Don grinned as he went to a kettle on a filing cabinet. 'The power of desks. By the way, I've been meaning to ask, you being kind of small, Jackie, and going out into the nasty world on your own, d'you have a gun or something?'

'There's one in the office safe.' She smiled. 'But I do know how to look after myself. In fact, being a titch has its advantages.'

'Yeh, I can imagine that.'

There was a knock on Jackie's office door and a head popped round. 'Jackie, sorry to disturb, need the camera for later.'

'S'OK, come in. Don, meet Col, our surveillance guy.'

Col eased into the room. A stocky guy with a shaven head, a ginger goatee to go with his earrings. Don reached over and shook a thick tattooed hand.

'Glad to meet you.'

'Same here, Don. Heard you was down on the Kate Connor case. Tough one, eh?'

'Looking that way.'

Jackie came over from the safe and handed Col a long lens camera. 'I expect you to get some good juicy shots.'

'Don't I always. Right perv, me.'

'I know.' Jackie turned to Don. 'Col's my special porn provider.'

'Ah, I see . . .'

'I'm sure you don't really need it, Jackie,' Col replied, looking at Don. 'Thanks anyway. I'll let you get back to business. Cheers all.'

Business, the so-called progress, it didn't actually take up much time. Two scant leads in that hundred square miles of teeming brick. Hardly worth the wages. But it was a tough case with cold leads. That was what Jackie kept saying. Cold everything, Don replied in his mind, apart from you. He was finding it hard to focus. The world was still an insubstantial swirl where nothing was solid. Kate was there, and his feelings about her death, but he couldn't concentrate.

Hers was just one face among many in a whirling crowd where each different face brought extreme emotions. He got a guilty glimpse of the man he'd thumped and then his mind wandered to lonely car drives where movement helped to wash those swirling emotions away. Jackie picked up on his distractedness.

'I reckon a bit of a break'd do you good.'

'Someone else said that.'

'Well, there ain't much more we can do today. As I said, I can check out my contacts in Social Services and the like to see'f Ricky Smith's in the system. You got this meet tomorrow, and that's it.'

'Yep.'

'So, if I give the secretary a list of my contacts to phone when she comes in this afternoon – then we both got a free day.'

'Sounds OK . . . I think I should come and work with you all the time.'

'You've only seen a part of me.'

'That applies to the both of us.'

'Anyway, flowers, we're going to buy flowers and take a little trip. It might help explain a few things.'

She parked the car by the lodge house, just inside the forbidding iron gates of the cemetery. Don helped with the flowers, a bunch of orange lilies and another of yellow freesias, all parcelled up in shiny cellophane. He noticed a change in the weather. Still overcast skies but now there was cold wind and he felt himself shiver.

'So who we going to see?'

'I'll tell you when we get there. I like to be quiet and still when I visit them.'

Don held back a little and followed her. Her black overcoat and woollen hat made her seem like a shadow walking into necropolis. The place was vast, acres of gravestones and the bare trees following hilly contours as far as he could see. The city scale of death. With Don trailing Jackie, they passed an old section of the cemetery, a crammed field of grey stone, a crop of ancient death leaning at all angles. The paths between were bright green with moss, indicating few ever ventured there.

'It makes you think.'

Don gritted his teeth.

'I don't like this place. There's too many ghost voices and it's making my head hurt.'

'What did I say?' Don whispered almost silently under his breath. 'Just shut the fuck up!' Little sound but the emotional energy was intense. Don moved closer to Jackie. They were coming up to a large building. It was the crematorium. Don tried hard to focus on what was on the outside. The wind in the trees. Skeletal nests exposed in branches. A long line of flowers at the back of the crematorium, each group numbered, a sudden drenching of colour indicating the death ceremonies for the day. One wreath was five feet long and said SARAH in yellow flowers. Pat did the same for Kate, after her body was released by the police and buried. Don shivered at the thought of the slang pit where she had lain all that time. He imagined he saw a face in the bushes looking down, a white bony blur of malice. They passed the crematorium and Don became more uneasy. Jackie had shut herself off and he felt his mind was starting to slip.

They went past another shock of colour, a cremation plot where regimented lines of bricks represented the dead; named bricks, thousands of bouquets, statuettes, poems and toys. The confusion of it made Don think a terrorist bomb had exploded and the colour was due to blood and body parts. He grabbed Jackie's arm.

'We there yet?'

'Just the other side of that hedge.'

'Sorry, feels a bit spooky.'

'It's OK. Give us the flowers, yeh.'

They moved to a grassy area where memorial bricks lined paths that went around a row of weeping willows, their dangling fringes swaying in the wind. Jackie stepped to one of the trees, got down on her haunches and laid the flowers down. Don stayed on the path warily looking around. Bad vibe place. The moan of the wind, the 'ting' of a wind chime, the rustle of dry leaves – portents like the humming sounds he got in his head before the voices. A hand thrust in his pocket to caress the sea bean. There were flowers here too, scattered across the grass, but these were weathered and sodden. Under the trees he could see what could only be grey ash.

'This place is horrible, a fucking boneyard.'

'It really is the future,' Don muttered just as he saw a squirrel with a flower in its mouth run up a tree.

Jackie stood up then and came over to Don. He was surprised when she put her arms around him but very glad. Living, human warmth. He held her tightly and scanned the sky looking for just a chink of brightness.

'Two years ago . . .'

Jackie hooked her arm into Don's and they walked back through the gravestones to the car. Two years ago Jackie had a mother and a son. They'd gone out driving, a special trip for the boy out to the Severn Valley and its steam trains. They never got there and they never returned. Going west on the A456, a winding road through fields and villages, someone misjudged a bend and slammed straight into them. Instant death. As simple and horrifying as that. Life flowing forth with optimism and then a violent full stop. Don was shocked. He didn't know how to react. He almost wanted to giggle.

'Jackie, that is . . . really awful. I . . . I don't know what to say.'

'What can you say? I haven't managed to find anything

to say about it myself cept that it happened and it's been pain ever since.'

Don put his arm around her shoulder and gripped hard. He wanted out of the cemetery fast. It made his head strain as though it was about to burst.

'Whatever I can do to help,' he said.

'Holding me's nice.'

Don saw the cemetery gates up ahead. He tried to increase the pace, conscious of the cold wind at his back, seeing white flecks blowing around as though some great chimney was churning out the remains of the dead.

It was snowing by the time they found a restaurant to eat in, a small Italian number out in the suburbs. The snow was nothing much, just a light scattering that would hardly settle. Conversation was awkward to begin with, Don wanting to say things but unable to find words. Jackie spoke of a father who only stayed around a year after Lester's birth. Her mother did a lot of the childcare then as Jackie worked. Five years and they were beginning to get on top of things. Don just looked at her sad eyes, was conscious of murky waters inside his head and the vile things floating in there. She talked about the emptiness, a six-month void of tears and hopelessness; and then a gradual glimmer, an hour of forgetting and the slow haul to making a day seem worth living.

'Guess that's where I am now, trying to take each day as it comes, knowing how to jump over the bleak moments that always show up.'

'Like hands wanting to pull you down.'

'Yeh, you get that?'

'You know some of the shit I've had.'

'Jesus, what a miserable bunch.' Then she smiled. 'OK, fuck this. Music, I know this little jazz bar. Music's good when you're down in the dumps, ennit?'

'Sure is . . .'

'After we nosh, OK, let's drop the sodding miserable and get in some nice vibes instead.'

The saxophone player was good. He would do long fluid solos in the vein of Charlie Parker and then suddenly go for grunts, whines and off-rhythm wanderings as though he'd departed from the band and was lost in his own dreams. Don liked such quirky detours, the propelling into uncertainty and the anticipation of returning to the tune. And he did come back, though not always smoothly, much to the relief of the rest of the band who seemed much more at home with convention.

'I reckon not bad.'

'Yeh, they're all right, but for me, jazz and blues played bad is still good, if you know what I mean.'

'Those notes that bend . . .'

'Reaches you somewhere, in the gut, back of the neck.'

They sat in a corner at the rear. The bar was a single room, white walled with wood panelling going halfway up. The band played on a small platform in front of a wall of posters – two ageing black guys, the young black saxophonist and a grey-bearded white bassist whose belly matched his instrument. Don was sticking to half pints, letting the music clear his head and trying to think of things to say that would reach Jackie. He blundered in – 'Got a daughter myself' – and quickly regretted it. More travail. The lost love on the brink of the ocean. Pain and resentment. More grief. Shit! Don scolded himself, and, she is alive! But all Jackie did was nuzzle up close to Don and whisper in his ear.

'For you and me, right, the past, it's pure fuckery.'

'Guess so, though sometimes I'm not sure what the past was for me.'

'What you mean?'

'You know, how the mind rewrites things.'

'Yeh, but I suppose that's how we move on.'

Don nodded as he saw one of the older jazz players pick up a mike and announce a song dedicated to the audience.

'So, Don, what you reckon we try and move on, into the here and now, no strings and all that. I think I could be up for it.' Jackie's sad eyes smiled into his.

Don nodded again. He felt a surge of relief and hunger as the mike squealed and the bass began to thrum.

'You know how I feel.'

'Shit, Don, I haven't had a smooch in a long time.'

The song began. It was 'Trouble in Mind'. Don smiled as they kissed, the words coming over as corny but apt.

'What?' Jackie murmured.

'We got us a moment.'

'Right . . .'

'The sun's gonna shine, eh? I'll believe it when I see it.'

Jackie's flat was over in Handsworth. A four-storey box set back from the road and bordered by trees. She lived on the top floor with a view of snow-dusted roofs and chimney pots; long lines of them slotting together between the trees like a patchwork quilt. Don felt comfortable, away from the brooding hotel room, amid peach walls and elaborately patterned rust red drapes. He'd just got into the wrong sequence of events, that was what he found himself thinking of the immediate past. From the train journey onwards, he'd taken a wrong turn and got lost. Sitting on the sofa in Jackie's apartment, he could almost see another world bright and fresh. He got up and put on a CD – Metheny and Haden's 'Beyond the Missouri Sky'. Yeh, he thought, just a case of fucked up synchronization.

Jackie brought in coffees and snuggled up close to him. 'Good choice.'

'Soothing.'

'Yeh. God, Don, it is nice to do this with someone. Something else I haven't done for ages. When you're on your own, things creep in.'

Don couldn't reply. The music was therapeutic and it felt good to sit with Jackie, but he didn't feel completely at ease. How long could he stay with that guitar refrain before some shit plopped into his brain and he'd go sliding down into murk? He brought out the sea bean and began working the groove.

'I hope that isn't a reminder.'

'Nah, it's my comforter now, you know, like how some people use mobile phones.'

'Crazy sod. Well let's not linger too long, huh, mister. I think it'd be rather nice to go to bed.'

'Don't do it, Don, remember the last time?'

As calmly as possible, Don eased away from Jackie and went to the bathroom.

'I told you, I don't want you blurting out when I'm with someone.'

'I'm only trying to look out for you.'

'Fuck, you're trying to control me, you're like the bloody thought police.'

'And what about her, what you might do?'

'I never did anything bad the last time.'

'You sure?'

'Don't remember . . . but Lily did ring me back.'

Don sat on the edge of the bath and pressed fingers hard into his skull. The bathroom was nice, a homely place with personal things and the fiery leaves of a pyracantha plant on the windowsill. He wanted to be at home and untroubled, not plagued by some stupid voice.

'How about another truce, huh? I promise I'll be on my best behaviour and tomorrow, well, then we'll have a major chinwag and you can put me straight on everything.'

'Well . . . *maybe, but it'll probably take all day.*'

'Whatever.'

'You OK?' Jackie said when Don returned. 'Your eyes, they look kind of strange.'

'Yeh? Probably just overtired.'

'Let's go to bed, then.'

Jackie stood up and took him by the hand. They went into the hall and then into a bedroom.

'Make yourself comfortable. I need to go to the bathroom myself.'

Don sat on the edge of the bed and kicked his shoes off. He fingered the purple velvet of the bedspread and let his eyes follow the curves of a Matisse print that was on the wall. There were two photos on the bedside cabinet. Mother and son, he guessed. More images of lost ones, piling up in his head, cluttering spaces everywhere and even covering the ground you walk upon. Don sighed. How do you force yourself to relax? he thought and then he saw the aquarium in the opposite corner of the room. He shuffled over to sit in front of it. A dozen or so small fish swam and idled around green fronds and a branch of wood. Some bright blue and crimson, others scarlet with pointed tails and ackee eyes, and a few others, silver and black, rooting within the shingle with frilled lips. Don became quite absorbed. Gliding movements and passivity. A strange suspension of life in water. Eyes that constantly probed outwards beyond the glass. Jackie returned, came round the bed and put her arms around Don's shoulders.

'Found me pets, huh?'

'Yeh, fascinating stuff. What are they?'

'I got some tetras, swordtails and a few cories.'

'Cories.' Don winced. 'Which are they?'

'The catfish type ones on the bottom.'

'Huh, I guess it's nice to put a face to a name.'

'What?'

'Nothing. You can see why they're good to have, sort of soothing.'

'I have been known to fall asleep just watching.'

'Yeh.' Don moved his head closer to the glass. 'Do fish sleep?'

'I dunno, you know, hard to tell. They don't really have eyelids and they just sort of float around all the time.'

'I guess you'd have to be a fish to know.' Don smiled to himself.

'Enough of watching them.'

'Right. They can watch us for a change.'

'Whatever turns you on.'

'You think we'll be all right?'

'To tell the truth, Don, I'm a bit scared.'

'Same here.'

'We'll just have to take it slow, huh, one touch at a time.'

'Yeh . . . I like that.'

'Funny things, bodies.'

'Yeh, but nice.'

'This nipple, why do I like it so much?'

'Cos it's mine and so very special.'

'It's like a closed sea anemone.'

'Don't eat it all.'

'Mmm, think I'll explore some more.'

The water in the undersea cave was warm and quite glutinous. It was a pleasure to swim in. With a little wag of the tail, he could slip through narrow openings, circle shiny columns and even loop-the-loop, go upside down by the red ribbed ceiling. Even if he misjudged a manoeuvre it didn't seem to matter, for the walls were soft and pliant. This gave him the courage to be more daring and he began to test out his speed, darting along corridors and corners as if he was born to it. Then he came to a cave where the water flowed fast and he thrust himself in and rode the flow. Scary, but exciting. He went helter-skelter down the twists and turns, picking up speed, and then suddenly shot out into a large lake within a cavern.

'Wow!' he said as he eased up in the calm water and let his fins dangle.

'The fish jumped over the moon.'

'Who said that?'

'It ain't so bad being mad.'

'Fucking normal if you ask me.'

11

I t's kind of like it's just come out, Don was thinking, right out in the open, and that can't be bad. Better than having unseen nastiness niggle away inside. He was driving back to the city centre, a slow rumble through morning traffic and Don checking out the various street scenes. Craziness, it's got to be everywhere. Locked behind doors and buried under sheets, like those pests that lurk beneath the shiny surfaces of life. Don got a sudden view of people leaving their front doors, bawling out their perversions and paranoias into the street like god squad touts who harangue the public about their sins.

'Whip me thin as a rake. I want to be trendy. Somebody whip me, please!'

'Hear this right, don't ever use phones. The germs them, they come down the line, enter your ear and eat your brain away.'

'When my dad died, I ate a fucking massive gateau. It was amazing, I felt really fine after that.'

'I like to suck the dirt from people's fingernails and then have semi-strangulation sex.'

Don laughed out loud as he crossed an overpass, then hit a line of shops: 'Depression – £1.60 a kilo. Stress now reduced to half price.' 'Magazines to make you feel small at bargain prices.' 'Executive Sod-the-World Pills with added smugness.' 'Ha, ha, great stuff!'

'Well, you're in a good mood.'

'Ah, the piddling little fish speaks. I had a good time last night, despite what you said.'

'A one-off. You won't be able to keep it up, in more ways than one.'

'I've accepted my fate, Cory, and I don't give a shit.'

'That's very irresponsible.'

'I'm gonna go with the flow, and I tell you, what a flow it was last night.'

'You will do it. When the time comes you'll get the urge and be a right vicious bastard.'

'Sod it, what do you know, the displaced groveller in fish shit that you are?'

'Oh yeh, and where do I grovel? Right inside your filthy mind!'

'You're on the way out, Cory.'

Don got a dirty-stop-out look from the woman at the hotel reception, a look that turned a little fearful when he grabbed his key and gave a broad smirk. Don didn't care. It had been a good night. Some warmth and tenderness, a revelation of frailty and not punished for it. The receptionist then remembered he'd got a message and nervously passed it over. Don shoved it in his pocket and went to the lift. The sex had been nice too; tentative, timid explorations that ended with a long sigh like a flurry of wind heard far off in the night. When morning came, though, there had been some embarrassment; unfamiliarity and uncertainty of what might have been said and its meaning. Don was getting used to such feelings and thought little of it. He just looked forward to the evening when they'd meet again. He paused at his hotel room door. Bad vibe place. Funnel into lousy dreams. Where under carpets nasty creatures lurk. Don gritted his teeth and went in. It seemed anonymous enough, cleaned up and prim, maybe safe for a short stay.

The note was from Shafaq asking him to get in touch straight away. Don hit the blower.

'Where you been, man? Tried a few time.'

'Took your advice and had a holiday.'

'Got a good buzz, I hope.'

'Yeh, but not in the way you think.'

'Right, well, I got this meet fixed up with **Mitch** for today. You still up for it?'

'Sure.'

'Four thirty, on the Small Heath Bridge. You **know it**?'

'I don't, but I'll find it.'

'Don't be late, man.'

'It just better be worth the cash.'

Don stripped off and went into the shower. **Sliding** the glass door shut made him feel secure. Turning **on** the water and he felt completely trouble free.

So, you go snouting around for titbits with the swans of the Corrib estuary. Ain't so bad. Stomach full, it's a short haul to watch the sun set over Galway Bay, see the dizzy lights of the ferris wheel rotate like a flying saucer about to land. Fine stuff. Then it's west along the shores of the Gaeltach to the warm waters of the Gulf Stream. Very relaxing. Up north then, following the tails of those fat baskers until we get to the Isles. I'm out there, Melanie, really, beyond the stiff marram and the crashing waves, canoodling with the sharks and sending high-frequency love messages in on the wind.

It never used to be the case that he found **showers** so soothing. Don shook off loose water and began **to dry off**. Halfway through, the phone rang.

'Yeh?'

'Don, it's Lil, hope you still remember me?'

'About there, I guess, the faintest lingering of **scent**.'

'You said you wouldn't mind meeting up **again** and, well, I'm close by.'

'Right.'

'Fancy a coffee in the lounge, bout five minutes?'

'OK, but not for long, huh. Got a meet later.'

Don finished drying and got dressed. Not really what he wanted, seeing Lil again, but he reckoned people were the next best thing to showers for keeping the voices at bay. He got tooled up and went off to the lifts.

How could he forget Lily? She stood out in the lounge like a bougainvillea on a slag heap. The bush of gold-blond hair, the black leather jacket and bright red top and, of course, within scarlet lips, those gold-capped teeth. Don felt a strange tingle of desire as he sat next to her.

'You look a lot better than when I last saw you.'

'And you look like the luscious Lil I remember, sort of, before I got pissed.'

'It was quite a wild night.'

Lily had some coffees already lined up on the lounge table, so Don scooped in sugar and reminded himself to keep his distance. His thoughts may have been read. Was he getting that transparent?

'Don't worry, Don, this isn't a come-on. Though I wouldn't say no to another night out with you.'

Don eased back with his coffee and tried to stay deadpan.

'Finding out you were a private investigator, it set me thinking, about a problem I've got.'

'Oh, right . . .'

Don listened, becoming conscious as he did so of Lily's body, her large breasts and wobbly thighs, parts he remembered touching during that drunken dream night with her. The problem Lily had was no surprise. A man, a man a bit like Don, pulled into a passionate fling one night in that somewhere place in the suburbs. Problem was, this guy was definitely in the reject bin but he wouldn't accept it.

'It's getting really awful. He phones all the time, turns up at my door, sends me silly little presents and I've told him, politely and with my choicest abuse, to piss right off but the bugger still harasses me.'

'Well, Lil, the way you go on . . .'

'I know, but this has gone beyond misunderstanding.'

'What do you want me to do?'

'Thought you could pay him a visit, do whatever you think's necessary to put him off.'

'I dunno. I mean, I've got this heavy case at the mo.'

'I'll pay you, and it'll only take a couple of hours.'

'Well . . .'

'That should be good for a crack.'

When Don left the hotel, the cold slapped him in the face. He stalled, realized he was still in hostile territory, and cautiously looked around the street. No obvious predators, no 'wanted' signs for a middle-aged mugger, just the shiny pole far down with the camera staring at him. Don stalked off to the side street where his car was parked. The clouds above were starting to darken, the cold was vicious and he just couldn't warm up.

Even in the car he shivered as he went through the map book trying to locate the venue for his next lead. 'Unrelenting': the word popped into Don's head and made his stomach knot. The city, the weather, the sadness. Don sought an image of Jackie as he switched on the ignition and drove off into the growing shadows. But the previous night was drifting away from him. There was the gaudy shock of Lily to worry about and the fact that he'd agreed to help her. And now, driving through the dingy streets, more disturbing creatures were stirring in his head. Desperate down-and-outs prowling, and hard thugs searching for a fight. The lust-driven sex cruiser on the move, nervously licking his lips and on the lookout for easy prey. And Don, stuck in darkness, heard the rattle of door handles in the corridor slowly getting closer. Nearing his destination, he spotted an open pub and promptly put his foot on the brake.

'Not many four o'clock drinkers, huh?'

'That time of the week when the money's running out. My lot'll have been down the bookies all day.'

'Looks like they had no luck.'

'Too right there.'

With his right hand, Don fondled the glass of whisky while his left palm smoothed at the sea bean in his pocket. He was the only one at the shabby bar, but it had all that Don needed.

'Bloody cold out there.'

'So I hear.'

'Probably best to stay at home.'

'I hardly ever go out at this time of year.'

Don could see. The barman, portly and ageing, had a pallid face and almost pure white hair. Could've been an albino. His pale forearms rested on the bar and his bored, watery eyes stared at the flickerings of a silent TV.

'Just passing through, are yer?'

'Yeh . . .'

'Not from round here.'

'Up north.'

'Damn sight colder up there.'

'Yeh, but you've got the Gulf Stream and that ain't bad.'

'Eh?'

'Good for a nice long swim.'

'You've lost me.'

Don sighed. Boredom and small talk. Could do with some of that, he thought. Little rituals reminding us we're not alone, which, along with sleep, help fill out the long hours of a life. He sighed again and raised his glass. 'Here's to a change in the weather.'

*

He decided to walk to the bridge, a couple of hundred metres up a side street, the pavement buckled and the lamp posts leaning, their lights inadequate blobs in a misty halo. Hunching up against the cold, Don tried to focus on the case and the guy Mitch who was supposed to know the nastiness that surrounded Khalid. He was finding it hard to grasp onto detail. Kate was some sort of broken flower; she was lost in the winds on a wild shore. And what Don was walking into, wading through, was a nightmare swamp that he was too scared to think about. The Mitch guy, he just wanted a name or a connection that brought him closer to knowing why the flower was broken.

The road suddenly dipped and he saw the bridge in front of him. A metal tubular bridge that spanned railway sidings and an expressway. It was ill lit, narrow and empty of people or cars. Don stood at its entrance and stared. Shadows on the walls shifted and the road seemed strangely rumpled like a long carpet someone had scuffed.

'*Don't like the look of this.*'

'Same here. What the fuck's hiding out there?'

'*What's gonna come along and get us?*'

'Shit, it is exposed.'

'*Got to be a set-up. The Snooper, he's out to scrub your mind clean.*'

'Or worse.' Don looked back the way he'd come. 'I'm gonna go and get the car.'

He went back up the buckled street, wondering why no one was around, all houses draped and their lights dimly muted.

It was when he'd got to the rise in the road that he heard the car. He turned and saw it coming fast across the bridge, the tuned up engine growling and a throb of bass thundering in its wake. Don sought shadow and a possible place to run. His hand was on his gun when the car came up to him and stopped. The engine idled loudly but the music was suddenly cut off and the passenger window wound down. Don stared at a sub-machine gun and then a face appeared.

'Yo, dushman, betcha didn't wanna see me, sinner?'

'Shit . . .'

'Yeh, guess that's what you're gonna do, right from that fucked up head of yours and all the way down; brain, guts and shit all over the floor.'

'You couldn't do it, Khalid, I got protection.'

'What?' Khalid laughed.

'Like you said, I got my own ghost gods and they're right slippery buggers. I'm sending them now.' Don raised his arms and waggled his fingers at the car as if casting a spell. 'They're gonna make you really unhappy, man, make you feel that what you believe is total crap and you'll be thumping walls and headbutting mirrors in no time.'

Don stared at the thin barrel of the gun as though willing it to shy away. He shook his head in a gormless fashion.

'Fuck, you are crazy, man.'

'And don't you forget it, there's a nasty slippery thing in your head right now and it's going to chew your brain to mush.'

Don saw a lorry coming over the bridge and heading towards them.

'You're fucking beyond saving.' Khalid pushed the gun further out of the car, his cross-eyes at odds with the gun's trajectory.

'Get away, he's going to do something!'

Don laughed. 'You're worried, ennit?'

'Move, run for cover!'

The lorry came off the bridge and shifted gear as it hit the rise. It was an empty flat-back and it bounced and rattled with the change of incline.

'Dive!'

'You're dead meat, mate.' Khalid growled.

The lorry's horn blared and its brakes screamed, then came the blast of rat-a-tat cracks that shattered the dark and sent sound waves ricocheting around the walls of the street. Don managed to dive in time, or rather he collapsed in a heap as though fear had sucked away all his strength. The bullets missed, sprayed an arc above him and before there could be a second salvo, the lorry had butted up to Khalid with the unseen driver's hand still on the horn. The car revved up and sped away. Don seemed like he was sleeping.

A rustling in the bushes. Sticks scraping against nylon. Wet leaves squelching. The Snooper was crouching over Don. He could see the brown stubbled face and the yellow cap hiding his eyes. Don felt the cold metal in his mouth.

'Don't you a worry, man, me ent gonna blow you brains out. Dis here is a sort a speshal gun, the fuck sucks steada shoot, gonna suck out all that shit in you brain an mek you free.'

Don pulled his head back and rubbed his hands in the leaf mould slush.

'How about I just puke it all up in your face?'

'Rain on the way again.'

'Yeh?'

'Don't know which is worse, rain or cold.'

'Winter.'

'Right, whatever shitty way it comes.' Jackie was stirring rice in boiling water, something to go with the curried chops. 'We gotta get to warmer climes, Don.'

'The sea'd do me.'

'Would you come, us, together and all that?'

'Dunno. How long you reckon we'll last?'

'Come on, Don, I'm fantasizing that's all.'

'OK, I'm with you, all the way, some hot ocean where we can scuba dive.'

'You ever done that?'

'Nah, can't even swim, but hell, I'd do it anyway.'

'That's the spirit.'

They ate in the kitchen on a table that was cluttered with bills, letters and flyers. Jackie just pushed them aside and plonked down the plates.

'It's nice to know you're not very domestic.'

'It's been a bit of a crash pad for me, but watch out, I might change.'

Don looked at her. Another song sprang to mind. 'What a difference a day makes.' A bit of a glow to her cheeks and a little more white in the eyes. The observation worried him.

'So tell me about this news you got on Ricky Smith.'

'It came from a friend of mine who works in a sheltered home for young men who can't cope too well on their own. He was there a while back. A handful apparently, throwing tantrums and getting into spats with the other guys. They kicked him out, sent him back to his mom.'

'You got the address?'

Jackie smiled.

'Crème de la crème. And look at me, dodging bullets and cross-eyed nutters.' Don had stopped shaking since his confrontation but he still felt the shock, like someone had tied a knot in his guts.

'Yeh, but that shit Khalid, the way he's acting, he could be the one.'

'That's true. Well, I'll keep at it, especially when it comes to that sodding two-timing Shafaq.'

'But not too heavy, huh? You got a mean streak, Don, and it worries me.'

Don stalled with his food. The comment came as a shock. *'Isn't that just what I've been saying, asshole?'*

Don did the dishes. It was an effort, a fumbling, clumsy chore that he couldn't concentrate on. His mind was hav-

ing a minor crash, thoughts splintering into whisper fragments – *blood flow, ghost glow, swallow* – a feeling that
something was moving within his head and touching brain
cells at random. He splashed water on his face and rubbed
with the towel, hard. He was glad to slump down on the
sofa and push up close to Jackie's warmth.

'This heaviness of mine, you know what it is, don't
you?'

'I think so.'

'Like you plough through the shit, feel pain, and mean-
ness starts seeping in.'

''Cept it's a job, Don, and you should keep it well separate.'

'Maybe, but this sort of job, there's no clocking off, is
there? You become part of the scene, you have to be as
bad as the bad guys or you're screwed.'

Jackie grimaced and shook her head.

'OK, maybe I can't keep on top of things like I used to.
This case, it seems to have got to me.'

Don heard her sigh as she leaned forward and reached
down for a small wooden box. She opened it. It was her
rolling gear.

'Ha, you're quite into weed, aren't you?'

Jackie gave off a forced smile. 'Maybe my way of
coping.'

'Shit, what a pair . . .'

Don sensed a change in mood, took a sideways glance
at her eyes and tried to imagine what it would've been
like in the days and weeks after her double loss. Those
long, long nights. He just couldn't go there and so put an
arm round her instead.

'That's good, a bit of here and now and nothing else,'
she said as she lit up the spliff.

Don tried to relax into Jackie's body. He stared up at
the swirling trails of smoke but still felt awkward and
tense. He found himself thinking of Khalid and that small

black barrel of his gun. There was a buzzing sound in his head.

'Reckon I'll grab a shower.'

'You want some of this?'

'Later.'

Don reclaimed his arm and eased off the sofa. Once in the bathroom, he locked the door and sighed loudly.

'You really are totally stupid.'

'Thought you might want to have a mouthful.'

'I mean, first you get suckered by some low-life scum and then you practically ask to be killed.'

'Maybe I want that.' Don began to undress.

'Didn't think even you would take guilt that far.'

'Maybe I don't care.'

'Yeh, that's more like it, avoid responsibility and blunder on until you really do it, really show your true side.'

'I'm just doing a job, Cory, and as I see it, you got in the way. I don't know how but that doesn't matter now. It only matters that I ditch you as soon as I can.'

'Spose you think that woman's going to help you.'

'Leave off.'

'There's a false situation if ever there was one, can't think what you'll do to her.'

'Just shut the fuck up!'

Don turned the shower on full blast and dived under. Once again it seemed to work, the noise and the drenching drowned out the unwanted voice that plagued him. He cleaned himself vigorously and dried the same way too. Once combed and in a bathrobe, he felt back on an even keel. He went into the living room. Jackie was eyeing him in a strange way.

'What?'

'Do you always talk to yourself?'

'Er, I mumble a bit, yeh, don't you?'

'Sounded like a full-blown conversation . . .'

12

Brooding clouds were gathering around the towers. Once more the eye-line was lowered and the city darkly cocooned. Rain pelted down. Don watched it trickle down the car window and gush into drains. He saw wheel spray, ripples on the road and barely visible figures hunched miserable on the pavements. Jackie was quiet, focused on the driving, with a frown that had been etched on her forehead since the start of the day.

'Once knew a couple, during a thunderstorm they stripped naked and fucked on the lawn.'

'Very elemental. What brought that up?'

'Dunno, looking at all this, it would make sense to go naked. I mean, you don't see fish with clothes.'

'This is true.'

'Wouldn't do it in the UK though, eh?'

'Nah.' Jackie cast a quick glance at Don. 'You were talking in your sleep last night.'

'I do a lot of talking, don't I? Anything weird?'

'You mentioned my name a couple of times, which was nice, and then some rambling stuff which was hard to make out. I picked up "Snooper" and something about a "bad ghost".'

'Don't remember a thing.'

'I am worried, Don.'

'I know.'

'Don't want you cracking up on me, don't think I could handle any extra shit.'

'Nah, don't worry, I'm all right I reckon, just going through a bit of a stressed phase. It would be great, you know, if you could just take me as I am.'

'Uh-huh.'

Jackie turned her attention back to the road ahead. They were heading somewhere east, on a circular route, churning the narrow roads and roundabouts on their way to Ricky Smith.

It was a long road, one among many similar in a vast estate on the outer edge of the city. A pre-war expansion, part of a remorseless growth across the green. Don looked at the ranks of bayed semis, the bedraggled privet and spanking new parking plots and felt a sense of dislocation once again: What the hell does it mean? Why am I here? Jackie kept the wipers going as they sat parked opposite Ricky Smith's house. This made the world outside seem more distorted as if waves were lapping around them, as though they had just surfaced there.

'What you think we should do, Don?'

'Not sure.'

'Just calling might be tricky.'

'Yeh, like we're social workers or something.'

'The guy is a bit loopy, prone to violent outbursts.'

'Wait for a bit, see'f he pops out?'

'I guess we got the time.'

'Can think of better places, though.'

'Well, you're with me.'

Don smiled. 'And it is fully appreciated.'

They got into a clinch then, within the steamed up glass, the air hot and clammy and the squeaking wiper blades keeping the flood at bay.

'You ever thought of seeing anyone?'

'What you mean?'

'About the way your head is, the bad dreams and stuff.'

'A shrink?'

'Such shit happens all the time, there's nothing wrong in seeking help. Went to someone myself when Lester died, just to talk things through.'

Don felt a sudden surge of panic and the sense of twitching in his brain went haywire.

'Nah, I'm all right, Jackie, really, just bad scenes and stress. It'll all work itself out.'

'I dunno . . .'

Don saw the door move in Ricky's house. 'Hold on, we've got someone coming out.'

The door was open quite some time before a young guy appeared. He wore a baseball cap and a thick, ribbed, blue nylon coat. Ricky was tall and the coat made him look bulky too. The shoebox he had in his hand seemed very small.

'What you reckon, Don? We don't want to flip him.'

'Yeh, let me have a go. The two of us might be too much.'

'OK, get to it, mister.'

Don climbed out of the car, pulled up his coat lapels and went bare headed across the road, his black hair soon shiny and flattened. He had to jump the gutter flow before he got into Ricky's wake.

'Hey there, you got a second, mate?'

Ricky didn't seem to hear and he gambolled on, over-inflated shoulders making him seem top heavy. Don ran and swerved in front of him.

'Sorry to interrupt but, well I'm lost, and I kind of hoped you could help.'

Ricky stopped dead in his tracks and stood stiffly with the box tucked under his arm. He was apparently twenty years old but looked sixteen, a round smooth face, mouth tight and eyes looking downwards. Don watched a steady line of drips come from the rim of his cap.

'We were heading for the city centre in the car.' Don shrugged. 'Ended up here.'

Ricky didn't reply straight away. The situation Don presented seemed to require some major thinking. Eventually he nodded his head and lifted his eyes.

'I've been to the city centre.' He talked slowly, with equal emphasis on every word.

'Right, so you know where it is from here.'

'Er . . .' This required more pondering. 'Well, there is a bus that goes there. Not sure which one, though.'

'Yeh, well I've a car.'

Don then heard noises coming from the shoebox. Scratching and tapping sounds. He looked at it and felt slightly threatened.

'Wow, that's weird. Never heard a box do that before.'

Ricky shunned back a little but then smiled. It was a half-moon grin that made his face seem even rounder.

'Bet you don't know what's in it.'

'Shit, dunno, not something horrible, I hope.'

'Nah.'

The rain was running down Don's neck and soaking into his shirt. The idea of getting into a guessing game was not appealing.

'You gonna tell me?'

'Take a peek.'

Ricky brought the box forward and lifted up the lid an inch or so. Don saw a small eye, which was spooky, and then the black head of a bird and patches of white.

'Phew, I was worried a bit there. Right, a magpie, is it?'

'You got it.'

'So . . . magpie, you going for a walk, keeping out of the rain?'

'I'm taking him to the police station.'

'Fuck, what's he done, been thieving jewellery?'

'He's got a broken wing. Kids, they threw stones and broke his wing.'

'God, some people.' Don looked at Ricky and saw that his mouth was now tight and angry. 'Look, you don't want the cops, you need a vet.'

'Don't know them.'

'Maybe we can help. I've got a friend in the car, maybe we can find a vet. Just wait here, man, I'll check it out.'

Don rushed back through the rain to Jackie. She wound the window down.

'Don't ask why, but we need a vet, preferably a free one.'

'There's one down in Aston I think.'

'OK, we're on.'

Ricky was happy to get a lift and extremely pleased to have somewhere to take the magpie. He didn't seem to notice that the lost travellers now seemed to know their way around. Don sat in the back with him, opening his clothes and trying to get the damp warmed up. He fingered up the box lid again. The bird had its back to him so he avoided the beady eye.

'Some day we're having, eh, magpie, attacked by idiots, rescued by –'

'My name's Ricky.'

'Don. Nice to meet you and that's Jackie up front there. So, rescued by Ricky, going walkabout in a box and now being chauffeured in a car. That ain't bad for a bird, is it, Ricky?'

'You think they'll fix him?'

'Bet they will, and find a place for him to go.'

'I want to look after him but me mom won't let me.'

'Right . . .'

Don tried to think of a way to change the subject, to try and get round to Kate Connor. He began to feel the coincidence would be too much, even for Ricky. They'd have to find some way to meet him again. He brought out his sea bean and began to soothe it. Ricky was intrigued.

'What's that?'

'Sea bean.' Don held it up.

'Oh yeh, seen one of them before.'

'Really?'

It was then that Jackie pulled up outside the vet. Ricky seemed apprehensive about going into the place, so Don braved the rain again and took him to the antiseptic smells of the reception. There was a long queue.

'Look, it'd be nice to know how things turn out. You got a mobile I can ring you on?'

'Yeh.' Ricky recited the number slowly to Don.

'I'll buzz you later.' Don lifted the shoebox lid. 'Nice meeting you, bird. When you get better, we'll have a right old chinwag.'

'Thanks, Don.'

Jackie had other business to work on for the rest of the day so she drove Don into town to collect his car.

'I thought you got on with that magpie really well.'

'Yeh, I'm quite getting into wildlife.'

'Ricky doesn't look a likely suspect.'

'You never know, he does have fits or something, but I agree, he's kind to animals for a start.'

'He might have things to tell, having known Kate, but whether you can get anything out of him . . .'

'Can but try. The injured bird is a good way in with him.'

'Want to meet up tonight?'

'Yeh, of course. I was thinking, actually – Mal Chariot invited me to Garvey's a while back. Want to go there?'

Jackie pulled up behind Don's hire car. Then they kissed again behind the windscreen wipers, that steamy refuge from the flood.

'Gonna see'f I can find Shafaq, I reckon.'

'Don't get mad and don't get broody.'

'Would I do that?'

Don heaved himself out into the rain and headed for his car. He suddenly felt tension in his shoulders and feathers tickling in his brain.

It was the same route as before, over to Café Nico and the winking pike, a cruise to the back street garage and then on to the Monument Arms. No sign of Shafaq, hardly anyone out in the deluge, people locked away in water-proof zones, no choice but to work, get domestic, cook up spoons, roll spliffs or go on weird mental trips, any distorted relief from the shit of living. Don got into the latter. Driving through the spray like he was some sort of sailor, it was hard to do much else than have a conversation with the fish that lived in his head.

'Guess this could be the future. Global warming, the seas rising and, from whence we came, we'll all go back to.'

'Good to see you know about evolution.'

'I can see how we got here. It's what we are now that has me fucked.'

'Don't ask me about it, this is one very bizarre world. A crazier jungle, I reckon, than the one I originally came from. I mean, well, just look at it all.'

Don did, peering through the windscreen at the blurred tower blocks, closely looming and then stretching away into misty distance.

'Just take it as it comes, Cory, that's the law of the city. Wherever you go, whatever happens, have your wits well tuned – to danger, and your own interests.'

'Huh, that sounds good coming from you. Khalid could've had you splattered if it wasn't for me.'

'I was spooking him. Anyway, those guns are hopelessly inaccurate and that truck driver turned out pretty helpful.'

'Whatever. Of course, then you go round talking to birds and let that woman Jackie imply that you might be cracking up.'

'Don't talk about Jackie.'

'The closer we get to retribution, the greater the need to sort her out.'

'Hey, who's talking about retribution?'

'You know you will do it.'

'Sod off.'

After checking out the pub, Don eased back onto the main road and headed to his hotel. The traffic crawled through rain and roadworks and he did what he could to settle his mind. He drifted away from himself – floated through drumming raindrops, past blinking brake lights and up towards the cloud swirl. There he could become immersed, lost, and swim the north-west waters. Thunderous breakers on the rocks. Endless winds across a scoured landscape. And in there, somewhere, that sad sense of yearning, the only certainty there was.

'Sort of nice place you got here, Mal.'

'Only sort of?'

'Well, can be a bit of a dive man myself. You know, years of finger marks on the chairs, ancient puke stains on the threadbare carpet and of course, any ceiling worth its while has gotta be nicotine yellow.'

'You white people sometimes disgust me, so friggin unhygienic.'

'A nice warm cloudy beer, a fat barman with dandruff and some homesick, tone-deaf, Irish old dear bawling "Danny Boy" with her false teeth out on the bar.'

'Man, fuckin disgustin!' Mal glanced over at Jackie and grimaced.

'He's just trying to get a rise out of you, Mal. Don't listen. It's his third whisky.'

'And that voice, you know, that broken, booze-ridden voice wailing at the dark and dismal end of the day, it's a fucking triumph.'

'Shit.'

Don smiled wearily. 'Jackie's right, don't take no notice of me, Mal.'

'Huh, so how come you tink you can tek the piss?'

'Sorry, it's meant as a compliment.'

'Yeh? Well, don't push it. I know we got tings in common but you is in my club now an you spose to show respec an give proper compliment.' Mal shifted his stiff shoulders around and winked at Jackie.

'It's a great place, really, I love it.'

'Better.'

'Blame my bad manners on Khalid. I had another encounter the other day.'

'Jeez, im sure got the hots feh you.'

Don looked around. The bar area was done out in dark wood panelling with black leather seats. Sober and functional, not much sign of the Marcus theme. The print of an old liner which could have been the freedom ship and some pictures of 1950s migrants with their baggy suits and wide-brimmed hats. The rest of the images were of black models, scantily clad but tastefully soft focus. In the next room there was a small dance floor and a few women were jigging to the tight clipped rhythms of R & B.

He turned back to Mal. 'I hear you're the supplier for my friend Khalid.'

'In some stuff, yeh.'

'Got a deal in the offing so things are a bit uptight.'

'Shafaq bin talkin, huh? Yeh, well, Khalid would like to cut me outa the chain, save a price hike an push a non-believer outa the system. Fat chance. The guy's a slime bag who nobody like. Is im you number one suspect?'

'Don't really know.'

'Well, I really hope you a do him. I'd be better off jus dealin wid Shafaq.'

'Another slime bag as far as I'm concerned.'

Mal raised his eyebrows. 'Dat a suprise. Anyway, better go an do the boss bit, so I'll check you later.' He got up and looked over at Jackie. 'Nice seeing you again, sis, but watch you step wid dis geezer, I mean, it a bit a suprise you is wid him, if you don't mind –'

'Don't worry, I've got him sussed. We're both refugees from bad pasts.'

Don nudged up close to Jackie and put his arm around her. 'You reckon you got me sussed, huh?' he said boozily.

'I have my doubts, but I think I can handle you.'

Don felt uncomfortable with this reply and the itchy sensation returned to his head. He tried to focus on the pink neon GARVEY'S sign that hung behind the bar. It did have some muffling effect but he still heard, *Little does she know.*

'You know you said we should get away from it all, together? I reckon I'm with you on that,' Don said with some desperation.

'Yeh? That's sweet.'

This 'humouring the drunk' remark did little to ease Don's sudden feelings of insecurity.

Jackie noticed his crumpled look. 'Come here, you. Just give us a kiss.'

They stayed about another hour in Garvey's. Had a smooch on the dance floor, a few more words with Mal and some young beauty he had on his arm. Then it was out into the night, the route back home through dripping trees and misty hollows to the bed by the aquarium. They made love with confidence as though there really were no doubts. It was only when he was half into sleep that Don felt a swell of panic, but he was too far gone to resist oblivion.

*

Though he was standing up, Don knew the man with the pale face was dead. In fact, he could see the bullet hole in his chest, a black gaping hole with something slimy and writhing deep within. Don felt himself turn rigid and begin to sweat. He was expecting the explosion of blood and he kept his mouth firmly sealed. The pale face staggered over and looked down at Don with plaintive eyes. Then long white fingers began to fumble around Don's mouth, maybe trying to prise his lips open. 'Dat's it.' Don knew the voice. 'You gotta gi im medicine, heaps a it, shovel it in. It the only way to clean im brain.' The man's fingers pushed through lips and began to scrape at Don's teeth. 'No! No! No! I'm perfectly fine! Jackie said so,' he shouted through gritted teeth. The fingers had a foul taste and Don shied away, fell down onto some lumpy surface, a kind of carpet under which strange shapes wriggled around. Then Don was running, he was down by the docks where the water was oily and black and someone behind him kept shouting, 'But you will do it, you will kill again!'

13

'Hope we're going to see some action.'
'You will.'
'That guy, he really screwed us, might've spat the bullets himself.'
'He was just making a few extra quid.'
'What?'
'Business, it don't have any conscience.'
Don was parked across the road from Café Nico. It was early, maybe the time when Shafaq would go get his breakfast. Don hoped so.
'Getting ripped off, Cory, happens all the time. It's the way the country's run and you just put up with it most of the time. Shafaq probably doubled his take for snitching on me, just business, but he had to be betting that Khalid wouldn't mess up.'
'Got that wrong – thanks mainly to me.'
'You're the genius.'
It had been good to get up early. Rising with Jackie, caressing her body through the silk slip she wore and getting into a conversation through looks alone:
'Yeh, so I'm sleepy, why are you so bright eyed?'
'Ah, enjoyed the sex, did we?'
'Don't let it go to your head.'
'Well, you know what my head's like.'
'Totally ga-ga, but it's nice chilling out with you.'

'Ain't it just.'

And on until Jackie left for work. Don didn't stay long after. The empty room, it soon started to twitch and he got to wondering whether the silent conversation with Jackie was yet another imagining in his head.

He looked across the road at the café. The rain of yesterday had moved on and there were plenty of people about. In among them was one Shafaq. Don quickly got out of the car.

'All right, Nico? Elvis still winking, I see.'

'Well, he does know a thing or two.'

'Yeh, clever buggers, fish.'

Shafaq was just about to turn round and clock the visitor who stood behind him. He was only halfway there when Don's gun nuzzled spine bone. Shafaq went rigid and groaned.

'You must've expected me since Khalid fucked up yet again.'

'Don't know what you talking bout, man.'

'Skip the crap, Shafaq. You owe me double and you're going to pay it right now.' Don prodded hard with the gun. 'Let's go outside. Be good and you might get to tasting that breakfast.'

'Dunno if I feel that hungry now.'

'Let's go.'

They went out onto the busy pavement. Don shouldered Shafaq along to a side street, turned into it and pushed him into a back-of-the-shops alley. The gun came out into the open then as Don eyed up a large garbage bin.

'Somewhere to dump you if the worst comes to the worst.'

'Come on, Don, I didn't shaft you, honest. Khalid probably overheard me talking, is all.'

'Huh, after what he put you through, shoot him anyway.'

'What? You come out with that laid-back slop after what I had to face.'

'That's it, you really ought to get worked up.'

'Honest, Don, I didn't –'

'Facing a fucking machine gun in the back of fucking nowhere!'

'It wasn't me, man.'

'What a lying creep!'

'That's right, Shafaq, you're a lying creep.'

Don moved up close and pushed him against the bin. Shafaq's expression continued to plead innocence.

'Hit the bastard!'

Don raised the gun and smacked Shafaq over the head.

'Right, and again. Don't forget how really dreadful that scene was.'

Don raised his other hand and thumped Shafaq right on the nose. Blood began to pour. Shafaq put his hand to his face and tried to stem the flow. Scared and anxious eyes looked at Don.

'Shit . . . OK, OK, you want me to fix another meet with the Mitch guy, right?'

'Didn't take much to get him squirming.'

'I'll do it, really, no problem.'

'Mind you, I reckon he still deserves something permanent to remember you by.'

'Fuck . . .' Shafaq shuffled uncomfortably against the bin and wiped his bloody hands on his jeans. '. . . And you know, anything else I can help you with.'

'A bullet in the kneecap, maybe.'

'Shit, man, you gonna talk to me?' Shafaq pleaded.

'A punctured eardrum.'

'Fuck, you're really weird, man.'

Don realized that he had just been staring, silent but for the words in his head. He shook himself and refocused his gun.

'Do it, Shafaq, get on your mobile now and get me a meet today, a cast-iron, dead-cert meet, OK?'

'Sure, sure.'

With some nervous fumbling, Shafaq did what Don asked. Luckily for him, he got through straight away.

'I'm proud of you, Don. This'll set you up nicely for when we finally track down that murderous bastard. I'm sure you'll know exactly what to do.'

'Shut it now, OK.' Don muttered quietly to himself.

Shafaq finished his call. 'It's on, man, you can go to his place at four o'clock. I'll write the address down for you.'

'Any fuckery this time and you know what'll happen.' Don prodded his gun forwards.

'Sh-sure, man.'

'Another thing. This deal being cooked between Khalid and Mal, I want to know exactly when it's going down.'

'What?'

'I told you, you owe me double.'

'But fuck, that's business and nothing to do with you.'

'It is now. Khalid is due some payback as well and I want to screw the bastard. It won't affect you, might even improve your prospects.'

'Oh yeh?'

'Really. Mal was saying only last night how he rates you. This could help you get out even quicker.'

'Shit . . . I spose I could really do with that.'

'Settled then. You buzz me the moment you know.'

Don let his gun dangle loosely in his hand and smiled. Shafaq, fearful and slightly disorientated, put the blood-smeared address in Don's hand and began to sidle away.

'You know what you're doing, then?' Don said.

'Yeh, yeh . . .' Shafaq backed his way out of the alley. As soon as he hit the street, he ran.

'Don't suppose he will want his breakfast now.'

'I must say, I like this new plan.'

'Just keep it to yourself, Cory.'

'Jesus, Don, d'you realize what you've just said?'

*

It was time to go back to the hotel and make use of some of the services Pat was paying for. A good shower, of course, was Don's main aim. Driving off, he tried not to think about the way his – this – 'alien voice' had controlled him. It just wasn't his style to sock a guy, unless as a last resort. What was he turning into? Don squeezed the steering wheel. Really, though, he was frightened to think about it. 'Thinking about it' didn't seem a solution. Somehow, he felt he had to catch the voice out unawares. And how the fuck do you do that? Don went up the sweeping curve of an overpass, the sky still leaden with clouds and office towers merging into them. His face was frozen with perplexity. One of life's big problems. How do you catch a fish without thinking?

Back at the hotel, he had a message waiting for him. Pat Connor had called. It had been quite some time since they'd made contact. Don didn't feel inclined to respond straight away. His failed encounter with the cash machine still made him wince. Instead, he went to his room and dived into the shower.

Tried following ferries across the Minch one day, just to try and get a glimpse of you. Dangerous business. The waves were pretty big and shit, I had porpoises snapping at my tail. Then the bloody gannets came, dive bombing from out of the sky. No place to linger for a maudlin fish, had to hide out in the rocks at Sgeir Inoe . . .

Don dried himself down and got dressed. The room still had a haunted feel to it as though someone had once died a terrible death in there. He quickly got on the blower.

'Hi there, Ricky. Don here, the guy who helped you with the bird.'

'Oh, right, I remember you.'

'So how's our magpie doing then?'

'They said I did very well to bring him in.'

'Yeh?'

'They said they could fix him up.'

'Great.'

'They said it would take a lot of weeks for him to get better.'

'Right . . . say, why don't we meet up and you can give me the whole story. I kind of liked that magpie.'

'Could do, I spose . . .'

'You had lunch yet? Bet you'd like a big fat nosh?'

Don managed to get a venue set up, though it wasn't easy. Ricky was vague about places and where they were. Some corner caff at the back of the old bus garage by the motorbike showroom was the best he could do. He'd have to check with hotel reception to see if they could pin it down. Don then rang Jackie and told her what he'd set up. She seemed impressed but also a little distant. They arranged to meet at her office after he'd seen Mitch. Don put the phone down. He gave the room one last stare and then left to pick the brains of the hotel staff.

Finding the caff wasn't too difficult. Down a side street in an industrial quarter and backing onto a railway embankment. Patsy's was an add-on annexe to a small tool-making firm. Don had to dodge forklifts in order to park. He caught a glimpse of molten metal in the grimy depths of one factory. But Patsy's was a bright new place, freshly painted walls and glaring red plastic seats. The fruit machine was making a racket. Ricky Smith was making it do so.

'Finally found you. How's it going?'

'Aw-right.'

'So you up for a good lunch?'

Ricky's big round face grinned.

'The choice is yours.'

And there was plenty of choice. The usual fry-ups but also lasagne, chilli con carne, curries and shish kebabs. The baguettes were the size of marrows. Serious workingmen's food. The young Asian woman serving, black ponytail pouting from the back of her baseball cap, eyed Ricky suspiciously as he approached the counter and tried to decipher the menu.

'It's all on me,' Don said to her.

'Bacon, egg, sausage and chips plus a Irn Bru.'

Ricky knew when to make the most of a good deal. Don went with lasagne and rolls. He steered Ricky to a table, the guy just about able to squeeze into the seats.

'So, our magpie friend, what's going to happen to him when he's better?'

'I want to keep him.'

'The vet doesn't agree?'

'Says me mom has to do it but she won't let me.' There was a hint of anger in Ricky's voice, like that of a spoilt child.

'Probably best if magpie went to one of these sanctuary places, some place with big cages and open fields.'

'They said something like that.'

'It'll be good, but sad, cos I kind of liked chatting to that bird.'

'Chatting up the birds!' Ricky laughed loudly at his own joke.

After the food arrived, Don thought he'd try and get in some probing. It was a case of coping with slurps of ketchup, loud chomping and forced burps.

'Had a funny coincidence today, Ricky. Strange. I had to pop in on business to the Beyond the Galaxy games place. I reckon you must know it cos I was chatting to this Carmelita woman and your name somehow cropped up.'

'She's a cow.'

'Yeh, well, managers have to be heavy sometimes. Anyway, that was just the start of it. I know this guy Mal, right, and he's got a daughter called Bridie, yeh, and she's friends with a friend of mine called Kate; and it turns out that they used to go down the Galaxy too. Strange, I tell you.'

'I know them. Bit sort of snooty but we was friends.'

'Funny how things like that happen, ain't it?'

Ricky gave a ponderous nod and then prodded a chip into his egg.

'The cow banned me. I haven't seen them again.'

'Yeh, well, I haven't seen Kate for a long while.'

'Someone told me that she *went away*.' Ricky put grave emphasis on the last two words.

'Really? So did you just meet her down the Galaxy or did you chill out at other places?'

Ricky now had an empty plate and a look that said he still wasn't satisfied.

'Apple pie and cream?'

There was a big grin. Don called out the order and then repeated his question.

'There was some blokes we used to go off with. Bad people. Me mom told me to stay away.'

'Really, so what was bad about these geezers?'

The pie arrived. Ricky gave it a gloating stare then took a dollop of cream on his finger. The finger slowly moved through the air before suddenly darting into Ricky's mouth. 'Yum.'

Don bit his lip. He was beginning to feel annoyed and there was that tickling sensation starting up in his head. He looked around the room to check out for cameras and gave his scalp a painful scratch. Then his mobile went beeping. 'Fuck.' It was Lily.

'Don, that bloke I was on about, he's outside my flat right now, just sitting in his car and looking up.'

'Yeh?'

'Well, you said you could help and I was wondering if you could nip over right now.'

'I'm kind of busy, Lil.'

'How soon could you make it? I mean, I could try and keep him around.'

Don sighed. He looked at Ricky, a fleck of cream on his upper lip. He looked out the window at cold brick and galvanized fencing. He cursed silently and then said, 'Give us the address. I'll try and make it in half an hour.'

'You really are a sweetheart.'

Don turned his attention back to Ricky. 'Sorry about that, mate. Going back to these geezers, what was bad about them?'

'Drugs. They was using nasty, nasty drugs and me mom say you should never touch drugs so I never went again.' Ricky's serious look was somewhat subverted by the cream.

'So who were these guys, any names?'

Ricky slowly shook his head. 'Bad people, don't want to know them. One had "angle" or something tattooed on his head.'

'Was that angle or angel?'

'Dunno.'

Ricky's bowl was empty. He pushed back in his seat, put his hands on his stomach and grinned. 'I'm stuffed. Want me to show you my favourite motorbike? It's just up round the corner. A massive Kawasaki. Brrrrm, brrrrm. I want to get a bike but me mom won't let me.'

Don kind of felt sorry for Ricky. Around twenty years old and still a child. But then again . . . He said he was too busy to view the bike but that he'd keep in touch. As he left the caff a train rumbled along the embankment up above and Don involuntarily ducked his head. The street was empty of lorries and forklifts and the cloud count had grown, so everything seemed darker. Don walked towards his car. The darkness flooded in. A bad guy probably with ANGEL tattooed on his head and well into drugs. An innocent young woman, protectively kept so by her not so good father, drawn maybe into a scene where only base instincts matter. Don had done his fair share of trawling through drugs scenes. The superficial charm and camaraderie; the paranoia and desperation that seethed within the heart of it all. Kate would be easy prey. *Want to write a letter to you up there on the Gulf Stream coast. Something about how maybe your mother made a good decision. That people here can wander down the wrong alleyway and end up lost and rotting amid the toxic shit that so-called progress leaves behind. But only maybe. I don't want to do myself down. Wherever we are, we're all in it together. Guess the wind and sea is as absurd as the convolutions of the city. You and me, Melanie, under the same sky . . .* Don switched on the car engine. He suddenly felt very angry.

It didn't prove too hard to find Lil's flat again. Following the map to begin with, then getting glimmers of recognition as he got closer, until he found the street itself and the barren tree he'd stood beside waiting for a taxi. Don sat in his car for some time before entering the block of flats. He didn't want to be where he was, or do what he was being asked.

'C'mon, Don, go for it.'

'This has got nothing to do with me.'

'*Too soft with women, that's you.*'

'Just crazy, I reckon.'

'*You think too much. Just get in there and react.*'

'Fuck . . .'

Don did move then, up the path, into the block and up in the carpet-lined lift. Lily's door was open when he arrived and he could hear voices.

'Look, Jim, how many ways do I have to put it? I mean, for fuck's sake. I just heard the lift. That's probably my boyfriend. D'you really want to meet him?'

Don moved on cue. Pushed the front door and headed down the hall past the nude dude to the kitchen where the voices were coming from. Much to his unease, Lil threw herself at him when he entered and plonked a highly scented kiss on his cheek. 'Oh, Don, good to see you.'

Behind the bush of blond hair, Don could see the hungry-hearted one, a thin-faced guy with short black hair and shadowed jowls. Unease within him too, but also an edge of determination.

'*Go on, what a little shit, go for it!*'

'And who the fuck's this?'

'Oh, right, this is Jim, remember the guy I mentioned?' Lil turned towards him and gave a smug smile.

'And what the fuck is he doing here in your flat?'

Lil didn't answer but let Jim swallow and try to assert himself.

'We're friends, that's all, and I just popped round.'

'That's not what I heard.'

'Jim was just leaving, weren't you?' said Lil with triumph.

'I heard you were a dirty little stalker.'

'*That's it, Don, get worked up, really get him scared.*'

'People like you ought to be taught a lesson.'

Lil nudged Don in the ribs and gestured that he should let Jim leave. The guy had certainly caught some sense of fear: his chin was quivering.

'*Don't make it easy on him. You didn't have it easy.*'

'It's the fucking start of the slippery slope. A bit of stalking, then sniffing underwear, snooping and then onto assault and rape.' Don pulled out his gun and grabbed Jim by the collar.

'Don, that's enough!'

'No, Lil, these fuckers, they've got to be caught early and taught a lesson, else they'll be out murdering young women.'

'*You're really getting there, Don. This is great.*'

Don pushed the gun against Jim's nose and began to twist round the collar so that Jim's dark jowls tinged red.

'For fuck's sake, Don!'

'I-I'll n-never c-come here again,' Jim managed to splutter.

Lil grabbed both of Don's arms and began to pull. 'Come on, let the little sod go! Shit, why are men such bloody arseholes!'

Don felt his mind go completely blank and he let himself be pulled off. Jim immediately broke free and ran out of the flat.

'What on earth got into you, Don?'

'Did the trick, I reckon.'

'I thought you were going to kill him.'

'Don't know what I was going to do.'

'Bloody hell. Phew.' Lil leaned back against a cabinet and lit up a fag. 'Don, I was going to ask if you were up for a date, but I don't think I want to see you ever again.'

14

Mitch lived north of Lil's flat, so Don retraced his path back towards the city centre and then turned left to B16 and, what he'd been told, bedsit land. He tried to keep his mind blank, to push Lily and his own crazy antics down into the reject bin. Feeling tired and baffled, he sensed that events were getting out of his control. All he could do was follow the trail of death and hope to survive. But could he keep on track? Might he just get lost, go off down a side road and never reach any destination?

'*You did great. No fun being a ghost, even a ghost god – all you can do is rant and rave.*'

'Oh yeh.'

'*I'm relying on you, Don.*'

'Not a good idea, Cory.'

'*You've gotta get the bastard.*'

'I guess I'm still on the way.'

'*You gonna give this Mitch a pasting too? I bet he deserves it. I bet he's some scumbag who wallows in drugs and shit.*'

'I'll do whatever I have to, I spose.'

'*Fuck em all, nobody really cares. This whole place is a brick wall.*'

'Shut the fuck up, Cory!'

Don did manage to find the place, just. There was one moment, on a large, sloping roundabout, where all he could see was a blur of city and a ridge of dark cloud, when he nearly lost his nerve. Three times he drove around it before he took the plunge and found his route again. The road Mitch lived in was full of trees, thick black pillars streaked with moss and bare branches scratching at the sky. Don rang the doorbell for flat 3 and got caught up in a word storm.

'Don't know why I'm doing – Shafaq is a pusher in every sense – I mean, I haven't seen the sod for over a year – that was the last rip-off – you can't escape, I mean you can go to fucking Timbuktu if you want, but who the fuck would, swap one desert for another – better to stick with what you know, except some shits you don't want to know – fuck, life is a bitch.'

This little rap from Mitch took Don up the stairs and into the bedsit. A single room overlooking sad gardens of overgrown grass and bleached and broken fencing. Don grabbed the sofa while Mitch fretted by a small kitchen cubicle, his hands playing some invisible string instrument.

'Don't let too many people in – you gotta be careful round here – thieving narcos and nutters let loose in the community and all sorts of sexual freaks after your stash – you want a coffee? I think I've got coffee or maybe only Coke, can't be bothered half the time –'

Mitch was sort of mid-twenties. Thin, from face down to feet, and long straggly hair that hadn't felt soap for quite some time. He stood nervously by the cubicle, his eyes roaming and his fingers twiddling. Don could never understand why people took speed.

'Forget the coffee, Mitch, this is only a quickie visit. I don't want to invade your space.'

'Right, fair point, got a lot to do, places to check, in fact I probably should be somewhere else now, I did write it down –' Mitch looked vaguely around the room. 'Fuck it, it'll come, so, why are you here then, man?'

'Just hoping your memory isn't too frazzled, you know, overheated trips burning up the wiring?'

'Huh, yeah, right, man.' Mitch looked as if he felt he'd been dissed but couldn't quite grasp how.

'Going back over a year now, to when you was in on the scene with Khalid and Shafaq and all them lot.'

'Fucking trash bags I tell you, just, like it was that scene that did – soddin glad I got out cept you don't really get out, gotta go somewhere totally freaky to –'

'It's all right, I got where you're coming from, Mitch. You're just so dead right about the trash and I'm kind of interested in cleaning it up a bit.'

'You ent a –? I mean, I don't want no fuckin –'

'Nah, man, this is strictly private and personal. I work for this guy from up north who wants to find out about his daughter – Kate Connor, I reckon you might have met her.'

'Me? Doubt it. Like, me and women, I've known my fair share and all but, those days, yeh, those days you watched out what bint you got close to, like a quick dip in the sack and come morning, fuck, fleeced.'

Don handed over a photo of Kate.

'Wow, look at that man, I'm in love! I mean, what's her name? I mean I could truly go for that, talk about fucking pure as snow and the fucking slags I meet.'

'What about Bridie?'

'That name rings.'

'What about a guy with "Angle" or "Angel" written on his head?'

'Shit.'

Mitch stopped dithering by his kitchen cubicle. He sat on a chair and got out his tobacco tin. Don could see the grey plastic of an electronic tag strapped to his ankle. Shaky fingers and over-focusing eyes knocked up a burn.

'You really are bad news, whoever you are, a fucking bad dream walking you are – like, man, I'm trying to get out, get halfway clean and you bring that bastard up out of the sewer. Shit.'

'Happy memories, eh?'

'Don, get on with it. This guy, he's useless, he needs a kick in the teeth to get him to the point.'

'Don't want to talk bout what he did – better to fuck off to Timbuktu – but if you wanna give him grief, fuck, you can have half me dole cheque.'

'Is he vicious with women?'

Mitch nodded.

'Got any mates he hangs around with?'

'Yeh, there's Angel Beck, and then Daz Harper and Mick somebody, they don't come any more shitey. I mean, the fucking things they –'

'And you know where they are?'

Mitch nodded again.

'What about the guy Khalid? You reckon he might get vicious with women and fuck with those that look as pure as snow?'

'Oh, man, this is too much, I gotta, shit, it's all in the past and I don't want – pure dangerous – the future is where I'm at, where I'm going, like I've remembered, this guy, said I'd see him for a game of pool, probably should've been there an hour back . . .'

'Jesus, what a wreck of humanity, you really should whack him one.'

'OK, Mitch, I'll get out your hair. Just tell me where this Angel hangs out?'

'This pub called the Lock. I tell you, he's a cagey bastard.'

Don stood up and looked down at Mitch who was now shaking more than ever, his hands trying to hold his legs still, and dropping fag ash onto the floor. He didn't think pool would be what the appointment was for.

'Thanks for the help, Mitch. You keep on going somewhere else, yeh?'

'*Is that it?*'

'You've gotta go somewhere, I reckon, but not get stuck in between where you're coming from and where you're going, neither here nor there, if you get my drift, like going round in circles and all that shit.'

'*Don, cut out this crap!*'

'Right, I am talking crap.'

Mitch looked up, his head shaking. 'Whatever, man . . .'

Don drove off to Jackie's office. He had the sea bean in his hand. Something to soothe, along with the steering wheel.

'*We're getting there, Don. I can feel it, we're gonna get the bastard.*'

'Huh, just a few more names rising up out of the sprawl, more bad blood.'

'*Yeh, but this could be it, this could be retribution time.*'

'It wasn't me who brought that word up.'

He gave his head a slap and worked his thumb harder in the groove. He was getting sick of words and voices, the jumbled mush of constant chatter. He fought to impose some space, find some little fissure between the jabbering and the traffic clamour where there was just feeling, just a sense of quiet mourning for a young woman.

Corridors. The only problem with Metropolitan Investigations was the corridors. Don felt a chill as he walked down one. Those doors that might burst open with a nightmare shock. The way the perspective threatened to swallow you. Don got through all right to Jackie's place but was met with a different surprise.

Pat Connor sat in the guest chair, his balding head reflecting office light and his mottled face looking weary and glum. A false grin flashed when he clocked Don.

'Well, here be the great man himself.'

'Jesus, Pat . . .'

Don then saw Jackie in the corner fixing up coffees. He got a nice smile but felt suspicious anyway.

'You want a coffee?'

'Sure.'

Don grabbed a chair and sat some distance away, facing Pat. Slumped down was more like it – Don suddenly felt exhausted.

'Bit of a surprise, eh, but I had to go down south so I thought I'd pop in to see how it was going.'

'You could've rang.'

'I tried but it's hard to get hold of you and I thought a meet would be better, more personal.'

The coffees came. Jackie sat behind her desk and smiled again.

'We're doing all right, that's right, yeh, Don? It's a dangerous situation but we've got positive leads,' she said.

'Too right, it's dangerous.' Don felt tenseness in his jaw. He didn't want this. Pat was back there, part of a blood-smeared past Don was trying to swim away from.

'I know I can rely on you, mate, so what's the score?'

A strange sea, cold and hard, on a brittle reef where armoured crabs pick and probe. Ain't much fun being part of the soft shoals, though it all looks good on camera. In the crevices, pain and perpetual anxiety . . .

'Don? You still with us, or haven't you arrived yet?'

Don unlocked his eyes from the window and the steady stream of traffic that cruised the motorway. 'Sorry, it's been a tiring day.' He took a large gulp of coffee and shook himself into life. 'Right. The score. Well, I reckon we've got quite a big suspect list now, maybe four or five, and it seems like Kate might've accidentally met the wrong crowd. Drawn from a fairly harmless scene at a games parlour and into something much more nasty – drug psychos probably.'

'Fuck . . .' Pat's sociable charm sank back to glum weariness.

'Nothing certain, Pat, I could be going totally up the wrong loop.'

'When's this likely to pan out?'

'Couple of days, I hope.'

'So that's the time I got to decide what to do.'

'Guess so . . .'

You know what he'll want eh, Don, great, let's get them teeth sharp.

Don clenched his jaw and looked over at Jackie. She smiled and then gave a kind of apologetic shrug. Pat spoke again.

'There was something else, Don. Since getting hold of you was a pain, I did give Jackie here a ring, just for an update, and we kind of got to talking.'

Threat bells started ringing in Don's head. He looked again at Jackie but she kept her head down.

'Like, Don, I did ask you back home whether, you know, you were up for things. That shit with Halligan, I know it got to you and –'

'I told you I was OK, that the break would be good.'

'Yeh, but from what Jackie here was saying, sounds like the gremlins are back.'

'Sorry, Don, but I did say I was worried about you.' Jackie's face was rumpled with emotion.

'Told you she was a bitch.'

'S'all right.' Don struggled to speak. 'I'm coping.'

'All they give you is pain.'

'I dunno, Don, like you been telling Jackie that it was you who shot the brother. Now come on, mate, you know it was me. You were there, he fell on you but it was me that had to pull the trigger.' Pat glanced over at Jackie. 'Self-defence of course.'

Don's eyes went back to the traffic flow. *Pale face looming. Big gob open wide. An explosion of blood. That slimy face flopping onto his own. A growl of death as personal as a love bite.* But could he remember what happened before that?

'It was all confusing . . .'

'Yeh, I know, Don, and it's come down here with you. I blame myself, too selfish in finding out about Kate. Even though you're the best, should've sent someone else.' Pat ran a hand over his face. He looked concerned, but Don was never really sure about him, he was such a wheeler-dealer.

They're playing with your mind, some sort of therapy crap.'

'Anyway, you know my contacts, you know what a hypo I am, so I checked out a few docs, got a few opinions – bout what to do.'

'I reckon I can sort myself out.' Don didn't hide his irritation.

'Yeh, I knew you'd say that and I know you'll get the old bargepole out to any suggestion involving docs or shrinks. I know you, Don, and I've come prepared.'

Pat leaned over to a briefcase by his chair. A podgy hand brought out three small boxes. Don could see they were medical.

'These guys, they said – well, fuck, don't they just talk? Technical gibberish and high-handed with it. Something like – "Well, it might be a minor problem and you might get through it on your own, but they reckon the drugs are good these days, though of course they should be the ones who dish them out" – shit, I'm not making any sense of this.'

Pat threw the boxes onto Jackie's desk. He gave Don a shrug.

'Whatever. Largactil, Stelazine and Dolmatil. They dampen the bad chemicals in your brain, but they do have side effects – make you dozy, numb feelings, give you the occasional shakes – shit!'

Pat leaned back in his chair and wrapped his arms around himself.

'Ah, fuck it, forget this, Don, it's a totally bad idea.'

'I appreciate you are trying to help but –'

They want to poison you. Let you do all the graft and then come in and fry your brain. Don't buy it, Don!'

'I reckon I can sort it. I will, really.'

Pat looked over at Jackie with an expression that said 'at least I tried' and then he stood up.

'This was only a flying visit, Don, me just stopping off on the way to a meeting down the Smoke.' He picked up his briefcase. 'I guess you probably will sort yourself, but just go easy, yeh? Quietly finger the geezer and I'll do the rest. After that, a fucking big holiday for you, mate.' He gave off a grin, a thumbs-up and was clearly glad to get out the room.

Don saw it then, going back in his mind, the gun in Pat's hand.

They didn't talk about it until later on. A silent journey back to Jackie's place. A ready meal on the cluttered kitchen table with Don talking about Mitch and the speed mind that was consciousness of the city itself. Fast, fragmented and confused. Don found himself getting into that jive, aware of something wriggling around in his brain, something angry and frustrated and wanting to take over. Jackie tried to keep up.

'Been down that road,' she said, 'those pill-popping party nights where you rattle on till your jaw aches and your eyes just bulge and feel bruised. And it don't stop, well into the next day, and you can't imagine that sleep ever existed.'

'Till you crash for twenty-four hours.'

'Right, let's crash now, on the sofa. I got me a spliff, far more civilized.'

'Sounds good.'

'Then you can tell me how pissed off you are.'

They got down on the sofa and Don did. Jackie took the flak, the less than convincing assurances Don gave that he would sort it, but she didn't apologize.

'It frightens me. This is getting out of my experience. You're a nice guy, Don, I like you, but there's this strangeness about you and this freaky talking to yourself.'

'Something's got to me, that's all. It'll sort itself. I reckon it was the Halligan business, you know, a major shock to the system that has to work itself through.'

'I dunno, the mind, it don't half go deep.'

'Yeh.' Don shuddered. He got a vision of a pond full of murky entrails.

Jackie looked at him closely. Suddenly he had an awful thought that she might turn into a shrink.

'Shit, don't you ever feel your world, your reality, sort of slipping at times?'

'Well, yeh . . . specially when Lester died. On my own, in this place late at night, I'd hear him speak, a couple of words maybe, just about audible, and I'd freeze up with terror. Then maybe you'd catch a movement in the corner of your eye and it's like you're convinced someone's in the flat – a ghost, a spirit or maybe just a desperate robber.'

'Right, then you doubt yourself.'

'Maybe, but I don't usually let it go that far. I get up, switch on the radio, put some washing in the machine and maybe have a shower.'

'Showers are nice.'

'I guess we have to find our own ways to move on from shitty situations . . .' Jackie stalled. 'Bloody hell, Don, this is miserable talk.'

'Too right.'

'We've got to bloody well lighten up here.'

Jackie then realized that she'd smoked the whole spliff.

Don smiled and shrugged. He didn't mind; weed was bad for wobbly brains.

'Let's dig out music.'

'Fucking great.'

'A bit of old Gregory would do the trick.'

'Fine, and by the way, talking of changing things, I have just the inkling of a plan.'

'Really, and what –?'

'Too early to say.'

Jackie stood up and put on an old vinyl LP. A scratchy version of 'Set the Captive Free' began to rumble around the room. She raised her arms and started to groove with the rhythm. 'Yo, this goes back a bit, eh?'

'Before my time.'

'Bastard.' Jackie pulled a face. 'Have you know, I was in a dance group at school for a while.'

'You are hot.'

'That's better. So, come on, you lazy sod, join me.'

'Shit . . . do what I can.'

Music drowned out all further words and blew thoughts out of the room. Jinking reggae rhythm, rippling organ and then on came 'I'm ready, here I come'. Jackie grabbed Don around the waist and they both got grooving with the beat. All body talk then and sweat – 'a bumping and a grinding' as the Cool Ruler would sing, their worried eyes trying to smile and that brain-fucked, shit winter outside was something somebody else lived. 'Fiddle-de-dee, fiddle-de-dum . . .'

Later, in bed, Jackie fell asleep almost straight away. Tired, dilated eyes smiled briefly before ganja dreams took her. Don wondered what they might be like and whether they were as disturbing as his own. Her dreams, he thought, that was getting close. He smoothed the sea bean, looked across the bed at the fish tank and watched the suspended creatures within, their ever-open eyes testament to some sort of being. Don wanted to close his eyes but he knew sleep was some time away. He knew what was going to happen, the humming sound in his head, and he waited.

'*You really have been a lame fucker, haven't you?*'

'Is that you in the bottom of the tank, the one eating fish shit?'

'*Can't you see what they're doing? Trying to make out you're not up to it. Trying to ease you out and put you in a nuthouse. And as for her! You know it, Don, she only wants what she wants and she'll scheme her guts out doing it. Before you know it, you'll be someone else.*'

'I don't mind being someone else.'

'*Won't work. You've got to get the shit out of you and that means blood and retribution.*'

'I just want to sleep.'

'*You'd do well by starting with her. Yeh? You could just lean over right now, take that pillow there, shove it on her head and suffocate her. She's only a tiny human, after all, and she'll probably thank you for it, an escape from all the misery she's —*'

'Fuck!'

'*Go on, Don, do it.*'

Don slapped his head and quickly jumped off the bed. He went to the fish tank, thought about smashing it, before rushing off to the bathroom. The shower went on full blast and Don sought out the ocean's edge where waves ate even the hardest stone.

15

Bedroom lights in the morning. The window almost dark, flecks of rain glinting. Cold out there. Don eased himself out of bed and looked through the glass. A smear of light on the horizon. He could hear Jackie in the kitchen. The sounds she made helped. It had been a sleepless night, one exhausting struggle with himself and his mind. He had just about stayed together but the malicious voices, the dodgy memory and those weird dreams, they seemed to be getting stronger. Don got dressed and went bleary eyed into the kitchen. Jackie smiled and dangled a slice of toast from her fingertips.

'Sure, several,' Don said.

'I don't think you slept quite as well as me.'

'Druggie.'

'I know, but you've got to have a bout of oblivion now and then.'

'Frequently wouldn't be bad, but weed doesn't always work that way with me.'

Don sat down and took the toast from Jackie. She put more bread in the toaster and then supped at a coffee.

'You gonna be OK checking this lead out?'

'Fine.'

'I'm gonna be busy most of the day – a child custody case with nasty vibes attached.'

'Great, we can compare who's had the nastiest at the end of the day.'

'Yeh, and let's talk more, go through some a that shit you been through, mebbe untie a knot or two.'

Don laughed. 'Masochist.'

The slate grey dawn had finally made it across the whole sky by the time Don got outside. Cold wind blew up the road and the trees shivered and cried. He slipped into the car. The beams of his lights were still useful, preferable indeed, presenting warm funnels he could follow. He headed off into the city, joining the car hordes whose lights pointed to towers emerging out of the winter murk. His first place of calling was a bank. Pin numbers had become completely lost to him, but he could handle a cheque, he could look at a pleasant face, catch a glimpse of character (the female teller had crow's-feet eyes) and almost touch fingertips when he hauled in his cash. Cory spoilt the moment; the bastard had woken up far too soon.

'*Gotta watch it, Don. The cameras, these places are stuffed full of them.*'

Don sighed and gave the teller a wistful smile.

'*It's important, you're close to action and you don't want your movements traced. Remember that bloke you socked.*'

Don headed out into the street. 'What the fuck . . .'

'*It's no better here, look, one of those fucking poles beaming right in on you. I reckon you should keep out of the centre.*'

'They're everywhere, they're even on police vans patrolling round. Cops might soon have them in their helmets and I've even heard there's gonna be talking cameras.'

'*Maybe you should think of a disguise.*'

'Whatever, I'm off to the hotel. I need a change of clothes.'

Don did notice that people were looking at him, that they thought him weird for talking to himself, but he really didn't care. Strangers, who gives a damn?

Don headed left up the busy pavement, looking down at ankles and ripples of wetness. Shit, he thought to himself sourly, digging in the city for clues, digging in the city of my head.

The Snooper was tapping on the glass.

'Come on outa dere, Don, you bin wallowin too long.'

'Go away, I like being watched. I'm doing my bit to help people relax.'

'Yeh, but me got sometin much betta for you to see. C'mon, man, no pressure.'

Don found himself in a small room. There was a large bank of TV screens on one wall and some sort of console in front of them.

'See, there you got it, man, on screen, on tape, one big whack a the city.'

Don saw it all right, a mass of stranger shadows floating through bleached brick landscapes.

'We got we two hunnered a dem at the mo, an dat's jus here, dere's many thousand more all over, mekin sure we follow the straight an narrow.'

Don moved his head at different angles and peered at the glare. He found it hard to make any sense of the pictures.

'You wanna check dat one, camera 26, a real beaut, could watch you screwin you girlfren a mile away.'

All Don saw was cloud and a heap of scrap metal.

'But the real speshal one is dis.'

Don's eyes followed the Snooper's sparkling gaze where he saw an irregular-shaped rectangle that beamed out flickering grey fuzz.

'Our prototype, state a the art.'

'Can't see a thing.'

'Look closely, man.'

Don did. Beneath the shimmering surface of dots and lines, he could make out some sort of image, a shadowy blur shaped like a leaf or a fish.

'Early days, man, but the future surely.'

'What is it?'

'Fuck it, Don, it's the inside a you head!'

It had happened again. A quick remedial shower in his hotel room, a lie on the bed and he'd dropped off. Don groaned, checked out that the room was not being pernicious and then got up. He dressed, glad of the rest but feeling queasy about his dream. Where did the Snooper fit into all of this?

How do such things get inside? Don looked into the mirror. 'Normal,' he said defiantly, without daring to look too closely.

The Lock had the décor of a 'family, friendly local'. The fake padded leather seats, the mock 'olde' wood trimmings, and displays of barge and canal paraphernalia. In fact, coming in from the drizzle, Don felt at home for a while with the fantasy of a 'warm snug with good English ale'. The feeling didn't last long. The barman looked like a UVF heavyweight, past his prime maybe, but still capable of baseball batting a kneecap or two. Don received a surly, suspicious look when he got in a half. The rest of the room seemed equally unfriendly, white men mostly, serious daytime drinkers and tough-looking wheeler-dealers who hunched together in groups, perhaps preparing fiscal strategies for the black economy. No sign of the man called Angel. Don gave the barman a world-weary look.

'Don't it ever stop raining in these parts?'

The barman hunched his shoulders. He seemed galled that Don had the nerve to speak to him.

'Grin and bear it, I guess. Nice pub by the way.'

'Not from around here?'

'From up north, down on business.'

The barman shrugged again. OK, you could feel him thinking, so next, what kind of business?

Don didn't go on. Three men had entered at the other side of the bar. Don stared at stout bottles before taking a sideways look. One guy – pale, bristled face; flabby and round, sweat beneath his gelled black fringe. Another – frizzed up hair, sallow complexion and blue manic eyes. Don sneaked a final look.

The last one was taller and slightly older, thirties maybe. A worn, pockmarked face, his hair a short fuzz at the front and a dyed orange ponytail at the back. Don strained to make out the tattoos. A couple of prison-made crosses at his temples and the word on his forehead crinkled with frowns. Don waited for a moment of relaxation. It came when the pint was passed over. 'Fuckin great, Maxie,' said the man with ANGEL on his head. The three then slouched off to a corner table. Don pointedly looked out of the window where beer crates and a brick wall were being washed by rain.

'And still the sky pisses.' He sighed. 'Reckon I'll have me a pint this time.'

He took it to a table next to the three weird ones.

'So, we got that covered for today, and tomorrow we do the Barrel and mebbe check out Hopton Tower,' Angel said, his voice sharp and no-nonsense.

'Yeh, yeh . . .' Manic-eyes replied. 'Whatever, eh, what's most important is we can doss for the rest of the day.'

'You'd be totally fucked without me, Daz.'

'Whatever . . .'

'Huh, talkin a fucked,' this was the black fringe speaking, 'you see that soft porn shit on telly last night?'

'I'm strictly hardcore.'

'Yeh, well, I was just crashing out really, would've watched anything, ended up watching these bimbos with tit jobs pretending to screw to the sound of some sort of sugar shit musak crap.'

'What's the point, Mick?'

'Pubes.'

'Ha, ha, here we go.'

'Sad Mick's at it again.'

'Just, like, when you see these bimbos in the buff, they've always got blond hair and dark pubes.'

'So, that's women for you.'

'Yeh, but which one do they dye, their bonce or their fanny? If they're fake blondes, why don't they dye their fanny? Or have they only got one job lot a artificial pubes that all the nude bimbos have to wear?'

'Fucking hell, you got nothing else better to think about?'

'Wait a min, Daz, the sad sod could be onto something. You know, like the black pubes business is about drawing attention to the fanny. Like – look at me, aren't I the one, displaying you my crotch.' The angel guy showed this by opening his legs.

''Cept they don't, do they? There's fuck all to see anyway.'

'Yeh . . . that's why they don't show cocks. With a cock you do see something. You do with mine anyway.'

'Fuckin hell, Mick, a shrivelled prune, mate. So tell us, you dye your pubes, or you shave em off?'

'Piss off.'

Don sighed at the next table and stuck to sipping his beer. Even Cory was bemused. *Shark shit, dollops of it,* was all Don heard him say to himself. It could be a long afternoon before he found a way to get talking to them.

'There's a fuck thing you don't see much of in movies, a smooth as a pebble cunt, cept in hardcore of course.'

'Right, you might see something then.'

'Now we're getting there. You like em shaved, eh, Angel?'

'No way, Daz, might as well have a hole in the wall. I like my hands groping in thick bushy undergrowth.'

'Something else you don't see much of, a real forest of pube. It's like they all get the barber down on them for a short back and sides.'

'Ha, ha, too soddin right, and with some of the fuckers, it's just like a thin stripe. Fuck knows how they don't cut themselves shaving.'

'Probably do. If you got up close, probably see all the nicks and scars and a five o'clock shadow.'

'Ergh, puts you off the old cunny that does, don't it?'

'Fuck, I prefer to get blowed anyway.'

'Wouldn't mind anything myself at the moment.'

'Ah, Mick, now we have it. You're so fuckin desperate, you even watch crap movies for a wanky turn-on.'

'No soddin way!'

Don remembered he had some fags. He hadn't been smoking much lately. He wasn't sure why. Vaguely, he felt that Cory disapproved and so had cut down. This brought on a sudden sense of annoyance. Jesus, how deep down does it get? Don defiantly pulled out a smoke and leaned over to the next table.

'Say, don't happen to have a light, do you?'

The guy called Daz, the manic-eyed one, responded, pulling out a red disposable and chucking it over. 'When you gotta have one, you gotta have one.'

'First of the day.'

'Fuck, that ain't bad.'

'Probably blow me head off.'

'Yeh, well, nothin like a good blow.'

This brought smiles from his mates and a co-ordinated movement of hands to the beers on the table. Don leaned back and felt the buzz rush. That'll be enough for a first contact, he thought. Too pushy and suspicions will be raised. He leaned over to his pint and began to finish it off.

'*What? You've got this nasty shit Angel in your sights and you're gonna call it a day? That's pathetic.*'

Don put his hand to his mouth and mumbled. 'You may live in my brains but the fuck you don't have any.'

'*Don't get smart and sarky with me.*'

Don stood up, said 'Cheers' to the weirdoes and walked out of the bar.

'*I really don't think you should leave.*'

Late afternoon and the slate grey was getting pushed off to the horizon again. Don stood on the pub steps and saw midge-like raindrops dance beneath the car park lights.

'*And you should pack in that filthy habit. It'll kill me as well, you know.*'

'You first I hope,' Don said as he went to his car.

Don got a glimpse of something way back. A sudden sense of warmth and security. In some attic room in the middle of winter, with the cold outside and a blazing fire within. Nothing at that particular moment to worry about. When was it, then, that things got under his skin? He shrugged. The thought was slipping away. But he felt some hope that maybe once there was a time when he really was all right. He was sitting on the rust-coloured sofa while Jackie threw dirty dishes in the sink and made her usual half-hearted efforts to clear up. There was something about her flat that did bring a sense of ease.

'That'll do. I'm shattered.'

'I told you, I'll sort it in the morning.'

'You certainly have your uses.'

'Don't ask me to change a plug.'

Jackie slumped down next to him. Her eyes looked tired and slightly furtive but Don didn't get much of a view for she buried her head in his shoulder.

'Tough day, huh?'

'I told you, a lot of travelling around and a lot of angry people. It gets you down.'

'Dealing with parents and kids, you know, does it bring back things, like about Lester?'

'That's quite astute of you, Don.'

'Just dropped into my head. A lot of things seem to do that these days.'

'Yeh, well, you're right.'

'A wobble.'

'Yeh, a standing on the edge of a cliff wobble. There's this shitty father who wants his son but no responsibility and he's making his ex's life hell. Still, I'm getting the evidence about the bastard he truly is.'

'Sounds like a lousy case.'

'Ah, just listen to him.'

Don clenched his mouth and strained his head back. Sod off! he shouted silently.

'You feeling better now, though, Jackie?'

'I'm OK. Every so often, there's a bloody great hole and you feel it wanting to swallow you. Just have to grit my teeth and wait for the moment to pass. Glad I was seeing you tonight.'

'So was I.'

'Face it, you're just pretending.'

'Checking out a bunch of druggie psychos is hardly a situation to make you feel any better, Don.'

'Right, cept if the bastards can be banged up.'

'Bullshit, Don, you'll do the other, you know you will.'

Don headed for the bathroom. Behind the locked door, he went to the sink and splashed cold water on his face. An image of the Connemara Sky Road suddenly came to him, Bóthar Na Spéire, and he saw crystal clear rock pools teeming with shrimp. Don grabbed the towel quickly and desperately wiped at his face as though he had covered himself with creatures that wriggled and bit. He began to mutter intensely beneath the towel. 'Fuck you, Cory . . . I'm gonna get you out of me if it's the last thing I ever do . . . get a fucking knife and dig you out. Can't you see, I'm getting somewhere, and I don't need this shit screwing me up. I fucking hate you!' He put the towel down. The mirror showed what it always showed – a vague sense of himself but blurry in the details. Don didn't punch it, though the urge was there. He felt a little better.

'You all right, Don?'

'Yeh.'

'Talking of things that come back to haunt you, what about you and this killing?'

'Right, Halligan's brother. It hasn't bothered me so much since Pat came down.' Don put his hand in his pocket and soothed the sea bean.

'That's good, though weird that you were so convinced you did it.'

'I dunno, guess it was the trauma of that blood. All I can see of it was him keeling over and then puking out this huge flow. It went all over me and straight down my mouth. Couldn't help but swallow. And the fucker, he was a dead weight, he pushed and pinned me down and I went crazy with panic. I managed to get him off with Pat's help. Then I was on my knees and retching like crazy.'

'Shit, enough to haunt anybody.'

'I've seen nasty things before, but this was like, like a kind of rape, I suppose, and I was really outraged and angry, viciously so. I wanted to kill the bastard all over again.'

'Maybe that's why you thought you had shot him.'

'Could be.'

'A kind of post-traumatic shock kind of thing.' Jackie paused and then smiled. 'Bringing out all that guilt in your conscience.'

'Right . . . I guess I'm a bit of a paranoid type anyway.'

'Huh, you have to be paranoid to survive.'

Jackie got up from the sofa and went into the kitchen. She brought back a bottle of malt whisky and two glasses. 'What I need.'

'I'd be happy to join you in a dose of oblivion.'

'I wasn't quite thinking of oblivion, somewhere a bit before, where it works as a turn-on.'

'Oh, right.' Don smiled, pushed in close and ran a hand up Jackie's thigh.

'Frisky are we?'

'Not as much as you, I reckon, you randy sod.'

'I've got a lot to make up for.'

Jackie gently squeezed Don's crotch and then poured out the whiskys. 'Well, here's to friskiness, for as long as it lasts.'

'A long time, I hope.'

'You reckon? The case, it could be wrapped up soon. You could be on your way to your next little fling.' Jackie's tone wasn't serious but the glint in her eyes was.

'Nah, that thought kind of makes me want to drag it out.'

Don's finger circled the outline of one of Jackie's nipples. It somehow made him think of the sea.

'Fuck, Don . . .'

'If we get through this shit together, maybe, you know, we could . . .'

'This isn't a moment to think straight.'

'Fucked if I know how to do that any more.'

Hands were roaming. Don's fingers were climbing the stepladder of Jackie's spine. A hot tangle and getting hotter, lust impulses smothering other instincts, like the ones that might want to play it safe.

16

'Where the fuck did you come from? I just can't work it out. I mean, I've never given a shit about fish in my life. I'm not all that keen on eating them, all those bones and the dodgy smell that comes off a them.'

Don was clearing up in the kitchen. He had his hands in hot soapy water, holding a scouring pad that felt slimy and disgusting. Through the window he could see roof land, bare branches and flecks of snow whisking around like bits of paper.

'Where, Cory? Were you in that gob of blood, or are you the ghost of the fish that lay in Kate's mouth? An aquarium, I've seen you in an aquarium. Jesus, since coming to this bloody city, there seem to be fish everywhere.'

'How'd you expect me to know?'

'Eh?'

'I'm in you, so you must've put me here. Give me an Amazon backwater any day of the week.'

'God, I really am mad.'

Don managed to get the dishes cleaned and racked. He threw away the slimy scourer and looked at the rest of the kitchen. A total tip. Piles of paper and unopened mail on the table. Jars, bottles and pans left out, along with CDs, clothing and various ornaments, bought but never really put anywhere. The detritus of so-called retail therapy maybe.

Don gave up on any thoughts of sorting it out. He had some time to kill, so sat down and lit up a fag.

'Maybe I don't need to know where you came from, maybe I can find another way of ditching you.'

'Maybe you just have to do it, Don, get your retribution and I'll be off down the sewers heading for home.'

'Retribution for what?'

'Come on, Don!'

'I really don't know what you're talking about.'

'Don't think, just act, eh, Don. That's all you have to do. You'll know when the moment arrives; and when you do get revenge, it'll be a massive relief and the end of your pain. In the meantime, just play it canny, tell that Jackie what she wants to hear and keep your head down when you come across cameras.'

The snow was sparse, a reluctant fall, most of it barely reaching the ground. Don thought back to those crematorium chimneys and shivered. Across from the car park there was a factory, its yard littered with strange machinery. To the side of the pub, Don could see the canal and the jutting timbers of the lock gates. He felt an unsettling sense of déjà vu, some place maybe he'd visited in his dreams, some bad vibe place for sure. Don walked through the cold to the warm snug of weirdo England. Maxie peered beneath threatening brows when he poured out Don's pint, his tattooed right hand seeming to want to crush the pump handle. Don just let his head loll and sent his eyes off at strange angles. So the bastard doesn't like me. He then heard familiar voices coming from a corner out of sight from the bar. Don grabbed his pint, took a deep breath and then wandered towards the voices. The manic-eyed Daz saw him first.

'Yo, got yourself a light this time?'

Don took a sup of beer and gave a thumbs-up.

'So you had your first fag yet?'

'Been a bad day, must be half a dozen.'

'That's the fucker with nicotine, one little glitch and you're puffing like crazy.'

Don wiped froth from his mouth and began to look round at the seats.

'Sit down with us, man, fuckin boring in here.'

'Thanks.'

He grabbed a chair and found himself sitting opposite Angel. Daz did the intros.

'I ain't seen you around here before.' This was Angel, intense dark eyes within a thin-stubbled face.

'Come down from up north on business, just here for a few days. Been looking for a decent pub, you know, something that doesn't try to be something else and rip you off in the process.'

'A spit and sawdust man like meself. So what's your line of business?'

'Buying and selling.'

'Right.' Angel smiled. 'Totally legit, of course?'

'Do I look like a dodgy operator?'

'Yeh.'

Everybody laughed then. Angel's laugh was high pitched and his nose crinkled into lines.

'Got you fuckin sorted then,' Daz said. 'So you got a spare burn? I've gone and spliffed all mine.'

Don pulled out a packet and handed it round. He then surveyed the bar and checked out the ceilings.

'This place ain't got cameras, has it? Was in a bar the other day which did.'

'Ner, Maxie's a hard arse, but he's no snoop.'

'Got em everywhere now.' This was Mick, his face shiny with sweat as though the gel he wore had covered his whole head. 'Ain't safe to do anything iffy in public.'

'Public! Private ain't much better.' There was an edge of

anger in Angel's voice. 'You arsehole, they can bug your phone, read your e-mails and your post. With this terrorist shit, they can get total surveillance on any poor sod.'

'It ain't that bad yet.'

'Don't you believe it, Mick. You could make some fuckin joke on the phone about how you'd like to wring the PM's neck and the spooks'd be onto you like a shot. You wouldn't be able to piss without them knowing it.'

'Or wank.'

'Sod off, Daz.'

'Fuck, Mick, I worry bout you. You're soft as shit.'

'Hold on –'

'Today, doing business, you were pratting around like a fucking ice-cream seller. No checking things out whatsoever for spies or set-ups. I tell you, if we get busted, it'll be down to fucking you and I'll fucking get you for it too.'

Mick's face had gone a slimy red colour and he was clearly looking for a hole to ooze into. Don sought to smooth things over.

'Yeh, well, they can shift a satellite nowadays to beam right on your house,' he said.

'That's true, and they got electronic chips they could fucking bung into you.'

'Gonna video your thoughts soon,' Don said with authority.

'Wouldn't be surprised.' Angel downed his pint. 'Get em in, Mick.'

Don didn't want one, but he went with the flow. He also felt obliged to take up Daz's offer of a twenty-quid deal. Well, at least Jackie would get into that. Another half an hour passed, more of the downtrodden woes of drug dealers and interpersonal piss takes, what you do on a shitty winter afternoon. It was Mick who took most of the flak. Don felt OK, almost comfortable, and nearly ready to raise the subject of young women. But not quite. Some-

thing slithered uncomfortably in his head at this hesita-
tion. He determined to remain resolute, although he was
getting booze woozy and not so sure what he'd do. It was
at some point then that he saw the red pebble: Angel jaw-
ing to Daz about some local jerk and in his hand, smooth
and shiny, a two-inch pebble the colour of blood. He was
even thumbing its surface just like Don did with the sea
bean.

'*Look at that!*'

'Stay cool, we don't want to rush this,' Don said to
himself silently. He was amazed he could sit there and do
just that. He then thought of one more thing to push up
the cred.

'Gotta go soon, guys, seeing this geezer Mal Chariot
about some scheme he wants to flog.'

'Fuck, you know im?' Angel did seem impressed.

'Not really, yet. He OK?'

'Better than most.'

'That's good to know. I haven't come all the way down
here to be fucked about.'

Angel looked around at his mates. 'You should come
round our place soon, you know, bigger choice a pick-me-
ups and all that, have a good time, see maybe if we've got
any mutual interests.'

'Right, sounds a possibility. When?'

'How about tomorrow afternoon?' Angel wrote down
the address.

Don smiled to himself. Suckers, he thought. What drugs
greed does. Could easily go round there late that night. He
could bung a gallon of petrol through the letterbox, write
a fiery note to go with it and save himself a pile of trouble.
He gave his head a heavy slap when he left the pub. What
the fuck is it with me?

Don headed off through the evening dark to Garvey's

where he'd arranged to meet Jackie. A cold evening with a slight sparkle of frost beneath the headlight glow. Cory was restless.

'Like your idea, Don. That shit has gotta be a major suspect; vicious in the eyes but quite capable of charm. Easily lead some poor girl on and then turn nasty. You're getting there, Don. But shit, do get a move on, this place is getting colder by the minute and it's hard to take.'

'You mean I can freeze you to death?'

'I am a tropical fish.'

Don focused on the clouds of exhaust fumes that rose up mist-like around the slow traffic. His eyes felt bleary with the booze. There really has gotta be somewhere else.

I can see it, Melanie, an early morning walk across the isle, me swallowed up and lost amid granite blocks and steaming lochans. It seemed an endlessly meandering road, took ages to get to you by the sea. Had my first insect bite of the day. Had my first doubts as to who the hell I was.

Garvey's was hardly up and running. A few early drinkers at the bar, staff polishing tables and stacking glasses. Jackie sat in a corner reading through paperwork. She looked tired and strained. Yes, there really has gotta be somewhere else. Don sat next to her and gave her a kiss.

'Another day of fraught family life?'

'Yep. Another day, for you, of hobnobbing with the depraved?'

'I'm a natural, one of the fraternity.'

'Sounds like you're making progress.'

'I've got strong suspicions about this lot. I'm meeting them tomorrow at their place. Might be able to get something solid on them.'

'That is good. And are you holding up?'

'Sort of. With bits of Sellotape and Blu-tac.'

'Daft bugger.'

Don got in some drinks while they waited for the restaurant to open. It was turning out to be a boozy day. He hoped it wouldn't be a binge. Jackie looked into his bleary eyes.

'Sod me, I should've hooked up with an accountant.'

'Oh, well, they wouldn't bring you twenty-quid deals.' Don pulled out the stash he'd got from Daz and pressed it into Jackie's hand.

'Right, thanks. However, I do have to say, an accountant, he might've got me a twenty-K car.'

'Get away.'

The food at Garvey's was good. They had the Caribbean chicken, salad and fried slices of plantain.

'So, Don, what about the big bust-up in your life, your ex and daughter?'

Don shrugged awkwardly. This was not what alcohol liked talking about.

'You think you're carrying something of that, you know, something from that scene that's doing your head in?'

'Wow, that's quite a heavy line of conversation.'

'Go for it, it's always good to get the crap out.'

'Well, the bust-up wasn't so bad a thing, had them before; and while they stayed around, it was OK with Melanie. I might have seen less of her, but when I did see her it was special and we had a good time. It was the Scotland thing that was hard to take.'

'Must've been.'

'I was on a crappy treadmill work-wise, and when the wrench came, it was like I'd lost part of me.'

'Huh, sounds familiar.'

'Yeh, but she's still up there, growing away from me every day. You know, there's always that regret . . .'

'You just can't stop lying can you, Don?'

Don shrugged again. Had he lied? He looked at Jackie

and she suddenly seemed a bit strange to him, like he didn't really know her, like she was just a somebody that he happened to be revealing personal things to.

'You went up there?'

'Yeh, big mistake. Apart from shit with the ex, that's when the distance really hits you, in every way. Me and Melanie talking, and neither of us understanding what the fuck we're saying. And shit, up there, the work I do is totally unreal. In fact, up there is unreal.'

'That would be very frustrating.'

'I dunno, try not to think too much about it.' Don knew for sure that was a lie.

He looked over towards the restaurant area entrance. The chicken leg he held fell from his hand. Mal was coming in and behind him, stocky and cross-eyed, was Khalid.

Since the room was hardly full, it wasn't long before wayward eyes clocked Don, and Khalid froze mid-stride. You could almost sense the squall of emotion.

'What the fuck is that dushman shit doin here, Mal?'

'Eh?' Mal hadn't noticed Don or that Khalid had stopped. He turned stiffly, looked around and suddenly got wind of the situation.

'That fucker – are you in with that? – I mean that fucker has got evil voices, he is seriously bad news.'

Khalid started to walk towards Don, his hand beginning to reach inside his jacket. Mal hurried to intercept as Don moved a hand to his own pocket.

'I'm gonna wipe you out, you gotta be wiped out, you're dirty dog shit, a disease against the righteous, a fuckin –'

'Come on, man, cool it, remember where the fuck you is – my yard!' Mal butted his shoulder against Khalid and grabbed the arm that was feeling for a weapon. Don smiled and narrowed his eyes in a silent taunt.

'You in with this shit, Mal? I mean, at a time like this, I don't want any crap going on.'

'I told you, cool it, man. You got it wrong, Don is jus a guest from up north, dealin wid some murder shit from way back dat have nuttin to do wid you or me. Dat is right, ennit, Don?'

'Sure. In fact I've deliberately tried to keep out of that walking loony bin's way.'

'Fuck! See.' Khalid pushed against Mal. 'Look in his eyes, man – bad shit – I can feel it. And I know he's got the ghost voices, I know he's gonna kill and he wants to kill me.'

'Fuck, you got it all wrong, man. Did'n me a tell you to stop usin so much? Dis paranoia, it ent good feh business, an we bein so close, Khalid, we don't wanna screw up now. Let's get in the office, chill out an go through dem details you was worried bout.'

Mal put his hand round Khalid's shoulders and started to edge him towards the back of the room.

'I'll fuckin get you first!' Khalid shouted.

Mal turned his head to Don and Jackie. He had a pleading look on his face that said, 'Just get the hell out of here, please.'

They lolled together on the sofa later, conscious that a hard frost was building up outside and happy not to be alone. Jackie struggled with spliff rolling on the horizontal while Don bathed his bleary eyes on the glow of the fire. Who was this Jackie, this warm somebody? He felt quite peaceful, as if Cory was dozing on the rug and Don was floating somewhere halfway to the ceiling and getting ready to ascend to the sky.

'You really do rub that Khalid geezer up the wrong way.'

'He thinks he's got a private line to my brain.'

'I hope he's not right.'

'So do I.'

'What you were saying earlier, about Melanie, got me thinking about Lester.'

'I didn't want to –'

'No, s'all right, I do it all the time, but tonight it kind of felt nice, like you might remember a good holiday, or some bit of serendipity from way back that makes you smile. That hasn't happened that much before.'

'That is good.' Don could see a thin wisp of spider's web on the ceiling that fluttered in the heat from the fire.

'Yeh, in all the crap, there always has to be some sort of hope.'

'Got to be.' Don was hesitant about levitating through the ceiling, it was bitterly cold outside. Bide your time and go for the sun, he thought lazily. He got out his sea bean and inspected it, looked at the little dimple at its core, the radiating veins of it and its heart-like shape. Jackie nudged him and he dropped down an arm to pick up the spliff. She began to talk about Lester, another world, strange characters, sunnier days remembered in the middle of the cold season.

17

The metal was sharp and rusty and it snagged on his clothes. *In between there was some sort of slimy substance like wodges of wet and mouldy newsprint. No matter how hard he climbed, he always seemed to slip back. But it was important to climb, he was desperate to climb because back there in the pit, among the bone white branches, hell was happening. Don wriggled and heaved against the repulsive slime. He reached out for mangled handholds and tried to see if the edge was in sight. It was a murky blur through tear-drenched eyes. Images of the four dark figures prevailed, four squat forms that stabbed and kicked and cut open the body. Don saw a finger pull out a dripping eye. A breast was like a water balloon they juggled around and threw at each other. A knife sliced between her legs and the pubis was a red juicy fruit thrown aside. Don redoubled his efforts. He thought he could be next. He was too scared to intervene. He was frightened of finding out whose body it was. Then his fingers touched sand.*

'You is not far from the top, man. A few more step and me can grab you hand.'

Don knew the voice. Him again.

'Come on, man, keep a pushin! It one bad bloodbath down there. Dem is deprave monster. Me neva see nuttin so bad, and man, me see a whole lot.'

Don made one more effort and finally caught hold of the brown hand of the Snooper. At the moment of touching, they were somewhere else.

'Man, did'n me a tell you, you got a whole lot a shit inside. Fuck, you is a cesspit.'

Don looked around. They were on a path by still black water. A canal or dock or maybe somewhere underground.

'Don, look at youself. Here look in dis mirror, come on.'

Don did and there was no reflection, no sign of himself at all. What he saw was water, swirling seaweed and ponderous grey fish snouting at the pebbled floor. He saw something else that made him shiver. A head of black hair swaying gently among the weeds.

The road was stained white with salt. Don saw puddles edged with ice. With Jackie already gone for the morning, he drove off from the flat and his dream fast. All this confusion, he didn't know how much more he could take.

'This could be it. I hope you've got your gun.'

'I'm not sure if I know what I'm doing.'

'Come on, the git with the stone, the mentality of those lot.'

'Why am I having such dreadful dreams?'

'Cos you're getting close, cos all the shit is building up waiting for you to do what you have to.'

'I reckon I should tell Jackie about you.'

'The fuck you won't! She's out to stop you, she wants you for herself, it's her you should get rid of.'

'She's everything you're not.'

'But you're nothing, right, you're a nobody, a worthless shit without me.'

'Fuck off.'

'You can't even see yourself in a mirror.'

Don eased his way under the giant struts of a flyover and then moved on towards a large roundabout, one he recognized from before when he circled it several times, feeling caught in between time. The feeling was different now, like he was being chased and all kinds of horrors were about to catch up. Don went round in one go. He looked up at the sky. Still an indomitable cover of cloud, the only shift being from damp to cold. The route to Angel's house took him past a familiar line of tower blocks, concrete monuments thrusting out of sparse green, high densities of strangers. Don wondered about all their dreams.

'They don't exist, Don, they can't, you've only got what you've got to make sense of it all, and most of that is me.'

'Yeh, yeh, fucking know-it-all.'

Up ahead was the Monument Arms. Don thought he recognized the guy outside, shifting his weight and clapping his hands to ward off the cold. He felt a burst of loathing and a desperate need to express it. Don mounted the pavement and braked barely a foot away from a shivering Shafaq.

'Glad I caught you,' Don said as he got out of the car.

'Oh fuck, you.'

'Yeh, the mad bugger who's got an axe to grind.'

'I told you, I'm onto it.'

'It seems to be taking a hell of a time. Khalid was threatening me yet again last night. One more time and there'll be blood everywhere.'

'Don't take it out on me. I mean, I know, the git is getting worse, and I said I'd fuckin help you, man, but it ain't happen yet! Fuck, just chill out, will you?'

Don pushed his fists in his coat pocket. He didn't really know why he would want to take it out on Shafaq other than a growing feeling that he had to take it out on someone. But *what the fuck is the 'it' I want to take out?* Don cast moody eyes across the four-lane road, the concrete and brick beyond.

'I mean, how do you find anything in that lot?'

'Yeh, right, the big fucking jungle, eh.'

'Shit, more like a bloody great sea. Look, don't screw me, Shafaq, I'm right on the edge.'

'It'll soon come, like soon, soon come. Them's just checking out a few details, man, and, as I said, you'll be the first t'know when it all go down.'

Don gave Shafaq one more glare, then got back in the car. He took a deep breath and realized he felt nervous. Not just about what went on in his head but what he was about to go into. He drove off. Half a mile and he turned left into a side road. It was a 1960s estate, a slum clearance dream that looked little better than what had been replaced. Low pay and benefits land, just a short hike from the fenced in apartments where Khalid lived. Don parked, went up to a blue door and rang the bell.

'Yeh, come in, man. It's the man from outer space.'

'What?'

'Don't mind us,' Daz said. 'We just reckon you got alien eyes.'

It was a small terraced house. All you might expect as a pad for single men. No carpet in the hall, nothing there but a spray-painted skull on the wall, its orifices home to writhing snakes. Don went into the living room. Angel was parcelling up small white powder deals on the coffee table. Mick was ogling a very large TV screen, the sound off, the picture looking like a Second World War submarine movie. He was going 'PING . . . PING . . . PING . . . PING' and then laughing to himself.

'Shut it, Mick, we got a guest.'

'I'm doing the sound effects. "What is that on the sonar, Seaman Jones, a ship or a whale?" Fuckin great.'

Angel raised his eyes and pointed to his head. Daz went off to make coffee. The room also contained a battered three-piece and stereo unit. In the corner was an aquarium.

Don saw three orange fish nuzzling the glass, their big yellow eyes seemingly pleading at him out of the dimness.

'Them're Mick's. He don't know it, but we're fattening them up for a Sunday lunch.'

'Sod off.'

'What are they?'

'Just goldfish. It's a cold water tank.'

'Fuck, you see that? That's probably what she had in her mouth.'

'You want a snort, Don?'

'Prefer a spliff, I reckon.'

'Whatever your poison, we got it. So how'd it go with Mal Chariot, then?'

'Let's say he had some interesting propositions. You don't deal with him, do you?'

'Nah, mostly this git Khalid. What an arsehole.'

'I've heard of him.'

'Absolute fruitcake. Had a set-to with him a while back. A woman thing, he goes too far with them. Pulled a knife on me so I nutted him one.'

'You lived to tell the tale.'

'Well, he shivved me in the arm at the same time, so we kind of called it quits. He don't fuck with me now, though.'

Daz brought in the coffees. From what he could see, Don's mug seemed to have a year's stains on the inside. A joint then came over from Mick. 'There you go then, Cap'n, a live torpedo.'

'Why don't you jump in your fish tank and play boats, Mick?'

Don drew in some dope smoke.

'So how'd you reckon you might stand with Mal, then?' Angel said as he collected his deals together and wrapped them in foil. He tossed the package to Daz, who put it in a shoulder bag.

'What d'you mean?'

'We could do a lot better if we did business with him. Being with the shitface Khalid, we're kind of fuckin tarnished, you know, can't get a look in cos everyone knows Mal hates the bastard.'

'I'll have a word. The business I got, it does him a favour.'

'Sound.'

It was strong dope. Don was getting awkward shifts in his perception. Daz's wild blue eyes seemed more like glass marbles. The TV screen seemed to grow in size and Don was drawn into the lens of the periscope and its view of choppy waters. He noticed that Mick was doing the same, lining up the sights and ready to press the 'fire' button. A loud coke snort from Angel pulled Don away. He saw the fish again. Not pleading, but pernicious eyes, he thought.

'So, Don, anything we might do for you?'

'Er . . .' Don shifted around uncomfortably. 'What about girls?'

'Right.' Angel smirked and winked at Daz. 'Away on business, chance to shag around.'

'Something, you know, young and . . . firm.' Don felt himself choke. This was raw-nerve stuff and getting perverse.

'Don't pull out now, when you go down the sewer, shit is what you get.'

'Right.' The smirk grew larger. 'Nothing better than a fresh young virgin, eh?'

'Well, it's been a while . . . you do all right?'

'Fuck, I'm a dealer, man, what d'you think?'

'Slags most a them lot, though,' said Daz. 'Thin as rakes and been had by the whole neighbourhood.'

'True, it ain't often you get a real fresh virgin. Fuck, when was it? That blond bint from last year probably. Quite a scene.'

'Don, I mean, Don, did you hear –?'

'Shit, Angel, listen to you.' This was Mick, his greasy face looking quite shocked. 'No offence, Don, but we don't hardly know you.'

'Yeh, you're right.' Angel grinned, making the tattoo crosses on his temples tilt up. 'Some things are best kept as secrets, know what I mean?' And then he winked.

'Get out your gun, shove it in his fucking mouth and make him carry on!'

'I can't . . . woh, this is a strong draw.'

'We always provide the best.'

'There's always our sexy Samantha,' Daz said.

'Yeh, no virgin, but young enough and well into shagging. Do anything for the candy man. Fuck, she can't get enough.'

Don began to feel queasy. The heat of the room, the smoke and all the eyes that seemed to home in on him. Even on the TV, the captain seemed to be staring at him. Don pulled out his sea bean and got his thumb rubbing hard. He tried to find a safe place in the room he could focus on. A mousetrap by the skirting board was all he could find.

'Hey, man, I used to have one of them. A sea nut I called it, and I used to do just that, with me thumb. Lost it ages ago, God knows where. Got this now.' Angel pulled out his red stone and smoothed his fingers round it. 'Relaxing, ain't it? Like them worry beads.'

It was like a ritual, the two of them, smoothing thumbs together in some strange bonding ceremony.

'Don, it all adds up.'

A silent 'shut it' was Don's response. He was trying to get some clarity into his foggy brain, fighting against the cannabis flow and not getting very far. Get them where I want them, was all he could come up with. He shifted in his seat.

'Gotta go,' he mumbled. 'Got another meeting and you pleasure-mad fuckers have done me head in.'

There was laughter all round and, 'Way to go, spaceman.'

'I will have a word with Mal. Are you up for business right now?'

'Shit, everyone's waiting for new supplies, some hold up in the system apparently.' Angel raised his eyebrows and pushed up his chin. 'For that, we'll give our sexy Samantha a call.'

'OK, great, gimme your number and we're on.'

The road seemed ten times wider than it normally did, five m.p.h. seemed like a ton. Don drove off towards Jackie's like he was a red-eyed geriatric. He was trying hard not to think of Kate, trying not to make the connection between Angel's grubby hands and sharp eyes and that optimistic smile that stood on his bedside table. The thought of a physical connection was almost unbearable.

'It is them, I'm sure, that shit almost came out with it. You should've asked him to give a name.'

'Leave off, that would've raised suspicions straight away.'

'Should've got your gun out, shot the bugger in the knee, that would've got them talking.'

'Too risky. I need to get them somewhere where they feel exposed, and maybe work on that Mick. He looks like a weak link, they all seem to take the piss out of him.'

'Fuck, Don, you're just about there. Retribution beckons, all that shit you've suffered, you can sling it back double and finish the bastards!'

'Gotta speak to Pat, and Jackie.'

'Fuck no.'

'He pays the wages.'

'You have other needs, Don, and they're probably greater than his.'

'Shit, Cory, I dunno. I mean, I do want to do something, smash some fucking thing to pulp but, I dunno, the Halligan business doesn't seem to matter that much now and Kate, well, she is Pat's pain.'

He heard a car horn, saw he had a whole line of cars behind as he tried to work out when to move onto a roundabout. Feeling blind panic, he drove out regardless of traffic, got more blasts from horns, but managed to get through.

'Shit, am I on the right road?'

'Look, Don, what fucked you up is what other people did and up to now, you've taken that crap. You owe it to yourself to fuck people back.'

'Yeh . . . when you put it like that . . . but you're just a stupid voice who thinks it's a fish. I should just admit that I am mad and go and section myself.'

'They'll pump you up with chemicals, throw a blanket over your brain and then you might lose me.'

'That's a thought.'

There is no effective way to tone down a high. Coffee doesn't work, but food can help. Don sat in the kitchen and scoffed whatever was available, the sweeter the better. In between mouthfuls, he told Jackie about what he'd learned.

'Still circumstantial.'

'Yeh, I need to exert some pressure, that or hang out longer with the scumbags hoping they'll spill more details.'

'Not a pleasant prospect, I guess.'

'Nah, I'm sad, weary and sick to death of the whole thing. I'd just like to wring their bloody necks and be done with it.'

'Very professional.'

'Not like you to be sarcastic.'

'Don, you look a mess and I've told you before, you've

got this bloody violence bubbling away inside and it needs to be curbed. Come on, think work, apply some reason.'

'There isn't going to be any physical proof after so long, is there?'

'Unlikely.'

'It's gotta be a confession.'

'Obtained without undue pressure.'

'Maybe, but it isn't my job to convict the buggers, just tell Pat who did it.'

'What will Pat do?'

'I dunno, he could go either way.' Don looked at Jackie. A frown. A lip being chewed. 'I know, it stinks.'

'If you want me to help you, pressure maybe, but no violence. We get a recording, give it to Pat and the police.'

'Deal.'

'*I trust you're being canny now?*'

Don grinned. It was partly due to the dope and partly to hide the interference from his secret other. Really, how could he tell her about that?

'You still up for eloping?'

'I'm in two minds.'

'Aren't we all.' Don grinned again. 'Anyway, this plan I mentioned, there might be a way to get some serious dosh from people who shouldn't have it.'

'Jesus, Don, stop there.'

They both looked each other in the eyes then. Dope eyes, tired eyes and pained. And something else, something you couldn't say because it would seem too bad, but yet secretly, you might do anyway.

'Fuck, you fancy a lie down?'

18

A fog bank over the mind. It hadn't been much of an afternoon nap, Don's bleary mind thinking unsettling thoughts, close to Jackie on the bed but feeling miles away. He eased up and went to find her. She was in the kitchen. Don butted shoulders with her as she stood drinking coffee and he fumbled around for words.

'I – I was thinking, just, while we were dozing, the case, it could get wrapped up tonight.'

'Yeh . . .' Jackie sipped coffee and kept her eyes intent on the mug. 'I had that thought too.'

'I was wondering, this hotel room, why don't I just book out today?'

'Uh-huh.'

'I'm pretty much living here anyway.'

Jackie's eyes pulled away from the coffee and she stared at Don. Signs of alarm and defences up. 'What are you trying to say?'

Don sighed and fought against his dopiness. 'It's kind of saying, "Yeh, I like being with you" and, "No, I'm not trying to force anything".'

'I see.'

'I was also thinking that if things go pear-shaped with the case, the hotel could raise problems, like if I have to do a runner.'

'It's nice to know you're thinking.'

It was Don's turn then to avert his eyes and stare downwards.

'I guess I can see what you're saying, Don, it makes some sense, but, I dunno –'

'I've only got one suitcase, you can kick me out whenever.'

'That's a lot harder than me just not opening my door to you, especially if things do go pear-shaped.'

'I know, but –'

Jackie went over to the window and stared out at frosty roofs. Daylight was beginning to slip away. Don noted her silhouette, dark and sad, like the time she walked into the cemetery. He went up and put his arms around her waist. They both looked out at coldness.

'Sod it, you might as well do it, Don. You're right, it doesn't make any difference to the way we are. We'll still have to make up our minds, about what we want to do.'

Don took a shower. Back in his element. He wanted to think about a future with Jackie but didn't dare. Fingers rubbed hard into his skull and coarse cloth scoured his skin. A punishing way to get himself sorted, get himself ready for a try at resolution. The cloth felt like sharp stones and he thought of walking barefoot over coral strands and shell beaches out there in the west where the water was warm and full of life. Painful, treading on the bones of the dead. After the shower it was more food, the dope effects now a hunger ache which he still needed to satisfy. Then it was on the blower. Jackie had suggested a place for a meet. A breaker's yard beside the blue brick viaducts of the old town. She still had the key from when investigating a parts scam.

Don spoke to Angel. 'Wow, some blow that was. I'm still flying.'

'Yeh, looked like you was heading for the stratosphere.'

Don said that Mal would give the gang a one-off go at direct dealing. It'd have to be that night though, at Enzo's yard. Just name the commodity and bring the cash. Angel seemed to swallow it without question – a cagey guy maybe, but it looked like caution had lost out to greed. He rang off saying that Samantha would like to meet a spaceman and would really dig the chance of alien sex. There ain't nothing that ain't normal nowadays, thought Don, or maybe nothing that ain't crazy.

He remembered Ricky and the bird with the broken wing. He kind of liked Ricky. Back on the blower again. 'So, how's the feathered geezer getting along, our Rick?'

'Don, ennit? Thank you for ringing. The magpie, he's almost fit.'

'Great, what you've got to be in this world, eh, Ricky? He should be up for a good old chat then.'

'Fuck, went there yesterday and he was squawking like mad.'

'I like it. And are you OK?'

'Yeh, just met this guy who collects old bikes. He's going to show me how to do em up. I could have meself a sort of job.'

'Great, check you later.'

Don kissed Jackie before he left to do some final sorting. Responsive and sensual, but still that worry in her eyes. Don didn't dare think too much about how she really felt. This was going to be one last push, crazy or desperate, and the hope was – the hope was that he'd get a result and not screw up. *In the winter, the waters are cold and you can die in seconds.*

Back then to the concrete canyons of the expressway for Don, heading into the city centre and his hotel. Check out time and an uncertain future. Don tried to look beyond the streetlights for any sign of stars but the brooding blackness of clouds still prevailed, the blackness and a damp, bone-chilling cold.

'*I hope you really have got this properly set up, Don.*'

'I got em where I want em.'

'*Just make sure the Jackie woman doesn't get all soft.*'

'She's just being what she is.'

'*I mean, prison's no punishment for scum like that.*'

'Probably true.'

'*Just home from home for them. You get your sex, your drugs and your rock 'n' roll in there all right.*'

'And TV movies.'

'*For those types, it's a bearable option, a similar lifestyle and no responsibilities. They should know what real punishment is.*'

'Angel's done time before.'

'*No choice but to give them pain.*'

'Like a bullet in the gut and a slow death.'

'*Now you're talking.*'

'Retribution enough for the shit I've had to take. Nothing else for it but to let go, wipe the buggers out and get myself looking forwards again.'

'*That's it, now you're getting it, it's a kind of final solution. Do it and you'll never be hurt again.*'

'We're a team, ennit, Cory?' Don caught a glimpse of himself grinning in the rearview mirror.

'*Drive on.*'

Don parked up at the side of the hotel and rushed through cold to the balmy, carpeted calm of the hotel foyer. He asked for his bill to be prepared. They didn't know who he was. Don was happy with that. Progress. He took his key and headed up to his room. He noted that his feelings of paranoia had gone too, that this was some empty shell of a place that would be soon forgotten. His room was not quite so neutral, though, the bad vibe feeling still clung. Don trod the carpet warily and avoided the mirror as he collected his things. He checked that he had his plastic hand ties and spare ammunition. From the bedside table, he picked up the picture of Kate. What they did to you. Tears welled behind his eyes. He sat down on the bed and felt a wave of sadness. He wanted to ask questions about the why of it, but that brought forth glimmers of murkier things, obscene acts down in the mud and slime. Don stood up. The hotel room had a way of bringing out the disturbing. Quickly grabbing his bag, Don left and tried to slam the door on all of what he'd felt.

He drove back out of the city. On the three-lane conveyor belt of cars, a million lights twinkling, a million thoughts jostling within that moment. Don tried not to think because he knew reason had left him, there were just too many reasons. He eased down a slip road and parked under the thunder of the motorway. Jackie was ready, waiting outside her office building.

'You got your gun, sweetheart?'

'Of course, what you need for a night out.'

'Got mine too. Now, just be calm, OK, Don? Let's be professional about this, get the guys the way we planned and leave the rest to the police.'

'Let's just hope it does go according to plan.'

'I had a chat with Col, remember, our surveillance guy. He's agreed to act as back-up. He'll be parked up the road in case we need him.'

'God, that's good. I'm impressed.'

'When it comes to work, I don't piss about. Wish I could say the same about my private life.'

'I'm really glad you're here.' Don looked over. 'Jackie, a fantasy thought: what if we do manage to pull it off, can scam an escape and go travelling, where you reckon we should head for?'

Jackie gave him a tight smile.

'Just to take our mind off things.'

'Well, no promises, eh, Don, but . . . first off, we could go and visit me dad, Earl, in Jamaica. It's been a long time since I've seen him, though I probably wouldn't want to stay there that long, so . . . Maybe hop a few islands, you know, Grand Cayman. Slip over to Mexico, whatever.'

'You gotta have something to look forward to.'

Don wasn't sure he meant that. It suddenly seemed like he was talking because that's what he was supposed to do, and Jackie had become something of a stranger to him then. In fact, he realized he felt detached from everything, with the car driving itself and the city again just some token backdrop for an electronic game.

'I spoke to Pat on the phone.' Jackie maybe sensed the detachment and was trying to keep in touch.

'Right. I was gonna do that after.'

'Said he wants to know for definite before he decides what to do. Didn't object to the police being involved if it's a cast-iron case they get done.'

'Sounds very sensible for Pat.'

'He told me a few other things, surprising things about you, which it would be nice to talk about later.'

'Fine.'

'I also spoke to this DS I know and said something might be going down. He gave me a mobile number to call if we get results.'

Don bit a lip. She doesn't trust me, isn't that great. I mean, I could – He stopped himself. No thinking, let go and just do.

'Fine.'

'I've got a recorder in my bag. It's a powerful one, so, you know –'

'Don't say anything I might regret.'

'You got it, mister.'

'This is the road, right?'

Don eased the rental down a dimly lit street that was bordered mostly by factories. Dark Victorian affairs with dust-filled windows and cheap signboards which advertised industrial processes Don did not understand. They passed under one of the big railway viaducts, the streetlight glistening green and slimy on the moss-covered walls.

'That's the place over there.'

Don pulled up and Jackie got out to open the padlock. There were two piles of derelict cars leaning against a tall chain-link fence. Jackie pushed open the rusty gates and Don eased the car into the drive, taking a winding path to the back of the yard where a shuttered Portakabin stood. He got out. It was bitterly cold.

'I hope this doesn't seem too cloak and dagger, Don.'

'Well, no cameras, no passers-by. You could get up to all sorts down here.'

To the right of the cabin was an area where cars were being stripped down and beyond that, an open shed full of metal boxes, presumably storing the parts. Aside from a mobile crane, the rest of the place was jammed with the smashed and maimed remnants of cars, stacked four high like monuments to a futile future.

'This is the sort of place I sometimes have dreams about.'

'Tell me.'

'Don't, Don, don't get into that. You got to focus now. Check your gun. Put that woman somewhere out the way.'

'Later, eh? Jackie, you reckon you should loll by the car or something, look like a bored tart, maybe roll a spliff?' Don smiled at the expression on her face. 'Don't worry, just an act to allay suspicion before we try and nobble the guys. This is all going to be acting.'

'The only way to survive.'

'I spose so, though I don't think I should smoke any blow just yet. I'll see'f Col's in position too.'

Don got out his gun and checked the chamber while Jackie spoke to Col on her mobile and then rolled up on the bonnet of the car. When used to it, just the right amount of light, he thought, a couple of shades above oblivion. Then they heard a car draw up by the gates, and voices – oaths, moaning and giggles. Three figures muffled in coats came round the car wreck silhouettes and into view. Don nodded to Jackie and set himself.

'*Give the fuckers hell!*'

'All right there, Angel, and you Daz, Mick? Glad you found the place.'

'Wasn't fuckin easy, but we did have that tosser Mick driving.'

Don gestured towards Jackie. 'This is Eva, by the way, picked her up at Mal's place.' Jackie rolled her eyes, gave off a nice sulky, contemptuous look and put the spliff in her mouth.

'Oh, right. So is Mal here then?'

'*Right, Don, go for it.*'

'Not yet but should be soon. I hope so, it's a cold bastard of a night.' Don ambled closer, pulled out his gun and waggled it around his finger. He looked skywards as if checking out targets.

'Shit, didn't know you had a stopper, Don.'

'There's fuck you don't know and there's fuck you do.'

Don then gripped the gun hard and suddenly pointed it at Mick's face. He gawped in utter shock. Daz and Angel's facial expressions changed too, from smug grins to anger.

'Fuckin hell, I knew something stank about you. Fuck, Don, this ain't on.' Angel put his hand in his coat. There was a glint of steel as he pulled it out.

'You can drop that, you bastard!' Jackie had her gun out.

'Fuck you!'

Angel started moving towards Don with the six-inch blade and then a shot rang out. Angel stopped in his tracks.

His head began to twitch and he threw away the knife as though it had given him a shock.

'Fuck, that was barely an inch from my ear.'

'The next one's between the eyes.'

Don was very impressed.

'This a fucking sting, is it? You the bastard pigs?'

'Worse.'

Don got behind Mick, pulled his arms back and cuffed him. He did the same with the other two. He was silent, his eyes strange, and no one could hear *Kill, maim, wipe the bastards out* chanting in his head. He went back to Mick, yanked on his greasy hair and pushed the gun under his spotty chin.

'God, I hate scum like you.' Don stared nastily into Mick's eyes. He hitched the picture of Kate out of his coat and pushed it into his face.

'What?'

'You know her, don't you?'

'Don't speak to the fucker, Mick.'

'Eva, if Angel opens his gob again, put a bullet in it.'

Don went back to staring, his eyes boring into Mick's mud brown pupils as he tried to let his thoughts speak – *'I would start with some small stuff. Break a finger, crack a rib, put a bullet through a vein and let it slowly bleed. Think of how much anger that would release, how much pain would be transferred. Then I could go for the big stuff – gut, groin, throat – fuck, that would double the release and still the bastard could be suffering alive.'*

Sweat poured down Mick's face. He started shaking. 'I – I – I don't –'

Don frowned, narrowed his eyes, rammed the gun under Mick's jawbone and screwed it around.

'All right, yeh, right, I knew her.'

'What's her name.'

'Er . . . er . . . right, yeh, Kate.'

'And you killed her. You raped her, smashed her head in and dumped her!'

'No way, I couldn't, it wasn't, I was – stoned, I wasn't even –'

Don cocked the gun, pulled it back and then began to drill it into Mick's temple.

'That feels good, don't it, Don? Connected, from the brain, down the arm and into your finger.'

'I – I don't know how she –'

'Mick, don't!'

'– how she ended up at our place. Angel, I guess . . . They, they were fucking in the bedroom and I – I got the shakes, I always get the shakes when things are iffy.'

'Who was in the bedroom?'

Mick tried to look sideways but Don pushed his gun harder, worked it at the flesh like a corkscrew.

'Er, Angel, I guess, Daz, and K – Khalid.'

'This is total shit, complete bollocks.' Angel sneered. 'You won't get anywhere with this.'

Don looked over at Jackie and she stepped forward and refocused her gun at Angel's head.

'And who hit her?'

'I dunno, really. They dragged her into the living room, all starkers, and were fooling about, you know, feeling her, pushing her between them, and she fell. Then she tried to make a run for it. There was a fucking chase to the door. Don't know who picked it up, the hammer, the one we used to use for crushing shit . . . Fuck, it just started out as fooling, high-as-kites farting about. And it was nothing to do with me. I was pissed off, that bastard Angel took one of my fish and put it in the bitch's mouth – my best fucking fish!'

'Well, that kind of confirms the death sentence.'

'You're right.'

Don stepped back from Mick and ranged his gun on all

three. They looked pathetic and sinister. Don had a vague feeling that really they were rats, predatory shit-eaters that had evolved backwards. Blowing away such scum would indeed be retribution.

'You all right there, Don?'

'Don't let her into it, she'll stop you doing what you want and take you over completely.'

'Yeh. Don't get involved, Jackie, this is personal now.'

'Don!'

'These shits don't deserve anything but bullet holes from their cocks upwards.'

'Don, come on, give me the gun and we'll contact the police, we've got enough evidence now.'

'I told you, didn't I? You should blow her away too.'

Don turned and pointed his gun at Jackie. He couldn't really see her face, it was blurred and she didn't seem like Jackie at all.

'Oh, fuck, you've flipped, haven't you? You've lost it, you stupid bugger.'

'I will do it, I have to.' Don wheeled the gun around again and aimed it at Angel's stomach.

'Don, listen to me!' Don recognized Jackie's voice, even though it sounded strange and desperate. 'I think I know why you're the way you are, you know, what's eating away at you.'

'You're not here now, Don, you're not in for callers.'

'I'm not in, Jackie, call back later.'

'Don, I spoke to Pat again, he told me about Melanie, that she's dead – that you completely refuse to believe it.'

'Melanie?'

'Can't you see? All the pain, all the weird thoughts, you've locked yourself in a nightmare.'

'Melanie . . .'

Don looked around. Everywhere was pitch black. He fired one shot.

19

'Is this one of them places?'
'*Yeh, that row of machines, you pull in right next to them.*'

'Have we been driving long?'
'*A fair bit, round in circles mostly.*'

'OK, I'm there. Now what?'
'*You've gotta get out now and feed the car with one of those hoses, but watch out, these places, usual cameras all over.*'

'Fuck, hold on, I've got a hat somewhere.'

Don fumbled down the back of his seat and pulled out a battered trilby from under it. He rammed it over his head, down to his eyebrows, the rim bent over his ears, and then got out of the car.

'Right, I got it, you pull the trigger like with a gun. Shit, there's someone watching in that booth.'
'*Don't worry, she's dead.*'

'This stuff smells awful, gotta be poison.'
'*Sure is, machines run on poison, but you're not supposed to dribble it all over the place.*'

'Ha-ha, what aren't you supposed not to do?'
'*Don't get clever with me. You better pay now.*'

Don prodded the hose away and walked across the forecourt to the brightly lit pay booth. He kept his head down, following blue streaks of petrol and black stains of oil. The woman at the counter yawned and checked his bill. Don barely glanced at her.

'I didn't know dead people yawned.'

'I ain't dead yet . . . Mind you, meeting the likes of you might drive me that way. Thirty quid please.'

'Oh, fuck.' Don stuffed a pile of notes through the grille and quickly walked off. He got in the car, started up and drove out into the wide main road.

'She ain't dead. She answered back.'

'Probably a machine, a robot thing.'

'What? Why am I listening to you?'

'Because you screwed up back there, feel guilty as hell and have no one else to turn to.'

'I'm in shock, I know that, but you –' Don shook his head and looked out at the long row of shops he was passing, the street empty and fragments of snow falling.

'OK, face it, you're the one that's dead, a no-body, a lifeless lump of fear and self-hate.'

'The fuck!'

Don stopped the car suddenly. He jolted forward, his hat brushing the windscreen, and then he opened the door and got out.

'You bastard!' he shouted loudly, his voice echoing in the dark alleys between the shops.

He began to walk. It was a strange place of glass cases and shuttered secrets. He stared at some of the bizarre objects – the plastic machines, the posters of bluer than blue sea, the posed cadavers draped in cloth – and, all over, weird messages and symbols that he could not understand. Then he looked skywards, caught flecks of snow on his eyes and saw the camera.

'Sod it, you'll never know me.'

The bullet he fired brought sparks, a fizzle, and then the box flopped lifeless against its post. Don smiled, walked on and tried to dig the gun sound out of his ear with his finger. A burglar alarm had also been triggered, a relentless jangle that blared out into the street.

'*Don, come on, get back in the car. You're gonna get picked up and locked away for good.*'

'You don't own me.'

'*I am you.*'

Don stopped. He looked at an unlit shop window and saw a vague shape reflected back at him. A crumpled form. Legs splayed and shoulders drooping. A squashed hat on his head and what looked like a toy pistol in his hand.

'That's me. That's Dad.'

He found himself driving again, along black tongues glistening with salt and flecked with snow. Going through brick labyrinths where those with twisted hearts lurked and threatened danger to the lost and innocent. The empty highways felt safe with the movement. The landscape became almost abstract, like it was just smudged and dripped paint, or the inside of another world that had never been seen before. Don tried to focus on the word 'Dad'. It was such a painful word, it stabbed at him and made him feel miserable. But he kept at it doggedly, stubbornly, and made it a shield against that other Don who called himself Cory and claimed the body they shared as his own. As he drove further, he noticed that the tongues grew wider and some even looped over each other and went into deep ravines where night juggernauts groaned their way on longer journeys. The surroundings changed too, taller, white and skeletal, and Don saw himself rising up between them until the tongue became circular and he began to drive round and round.

'This is it,' he mumbled. 'Nowhere else to go.'

He carried on circling the roundabout. A place that was neither past nor future, sitting amid towers of bone, the hub of glittering highways that disappeared into distant nothing. But after a while the movement seemed futile. The pain of that word still gnawed. Don looked for a place to hide, saw a chunk of black in the landscape and a stony drive that trickled down into it. The car turned, bumped and slid its way downwards until the iron gate to darkness was reached.

'*You really have reach dead end.*'

'*Go away, Cory, you're out of my life from now on.*'

'*Don, come on. It ain't him, you gotta know who dis is now.*'

'*Fuck, the Snooper, all I need.*'

'*Call me Horace.*'

'*You must be joking.*'

'*Look, me got a pile a home videos to watch – an you will watch em.*'

'*Fuck . . . spose you might as well go ahead.*'

Don knew it had to be himself. He had become someone else's property. The subject had become an object to be scrutinized and laughed at. He was in his kitchen back home, the third-floor flat where he could look out the window and watch the skies constantly changing over the city. Summer skies then, deepening in colour as dusk fell. The phone call just stopped him rigid. It was Angela, his ex, ringing from Scotland. 'It's maybe too soon to worry, but Melanie, she went sailing with an ecology group and she hasn't returned.' Despite the quality of the picture, it was easy to see the blood drain from Don's face and all his muscles go taut.

'*You did'n believe anytin bad coulda happen then, did you, man? But no one would, you have to think for the bes.*'

'*I couldn't just stay there and do nothing.*'

'*Yeh, we got a pile a footage a you down at the station, walkin roun an roun, too borin to show.*'

'Shit, had to get the night train. Couldn't sleep. Hours of rattling through the dark and then all those bleak mountains appearing at dawn.'

'You did'n answer you phone, did'n wanna hear from Angela, you was in denial then, man. Look a dis, here you are at Uig, a walking ghost already.'

Don recognized the scene. The blue bay surrounded by bare hills, the lines of croft cottages and the deep quay where the ferries berthed. He had hated that quay, the sheer drop down to threatening water.

'There you go, there's Angela now tellin you Melanie fell overboard at a point dat was tricky wid currents. She had she a life jacket, an they kep tryin to pull her in but she got drawn toward rocks an they los sight a her. They stayed out till dark but they still could'n find she, nor the lifeboat that came out to help.'

'I remember now. I can see the helicopter out there searching in the morning.'

'Yeh, an dere's you getting angry wid Angela.'

'Fuck.'

'You ent really spoke to each other again.'

'This is a really bad movie you're showing me, Snooper.'

'It don't get any better. We got a reel a you jus walkin long the coast, up an down, an den dere's dat boat you hire to look for youself.'

'I thought she could've scrambled up on a rock.'

'Man, the water up there, it very cold. They said you daughter, she could'n survive but a few hour.'

'How many days was it?'

'T'ree.'

'Even now, after so much time, I think she's alive and want to travel up and see her.'

'Yeh, it doubly hard, man, when the body ain't found.'

'I don't want to watch any more.'

'*Right, so now you know what me bin a sayin, what a bin goin on!*'

'*I don't know what I know . . .*'

Don opened his eyes. The barred iron gate sat before him, clearer now, his eyes used to the light and a hint that dawn was on the way. Snow had turned to rain and beyond the gate he could see a field. He got out of the car, his limbs aching and the muscles in his head tautly drawn. The air felt slightly warmer. Don let the drizzle cool his face, wake him up a little, before he went to the gate and climbed over. Mist rose up from the grass and rough weeds of the field. A railway ran along one side of it and a motorway the other. Don could hear engine sounds beyond the embankment as he walked into the field and felt the wet seep into his shoes. He had seen the truth, those unbelieving eyes anxiously straining on a rocky shore, but he didn't know if he could accept it. Still there was the thought he could get on a train on that railway line and go and see her. As he progressed further into the field, he saw a mirror streak of water, a flooded hollow with tall plants growing through. He headed for it.

'*Face it, Don, I'm all you've got.*'

'No.'

'*Who else is going to look out for you, cover over the cracks, warn you of the bastards that are out to destroy?*'

'I'm a bereaved man who can't grieve.'

'*Fuck that pain shit. Together we make a team, we survive and get the job done.*'

'You gotta go, Cory.'

'*You like me too much.*'

Don reached the edge of the water. There was still a faint crust of ice at its edge but the drizzle made no mark and he could look down and see the black silhouette of himself, head disappearing into a dark sky. He put his hand in his pocket and felt the sea bean, soothed it with his thumb.

'Murder,' he muttered. 'Gotta somehow murder you, Cory. Fuck, somehow gotta murder part of me.'

Don started to press hard on the bean, then squeeze and dig his fingers in. He pulled it out of his pocket, thumped it in the palm of his hand, then threw it on the ground and stamped. Wet and muddy, he picked it up still unbroken and then pushed it down into the cold water. Crazy, but if I could somehow put you in there, keep you there, strain my brain hard and try to believe that you're out of me now and in this shit – then I might get the space to push you away for good. Don pulled his hands out of the water. They had become numb with the cold. He wrapped the bean up in his handkerchief and thrust it back in his pocket.

'*You don't think that'll work, do you?*'

Don didn't answer himself back.

'*Now who's the madman?*'

Don clamped his mouth tight and tried to imagine that the sound came from his pocket. Just a gesture maybe, but a start. Then he turned back towards his car. He was shocked by the view. All laid out in front of him, city lights blazing, one hundred square miles of concrete and brick. On the horizon, where the plain of lights was dim, was a streak of grey – another cold, wet winter dawn. In the car, he saw his phone on the passenger seat. The light was blinking. He'd had the sound turned off all night. He picked it up, hoping to hear from Jackie, trying to remember what had happened when he'd left her.

'Glad you up, Don.'

'Wha? Who is this?'

'Shafaq. Bit early for you, huh?'

'Why are you, er . . . ?'

'You wanted me to ring, badly, about the deal? Well, jus got back from an all-nighter and things're set for later today.'

'I'm getting there now.'

'Mal and Khalid got the finals stitched up a few hours back. Be at the multi-storey car park on Halward Street, top floor at midnight.'

'Right, that's good. You know what kind of size of deal it's gonna be?'

'It's gonna be big, two hundred K probably.'

'Fuck . . .'

'Said I'd do it, didn't I?'

'Yeh, and many thanks. I reckon it'll leave the way clear for you, Shafaq. Whatever happens, Khalid is gonna go down.'

'You know something?'

'Yeh, reckon I know too fucking much.'

'You are a scary bastard, Don, but I guess it's just the pressure, the pressure we all fuckin get.'

'You're dead right there.'

'You gonna tell me how things're gonna go down?'

'Maybe later, Shaf. I'm too shattered to speak right now.'

Don started up the car and began to reverse slowly up the stony drive. What happened at the scrap yard? Did he really leave Jackie all alone?

'Huh, and you think you can get along without me?'

Don gritted his teeth and thumped at his thigh pocket. He tried to believe that this dawn really would mean a fresh start.

20

He got through to her on the phone. Just a few words – Jackie was safe. Don smiled with relief and put his foot on the accelerator. She was at her office and he desperately hoped he hadn't messed up everything between them. It was getting near morning rush hour, Don heading into the city on those wide tongues that were starting to glisten with hints of dawn and be hosed down by car headlights. He looked at the outlines of zombie drivers, impassive and solitary, working their small machines through the big city machine to their places of labour. It still didn't make any sense. They seemed utterly apart from him.

Maybe, he thought, if I can hold onto that wound that is really me, my – my daughter's death . . . Don winced. Maybe things will become different. He then felt that awful squirming sensation in his head as though Cory was fidgeting, so he thumped at his pocket again and tried to concentrate on the road. Ten minutes and he was able to turn off the expressway and park under it, next to the office block. Then it was the stairs and the long corridor, Don feeling the spookiness of the place and a growing apprehension at seeing her.

'Shit, Don.'
'Jackie, fuck, hope you can forgive me.'

They embraced, powerfully, bodies pushing hard against each other. Only the desk lamp was on and it sent distorted shadows around the room. Outside, he saw flickering car lights beneath the grey sky.

Jackie stepped back and looked at Don. 'You do look different.'

'I don't know whether I feel it.'

'I thought I'd lost you.'

'Could've happened, I guess.'

'You know where you've been?'

'Nah . . . well some of it. I reckon I've been trying to face up to what you told me.'

'You had to do it, Don.'

'But Jackie, I ditched you. I ran off not knowing what the fuck I'd done and left you alone with three godawful bastards.'

'You didn't have to worry, Don. I know I'm a titch but I am experienced and know how to handle myself. It worked out OK, and anyway the buggers were cuffed. What you did was fire a bullet into the back of a wrecked van. It kind of went between me and Angel. Don't know who the fuck you were aiming for, but I'm trying to think it was random outburst.'

'My head was full of all kinds of things.'

'I ain't gonna take it personally, yet.' Jackie gave a reassuring smile. 'You just sit down and I'll make coffee. Jesus, your feet are soaking.'

'Don't ask . . .'

Jackie had handled it. She'd brought in Col and phoned her DS friend and then the police came. There was only one tricky moment when Angel made a run for it and got a bullet in his thigh. 'Totally lucky shot.' The tape also came out all right, enough information to start an investigation, though there was some curiosity about the guy who asked the questions. Jackie had stayed at the station while Mick was given a second going over. Some variations in his story but nothing much to raise doubts about it. With the police, on his own, he said Khalid had picked up the hammer. It looked as though he would be a star witness. The police were probably at the house now, doing a search.

'I gotta thank you, Jackie, and apologize again.'

'Hold on, don't apologize too much because I'm going to take the credit for this bust.'

'It's yours. What about Khalid?'

'They'll pull him in at some point soon, I guess.'

'Not too soon, I hope.'

'Why? One guy I'd've thought you'd definitely want locked up.'

'Tell you later. Did you ring Pat?'

'Yeh. I think he's glad the police are involved. Saves him an awkward decision. Wants to speak to you, though. I think he's pleased.'

'That can be later too. I'm whacked.'

'Shit, so am I.'

They looked at each other through the half-light. For Don, Jackie didn't seem so far away, that beautiful stranger he'd been with, but sometimes never believed totally real. He noticed the mole on her cheek, the ageing lines on her neck and a broken nail on her forefinger.

'You know what I'm thinking?'

Don yawned. 'Let's do it.'

He closed his eyes for most of the journey back to Jackie's place. Nothing new to see and plenty to forget. Don half dozed and was glad of that escape. *Such are the journeys I've made along the western coast, many thousand miles, Cape Wrath to Slyne Head and back again searching. How many eyes have looked in upon you; curious, surprised and frightened eyes delving the crevices to find you sleeping? Sometime, maybe, one fellow traveller may report a sighting, and I can seek out that rock and find you once more . . .*

'Come on, hon, home.'

'Right . . . shit, I need a shower.'

'Huh, you and water, you could be a –'

'Don't say it.'

They trudged dozily up to the flat, Don's limbs now aching bad and his feet feeling like ice blocks. He headed straight for the shower, glad to be sluiced naked, letting the lousy night get washed away and feeling sad, but warm and secure. In his element indeed. Then it was the bed, Jackie already in there, and two warm bodies began to intertwine.

'I don't remember any dreams.'

'I like remembering dreams.'

'Huh, mine you wouldn't.' Don turned over and flopped an arm over Jackie. 'God, I don't want to move.'

'It was nice cuddling up. You were different, almost completely with me, I'd say.'

'Yeh? Maybe it's the real me coming out . . . What a scary thought.'

'Nah, it's a good thought. Nothing buried, all our sodding skeletons out in the open. I reckon that should make things even better between us.'

Don looked at Jackie. 'A nice thing to say but I find that scary too.'

She shook her head and smiled. 'Anyway, come on, tell me, what's this plan you got up your sleeve?'

Jackie had made breakfast in bed, at three in the afternoon. Different. Don thought it summed the whole situation up, something way out of normal where the day starts with darkness and ends with oblivion at dawn. He nibbled his toast and tried to look a bit sheepish.

'According to my source, Khalid and Mal, they're doing a deal at midnight, on top of the Halward Street car park, two hundred K for drugs.'

'Uh-huh, and you were thinking?'

'Somehow Mal gets delayed and two unknown desperadoes, they jump out of the dark and mug Khalid, grab his bag of cash and then go joyriding down the M6 to catch an aeroplane.'

'Bloody hell, Don.'

'The thing is, these desperadoes, they ring up the cops, tell them – this suspect for rape and murder, they tell them where Khalid is.'

'Don, that is a really crazy idea, a very dangerous idea . . . and could be, I suppose, a brilliant idea.'

'It's worth a thought or two. If we forget the possibility of failure, and think just of what success would bring – much of anything we wanted, I reckon.'

'Midnight. We're gonna have to decide now. That's great, Don.'

'Yeh, tight, I know. Well, we can let it pass or just say "Fuck everything" and go for it.'

Don drank up his coffee and then began to crawl his way out of the bed. 'Whatever, just think about it while I go and give Pat a bell.'

Don tried not to think while the phone rang. A fear of thinking about the night before and a fear too of what might happen yet. Better to hold onto what is and let it all ride.

'Well, hello there, Don, glad to hear from you. How're you feeling?'

'Shit, it was a tough night, Pat, but I reckon I'm feeling better.'

'You did great. I'm really pleased. It's big thanks from me and a bonus.'

'I guess it didn't turn out too difficult in the end, well, not with the heavies. One guy snitched on the lot of them and the thing just opened up. Still a nasty one out there to get, but I've got a strong line on him.'

'Really good, and you've got them stitched up with the police. I tell you, my first idea was to come down there and fucking blast the bastards, slowly, a bit at a time. Jesus, it's been so long not knowing what happened to Kate, and then the horror of finding out what really did happen to her – fuck, the gory notions that went through my head. Still there, to be honest.'

'I reckon I know, and have always known, how you feel.'

'Yeh, Melanie. Fuck, Don, I guess I shouldn't've let you do this job knowing what was really screwing you up, but I was damn strung out myself and I guess I saw Kate's death, you know, it was a way for you to . . .'

'I suppose it has been in some weird way.'

'Well, sorry pal, hope you don't feel I used you, and sorry to Jackie too, cos I should've told her sooner. How d'you feel now, in the head, like?'

'I dunno, I kind of hope I'm on the mend.'

'Sounds good, that you're getting through. I owe you a thousand, mate. Bringing the police in, yeh, it's all right that they rot. Doing the aggro, that always haunts you a bit, like with the Halligan business. Anyway, I got contacts, I might be able to arrange a bit of nasty persecution for them in the nick.'

'Shit, you always have it both ways, don't you, Pat?'

'I try my best. So, holiday, Don, a fucking good one, with Jackie I hope. I mean, the contribution she made and the concern she's shown for you.'

'I'm setting it up.'

Jackie was sitting at the kitchen table looking pensive, her sad eyes linking directly with Don's heart. He sat down. He did feel sad, deeply, the cold ocean of the north-west inside him. A silent union then as the world turned totally dark outside.

'We'd have the element of surprise.'

'Sure, unless Shafaq rats us up again – don't think he will, though.'

'We could put Mal off right at the last minute so there'd just be Khalid's lot.'

'Yeh, and then be quick and decisive.'

'He's a raving maniac.'

'Unpredictable.'

'Vicious as they come.'

'But not that bright in the brain department.'

Jackie looked around her, at the cluttered kitchen and the lounge beyond. Her mouth was held tight and Don sensed bitterness within. Maybe a moment remembering all that's been lost. A moment when the trappings of life, the pretence that goes with them, are dropped and you see existence as it really is. Don sighed.

'Baz is out of hospital now and will be back at work in a few days. Nothing much I'd want to keep here, never one for all this possessions shit anyway, but I would have to do something about my lovely fish.'

'That sounds like a bit of a yes.'

Jackie smiled but shuddered too. 'It's a frightening prospect. Let's just prepare for a maybe, huh?'

They went off to the office, a journey through a cold damp evening where everyone else was travelling in the opposite direction. Endless flares of lights in Don's eyes as they passed the slow crawl, the hour of workers returning home. And in the distance, there they were, the tall shining towers of labour. It all seemed horribly clear to him. You go in and you come out, every day, endlessly.

'You can't say you would miss this, can you, Don?'

'Nah.'

'So how're you feeling about Melanie now?'

'Not sure . . . trying not to think too much. Sort of numb, I guess, maybe still wanting to think that she might be alive.'

'Yeh, numb, I was totally numb, and helpless with shock at first. Fuck, dunno how long that lasted but then I remember getting really angry. You know: "Why me?" and I'd get angry at anything – bad drivers, burnt toast, spiders on the ceiling – in fact any silly thing that irked me.'

Don gritted his teeth and felt his eyes moisten in the dark. Did he want to go through that? Wasn't it better to just believe for the best?

'Then of course I had a bit of a guilt trip. I always did encourage such days out with his gran. And then . . . perhaps like you, I was hungry for seeing Lester, feeling lost and waiting for him for days on end.'

'You got badly depressed.'

'Certainly did, still do when anniversaries come around. Mind you, feeling pissed off – there's any number of piles of shit around that can cause that. It's just life, ennit?'

'Fuck, Jackie, we really do have to get away.'

'I ain't too bad, just a thin streak of bitterness – like a cup of coffee, I need a bit of sweetening up.'

'I reckon that's why I'm here, to give that a try.'

'That has to work both ways, Don. You'll need a shoulder more than me, I reckon.'

They parked under the motorway next to Don's car. Traffic noise thundered up above as though it was in-built in the structure. Jackie leaned over and kissed Don.

'Well, I guess we'll do what we've gotta do,' he said.

'Right.'

'I'll sort my shit and you sort your shit and we'll meet up for – mmm, maybe a bit of action?'

'I'm almost convinced, Don.'

There wasn't much for him to sort out. He'd packed his

bags, so all he felt he could do was check the venue. Back on the road, sick now of being between places amid the petrol rush and bland landscapes, always uncertainty, always one more damned hurdle to cross. He bought a ticket at the car park kiosk. The sallow-faced old guy in there hardly noticed the exchange as he watched a portable TV. The gate dutifully went up as if the guy had just willed it. Don drove on and up through the grimy concrete spiral until on floor four he saw city-lit clouds loom above. He got out and went to the edge.

'It isn't too late.'

Don groaned and folded his arms tight.

'Khalid, he's the main bastard anyway . . . and now, well, the anger, it's still there, isn't it, quietly burning away? Don, face it, take it, you've another chance to wreak your revenge!'

His hand went into his pocket and he squeezed the sea bean. The gesture seemed pointless. Don tried to focus on the view, that vast starlit expanse, but it seemed as un-yielding as ever and made him feel uselessly small.

'No harm to go a little too far, eh? Sneak it in, Don, make it accidental. Only you and I need know.'

'No.'

'Come on, I look out for you, I keep you safe. It's just a taste of retribution and then we can go off together and look for her. After all, I do know the ways of water.'

'This place, my head, is no fucking place for a lost soul like you. I know it now, Cory, I know I've gotta murder you!'

'There's peace in the ocean.'

Don dragged himself away from the wall. Murder. What an irony to have to turn it in upon myself! He looked across at the open flat space where just a couple of cars were parked. 'Business,' he muttered, 'just calm, cold fucking business.' He tried to imagine the scenario for the midnight meet, walked around, stamped his feet down hard and clenched his muscles. Then he returned to his car and parked it close to the exit slip road. Don wrenched up the hand brake. The next thing he checked was the lift, a gloomy, smelly cubicle that he wouldn't dare use, but the mechanisms could be sabotaged. One more look and he went off down concrete stairs, his footsteps echoing and unseen things wriggling around in his head.

'She is dead. I am alone. There is a future.' Words continually repeated as he stepped out into city streets, looked for a taxi and a way back to Jackie's arms.

21

'At least it ain't raining.'

'No, but it don't seem far off.'

'Yeh, black clouds on the horizon. Remember that time I took you up on Beacon Hill, Don?'

'Yeh, better view than this, though.'

'That's when I first found out you was a dodgy operator.'

'Ha, well, I'm glad you've stuck with me, and I'm glad you've decided to come here tonight.'

'Probably against my better judgement. I'm scared shitless, Don.'

They were in Jackie's car on top of the car park looking out over the city, glimpses of streetlight sprawl between thrusting office towers. Ten minutes to midnight.

'Better ring Mal.' Jackie switched on her mobile and thumbed in a number while Don looked around at the scene. Car ready to block exits, lift buttons firmly jammed and CCTV sprayed over. Nothing else he could think of.

'Hi, Mal. Jackie Lee here, sort of out of the blue . . . Yeh, everything is OK and no, I didn't know you felt that way, you naughty man . . . Something you should definitely know about, from this cop contact I got . . . You got business tonight, right? They know it, Mal, they know it and they got your meet covered and ready to bust. This cop, he seemed to imply they got Khalid's mob infiltrated . . . I'm sure, he's a good contact, Mal.'

Jackie clicked her phone shut and shivered. 'Oh, well.'

'He bought it.'

'Seems like it. You scared, Don?'

'Certainly am. What else can you feel with Khalid? Look, if I go a bit ape-shit with him, don't worry, yeh, I just seem to have a way of hexing him.' Don wondered why he said that.

'Don, something you've never showed me, you got a photo of Melanie?'

'Er . . . yeh, there is one in my wallet, but I can never bring myself to look at it.'

'Go on, show me.'

Don hesitated but eventually took the plunge, dragged out his wallet and passed over the worn snapshot.

Jackie's hand shook holding it. 'Wow, a raven-haired beauty and your eyes. Sixteen, yeh? Lovely.'

Don felt the sadness, that sudden glimpse of deep water, but it was short lived. They heard engine sounds coming from below and then saw headlights swooping along dingy concrete walls.

It was an old model black Merc, bass thumping behind tinted windows and a fair bit of exhaust churning. The car swung over to the opposite wall, stopped and went totally silent.

'You really want to go through with this?'

'Shit no, Don, but I guess . . .' Jackie squeezed Don's arm and looked into his eyes. He saw fear and a need for reassurance.

'Whatever, I'm with you.'

'You gotta take risks, ennit?'

'To get that little bit more.'

'So I guess we just gotta say "Fuck it".'

'OK, well let's say that then and do it.'

'Hope he doesn't recognize me . . .'

'Here's good luck.'

Jackie quietly got out of the car and began to walk slowly towards the Merc. Don got out the same side, low down, and began to edge his way round to the side. When Jackie got close, a window wound down.

'Hey, looka this, guys, we got a midnight bint on the prowl.'

'You Khalid? Got a message for you from Mal, something about –' Jackie began to open her handbag.

'Eh, hold on, I don't like people doin that. Wait a sec.'

Khalid got out of the car. He had a briefcase handcuffed to his wrist and a gun in his other hand. The driver also got out, a white guy Don recognized as being one of his subway attackers. Don began to ease his way to the rear of him, saw Shafaq sitting in the back seat and motioned to him to keep quiet.

'OK, darling, let's see what you've got in the bag, no surprises, I hope, for your bleedin sake.'

Khalid moved forward. Cupped in her hand, Jackie had a canister of mace. She brought it up and sprayed his eyes barely six inches away. The uproar was instantaneous. Khalid recoiled and screamed. He hit the car, stumbled and fell, then thrashed about on the floor. As the driver began to move, Don pounced too, sending his gun butt head-wise. He felt the hard thump jar his arm. The guy slumped on the car bonnet and then did a slide floorwards.

'Fucking bastard bitch fuck! Shit fucking cunt slag!'

As Don got round the car, he saw Khalid struggling to stand, his crossed eyes bright red and streaming tears, one hand flailing around for something to grab and the brief-case banging the car. Jackie had her gun trained on him but didn't seem to know what to do next. Neither did Don. He saw Khalid still had his gun, unable to see perhaps where to fire it or maybe not realizing he did still have it. He wiped at his eyes and the case banged against his chest. Then he got on his knees, lurching right and left, with two pairs of worried eyes following every movement of the gun.

'Shit, Don, what do we do? This is fucking horrible.'

'Fuck, I'll try and get behind him.'

'Bastard poison bitch, where are you?'

Khalid started blindly pointing his gun. It suddenly fired. Two yards wide but very scary. Don just dived straight at him and flattened him back on the ground.

'Who the fuck?'

'Yes, bloody hell, Don, yes! Now's your chance!'

Don got the gun hand and started bashing it against the concrete while Khalid's case thumped his head.

'Fucking hell, I fucking know you! You're the fucking dushman, the devil voice fuck!'

'Throttle him, put your thumb on his windpipe, just punch the life out of him!'

Khalid continued to struggle violently and seemed to ignore all pain. His hand was a bloody mess, his eyes burned but he fought on relentlessly. Don squirmed round and managed to get a foot on the gun hand. He pushed up on one knee and looked down at the wet, frothing scowl of Khalid's face.

'Yes, now, Don, one shot between the eyes. For the one who raped and killed your daughter.'

'No! It's fucking you, Cory, I want to kill!' Don thumped Khalid on the jaw.

'A piss punch, you shit evil.' Blood seeped from Khalid's mouth. 'I'm gonna have you, gonna fuckin slice your heart out!'

Don didn't notice, but Jackie did. The briefcase hand had found a flick knife. It had just slid open before Jackie grabbed the case and pulled his arm back. Don punched again. Khalid slobbered and laughed. Another punch and then again.

'Go on, this is great!'

'REALLY, CORY, IT IS YOU I WANT TO DESTROY,' Don growled between clenched teeth.

'What? No, you can't do that!'

Don punched. He wasn't sure how many he sent through the dark. All he knew was he was hitting flesh, the yielding flesh of a creature that he saw as part of himself. Jackie called to him, shouted for him to stop. He saw Khalid then, senseless, a groaning, twitching unconsciousness like that of a sedated wild animal. Don looked at his aching and bloodied fist.

'Shit.'

'Don, how the hell do we get the damn case off him?'

'I'll search for the key. You go and check the driver, cuff him and see'f Shafaq's still keeping his head down.'

Don searched. His fingers fidgeted through sticky clothes. They felt warm, repulsive flesh. Don hated the intimacy. He could smell sweat and mace, he feared a sudden eruption of blood. No key. Khalid still writhed and muttered and Don sensed it wouldn't be long before he regained consciousness.

'Any luck?'

'No. We'll just have to try and shoot the bugger off. You or me?'

'Shit, I'm shaking like a leaf.'

'So am I, but fuck it.'

Don stood up and pulled the briefcase out across the ground. He focused his gun on the metal chain. The barrel shook.

'This really is the moment, don't blow it.'

'Fuck you, fuck me!'

Don shut his eyes, fired, saw Halligan floating, saw Khalid ogling, saw fish shoaling and ripping a dead woman to shreds. He fired three more times.

'Jesus, Don, you've shot his wrist.'

'Only that?'

'You've broken the chain too.'

'Thank the fuck. Check for the dosh, eh, and then let's bloody well go.'

Khalid was coming round and tried to lift his head up. Don stared at the rumpled figure and the bloody wrist with the half chain that twitched in red ooze. He tried to think that it really was a smashed fish bludgeoned on a chopping board, all guts and scales; a scarlet smear left in his brain after surgery, a broken chain that had set him free. Then he stepped over and kicked Khalid's head back down. He picked up the dropped gun and went to the back of the car. Shafaq sat hugging himself, his serious eyes focused on far horizons as though that's where he wanted to be. Don gave him the reason to do that.

'Go, man, you won't wanna be around when we've left, the cops are coming.'

Don then took the ignition keys from the Merc.

'We got lots of money, Don.'

'Let's go, huh.'

Jackie ran to her car and got it going. Don picked up the flick knife and shivved the Merc's tyres. He couldn't be bothered moving the rental car to block the exits and so rushed to Jackie and got in with her.

'Fuck, let's just go, sweetheart.'

Jackie swung the car into the exit ramp and sped precariously down and round the gloomy spiral. She braked at the gate, though. The old guy was still watching his portable and didn't look as he sent up the bar. Jackie zoomed off into the night streets.

'Shit, I'm still shaking.'

'Better ring the cops, tell them where Khalid is.'

Out came Jackie's phone.

The streets were empty, just cold, damp, nothing zones. Jackie was heading towards her office first of all, part of the 'maybe' plan she'd thought about earlier in the day. Don could see growing relief and a nervous flicker of happiness on her face but he felt he was going the opposite way. Sadness, like a sweat stain, was beginning to seep all over his body. He fingered the photo of Melanie in his pocket and wondered if he could sneak a look. Nah, too much already for one night.

'How you feeling, Don?'

'Not that great.'

'You had those weird eyes.'

'Yeh . . . well, you really wouldn't wanna know what was going on in my head.'

'I don't ever want to see them again.'

Don wondered about that. Was Cory still lurking inside him, perhaps holed up in some crevice in his brain? What if he wouldn't go? What if some other violent obsession came out? Don fingered the sea bean and felt the photo again. He pulled it out. Just a fleeting glimpse and it was like only yesterday that they spoke.

It was only a quick trip to the office. Jackie had prepared a number of e-mails during the day that would announce her departure and the arrangements she had made. The principal one was to her boss, Baz. She switched on the computer and sent them all off. Then, a brief look round the room and she was ready to go.

'Bad memories mostly and hassle.'

'Bet you wish you could take the office view.'

'Sod off.'

Then it was the short journey to Jackie's flat. Here was a second set of arrangements, primarily envelopes filled with cheques.

'Bad debts, money for people to sort out loose ends of business, that sort of thing. The next door neighbour will let people in.'

'What about the fish?'

'The aquarium shop – giving them one hundred to take it away and find them good homes.'

Don ventured over. They just float and feed really, but the eyes, those ever-open eyes, they seem to bring in upon themselves whole worlds of experience. He tapped the glass and watched them dart away. Just stay that way, he thought.

Jackie came and put her arms around him. 'Shall we go?'

'You sorted?'

'Good memories but also pain. I can leave it all behind.'

'Right.'

'Bye fishes.'

They drove out of the city and didn't speak. Two faces bathed green by the dashboard glow, faces flickering with passing streetlight as though streams of emotions were flowing through them. Few else out on the road but for the odd insomniac and night worker. Deserted and quiet. Pure deception. Those hundred square miles and so much craziness within.

Don thought he recognized the road they were on, the petrol station they passed and some of the configurations of brick and concrete. No names or belonging. When they started going uphill, he knew it was the same road. Curving tongues and skeletal towers; and then, up ahead, the roundabout and the black field where he'd faced up to himself. But no stopping. Jackie confidently surged around the roundabout and took the motorway link. Barely a short look back from Don and they were on it, the three-lane night corridor to a new future. Jackie flipped on a CD. Don knew it straight away. Cherry, 'Orbit of La-Ba', him and Dewey Redman cooking up a wild exotic dance on trumpet and musette. Then rain began to dribble on the windscreen.

22

First three impressions of Jamaica. When he got off the plane, Don felt he was stepping into a hot oven, a ceaselessly hot oven as it turned out. Second, the roads had more holes in them than a colander. And third, the nights were very noisy. Don and Jackie were standing by the roadside at Hampton village waiting for an unofficial taxi to turn up. Fourth impression, Don thought as he looked skywards, cloudless blue sky.

'You sleep all right, hon?'

'Eventually. Reckon I dreamed about you.'

'A good one, I hope. What a racket all them frogs and crickets make. I got off and then a donkey woke me at dawn, saw a lizard on the windowsill which I had to shoo off.'

'Things couldn't get more different,' Don said, looking at a grove of banana trees and seeing little green fingers poking from beneath glossy leaves.

'Yeh, it really is what we need.'

'Your dad seemed very pleased to see you.'

'He did. He's gone off apparently to arrange a party for us tonight at the bar.'

'You mean that bar?' Don looked up the road at a small wooden shack barely ten feet across. Rough wooden poles held up a blue plastic sheet at the entrance.

'You just get your drinks inside, the party's in the road.'

'Of course, where else? Well, we should foot the bill, I reckon.'

A battered grey Volvo growled up to them and came to a stop,

'Yoh, you headin feh Mo Bay? Right, hop in den.'

They squeezed into the back seats, saw a crack across the windscreen and a CD player on the front seat plugged into the dashboard. Beenie Man was telling the world that 'real gangstas don't play'. Don didn't want to know anything about that any more. A lean, grey-frizzed guy looked at them through the rearview mirror.

'Eh, you Earlee's daughta? Yeh? Great, me hear dat you had a come over. Word travel fast roun ere. Name's Taylor, very please to meet you. An you is?'

'Don.'

'Nice, truly.'

The car clunked into gear and groaned off along the narrow road, a road full of bends, holes, hills and over-arching greenery that had seemed very perilous to Don when they'd come up it the previous night. The daylight didn't change this perception much.

'Was in Inglan meself, sis, feh twenty-odd year, work as a guard feh British Rail, come back, wha, coupla year now.'

'Glad you did?'

'Ha, jus look aroun you, sis.'

They were coming over a ridge and heading steeply down into a green valley, green of every shade, punctuated by white limestone rock and big red flowers on the tulip trees. In the distance, the blue of the bay and misty hills beyond that.

'Don't miss anything?'

'Jus me sons. They bin on visits but dem won't stay. Don't like mosquito, bad public service, murdah rate, lousy TV and ting.'

'They'll learn to appreciate it.'

'Mebbe, but me miss em still.'

'Yeh, but ain't that just the curse for all parents,' mumbled Don.

'You a dead right dere . . .'

The car bumped its way on down past wooden shacks on stilts, breezeblock cottages and small settlements where people stared and Taylor thumped his horn; then down to Granville where kids in brown uniforms came out of school for lunch and old women flogged banana and yam by the roadside.

'We're gonna have to start changing into dollars, a bit at a time, yeh. Dad said he'd help out too.'

'I hope the dosh is safe.'

'Earl's got a good hidey-hole. We'll be all right as long as we keep quiet and don't flash too much around.'

'Right. Well, I need to buy some cool clothes. Can't wear these all the time.'

Don was wearing one of Earl's shirts, a blue flowered cotton number with the word 'calypso' printed all over it.

'I think you look quite stylish, mister.'

They entered Mo Bay. Here, wide busy roads and white dusty buildings. Taylor pulled to a stop.

'Dis the Toyota garage, where we a normally stop. But if you want fi go further me a tek you, extra dollar a course.'

'The beach, that's our first stop. Earl said Doctor's Cave was good.'

'Doc Caves it is.'

Then it was off down Barnett Street, Don clocking the jumble of shops, people bustle, pigs in the road and cops on corners with sub-machine guns. It was all very strange. He felt a bit like a refugee, a rich one maybe, but still one of the millions across the world, neither here nor there, all out to escape some lousy shit or other. Some things haven't changed then, he thought. They crawled around impromptu stalls, down past Sangster's and the fire station, then hit the sea road and the Strip. This was fast food and hotel land where tourist and hustler pitched their butts. Far up on Gloucester Avenue and the beach entrance was reached.

Don gingerly trod the hot white sand in his bare feet, two tumblers of iced orange juice in his hands. The heat was almost solid, a force in itself, and each step was an effort to make. He felt quite numb and overwhelmed. It was as if nothing else could ever have existed. This was good. Jackie lay back in her bikini on a lounger. She seemed equally flattened. Don sat on his and handed over the drink.

'There's a stunning Russian woman back there, must be seven feet tall.'

'How'd you know she's Russian?'

'An imaginative guess. You reckon she might be paying for a stud?'

'It happens. Fancy her, do you?'

'Well . . . it's more like having a sense of the new and the opportunities it could bring.'

'I see. Gonna have to watch you in more ways than one, am I?'

'What you mean?'

Jackie frowned. Don got a glimpse of fear and grief. 'You know,' she said.

He did know but was trying hard not to think about that. He felt a shiver deep inside.

'Just trying to think of things positive, you know, love maybe and all that.'

'S'all right, I know. It's gonna feel a bit strange for a while, I guess.' Jackie looked over and into Don's eyes. He felt reassured, her look saying that things really were OK.

'Yeh, think I might give that guy over there a hundred quid.'

'Why?'

'The fuck, he's smiling.'

Jackie laughed and shook her head. Don felt in the pocket of his shorts, these too borrowed from Earl.

'I'm going for a little walk by the sea.'

Don eased himself up once more and plodded across the hot sand. In front of him was the blue bay, the water languid and rippled with sun. On the far side, a white liner was berthed and beyond that, green hills blurry in the heat haze.

He paddled along the clear water's edge, heading for a quay where tourist boats pulled up. Twenty-four hours before, he couldn't grasp anything beyond relentless cold and dark. Could things be so easily shed? The pain, he knew, still lurked and would for a long time. But what about the state of his head? Was it still lodged in there, that crazy fish, just lying low and waiting for the right moment to crawl out? He slapped his head and wondered whether he'd ever go a day without fearing that the voice might speak.

'Hey, mister, you got a camera?'

A young black woman was sitting in the sea, the waters lapping around her legs making diamond sparkle on ebony. She looked back at Don with a big smile.

'Sorry,' Don said, 'something else I gotta get.' He shrugged. 'Then again, cameras . . .'

'Just wanted a picture a me, here, in the middle a all dis.' She gestured with her arm.

'Nah, you don't need a camera. Just look at it closely with your eyes, click them shut and it'll be printed in your mind for ever.'

'Ha, nice one.'

'See you, and be careful if you go swimming out there.'

Don moved on and stepped up onto the wooden quay. At the end, he looked down into the water. Pure and clear. No fish that he could see, just ripple shadows dancing across the coral rocks. He put his hand in his pocket and pulled out the sea bean. A final squeeze, a last soothe along the groove with his thumb and then he threw it as far as he could, out beyond the swimmer's boom and into the currents of the bay.

THE CITY TRAP
John Dalton

'*The reason I don't have much of a track record is because the people who come to me don't have any money.*'

'*Whatever the rates, I have the money.*'

'*So what's the job?*'

'*The biggest thing you've ever snooped into.*'

Des McGinlay's first big case should be easy to resolve. But he's fending off the 'big wallow' – desperate to pull his life together as he picks through the wreckage of others'. Vin, who loved the murdered girl, is being set up as the fall guy; Bertha, her grieving mother, wants Des for a lucrative future. Lowlife sharks are circling – sucking Des into their vortex – and at street and canal level, down in the pubs and blues parties no one is playing by the rules.

'Dalton evokes a strong empathy for the downtrodden, taking pride of place among British crime writing's dirty realists. The slick tale unfolds like a whiplash, with thin glimmers of redemption shining out. A powerful new voice' *Guardian*

'Dalton's debut grips you around the throat from the start and doesn't let go' *Nicholas Royle*

ISBN: 0 9535895 6 0

www.tindalstreet.co.uk